Novels by Margaret Yorke

SUMMER FLIGHT
PRAY LOVE REMEMBER
CHRISTOPHER
DECEIVING MIRROR
THE CHINA DOLL
ONCE A STRANGER
THE BIRTHDAY
FULL CIRCLE
NO FURY
THE APRICOT BED
THE LIMBO LADIES
NO MEDALS FOR THE MAJOR
THE SMALL HOURS OF THE MORNING
THE COST OF SILENCE
THE POINT OF MURDER
DEATH ON ACCOUNT
THE SCENT OF FEAR
THE HAND OF DEATH
DEVIL'S WORK
FIND ME A VILLAIN
THE SMOOTH FACE OF EVIL
INTIMATE KILL
SAFELY TO THE GRAVE
EVIDENCE TO DESTROY
SPEAK FOR THE DEAD
CRIME IN QUESTION
ADMIT TO MURDER
A SMALL DECEIT
CRIMINAL DAMAGE
DANGEROUS TO KNOW
ALMOST THE TRUTH
SERIOUS INTENT
A QUESTION OF BELIEF
ACT OF VIOLENCE
FALSE PRETENCES
THE PRICE OF GUILT
A CASE TO ANSWER
CAUSE FOR CONCERN

Patrick Grant novels
DEAD IN THE MORNING
SILENT WITNESS
GRAVE MATTERS
MORTAL REMAINS
CAST FOR DEATH

Collected short stories
PIECES OF JUSTICE

THE PRICE
OF GUILT

Margaret Yorke

sphere

SPHERE

First published in Great Britain in 1999 by Little, Brown & Company
This paperback edition published in 2000 by Warner Books
Reprinted by Warner Books in 2002
Reissued by Sphere in 2013

A CIP catalogue record for this book
is available from the British Library.

ISBN 978-0-7515-5209-6

Typeset by Palimpsest Book Production Ltd, Falkirk, Stirlingshire
Printed and bound in Great Britain by Clays Ltd, St Ives plc

Papers used by Sphere are from well-managed forests
and other responsible sources.

MIX
Paper from
responsible sources
FSC
www.fsc.org FSC® C104740

Sphere
An imprint of
Little, Brown Book Group
100 Victoria Embankment
London EC4Y 0DY

An Hachette UK Company
www.hachette.co.uk

www.littlebrown.co.uk

The Price of Guilt

1

The man and the boy sat side by side in the Underground train, pressing together as more passengers entered, filling the centre gangway and the spaces by the doors. Louise, whose left arm was in a sling, manoeuvred her way between the seats, thrust along the carriage by the pressure from those behind. She stretched to reach a strap, difficult because as well as her broken arm she had several fractured ribs, and was amazed when the boy stood up to give her his seat. Accepting it, she thanked him gratefully. Her journey had already involved an hour by main-line train and another tube trip. She exchanged shy smiles with the boy, who stood so close to the man that they were touching. There were other men with children in the train; it was half-term, and fathers were enjoying quality time with their offspring. Here was one lad with old-fashioned manners, she thought: Colin would have approved.

She must not think of Colin. Distracting herself, she spoke to the boy.

'Are you going to do something nice today?' she asked him. His head was now much on a level with her own; he'd be about ten, she thought, not good at guessing children's ages.

'He's going back to his mum,' said the man. 'In Reading.'

So they were probably bound for Paddington, as she was.

The boy was leaning even closer to the man. His face was pale.

'He wants to stay with me,' said the man.

'Oh dear!' Here was a sad domestic drama: separated parents. Louise did not want to seem too curious, but she asked where the man lived and he said it was in Southwark. Louise, not good in London, thought that must be near the restored Globe Theatre, but did not hazard a comment about it in case she was wrong.

'I expect you often come for weekends, don't you?' she said to the boy, who did not reply. 'It will be easier as you get older,' she added. For things were, weren't they? You could certainly talk to strangers more freely; your motives were less suspect. Or were they? What were hers, now? Mere interest? A few weeks ago she would simply have thanked the boy for surrendering his seat, then sat in silence; today, she had spoken easily to both boy and man, and the man had responded with an obvious cry from the heart, which had pierced her own.

So much had changed so quickly.

At Oxford Circus, when a lot of people left the train, Louise was able to move up a place.

'Here's your chance,' she said to the boy. 'Have my seat, quick.'

The boy slid into it, not looking at her, nestling up against his father, who glanced at her and smiled briefly, then whispered something to the boy. Louise looked away, studying the advertisements above the opposite seats, visible because fewer passengers were standing now. It was years since Louise had last been to London; she felt quite strange, fascinated by the diversity of people around her. It was stimulating. She should do it again. Perhaps she would, depending on what happened today.

As the train halted at Paddington she stood up, ready to leave. The man and the boy rose behind her.

'Are you all right, with your arm?' the man, Andrew Sherwood, asked. 'Can you manage?'

'Oh yes,' she said. 'Thank you.'

Even so, he and the boy saw her down to the platform and then, with a muttered goodbye, strode off. Louise followed more slowly. They were probably catching the same onward train, she thought, but she would not embarrass them by sitting near them. Their misery was blatant; they needed this precious time together.

There was nearly half an hour to wait before their train left. Louise saw the man and boy go into a snack bar, and she chose a different place to have a cup of coffee. Her shoulder-bag, old and shabby, was slung across her chest; the plaster on her injured arm allowed her to use the fingers of her left hand to a limited extent. She was growing more adroit daily but the rib injury was causing her more discomfort than the arm.

The solicitor's letter, which was waiting for her when she left hospital, had come as a complete surprise. Colin hadn't known about it. He would have read it and would have insisted on accompanying her to see Mr Barnes, with whom she had an appointment today.

But Colin had gone. After her accident he had mysteriously disappeared, leaving no note and taking the car and all his clothes. That day, Louise had been at the hospital where she helped in the shop once a week; she was to return within a few hours in an ambulance. She had done an extended shift, standing in for another helper who was ill, and Colin knew she would be later than usual. He had driven her there, as he usually did, and he always collected her. Some of the staff were impressed by this apparent dedication, but Louise knew that he did it to make sure that she was where she said she would be, not at liberty, roaming around the town with people he did not know. Louise was not allowed friends. Since his retirement, Colin drove her to Tesco's once a week and supervised her purchases, thus sparing her, he said, the bus trips she had hitherto been obliged to undertake.

The evening she was knocked down by a hit-and-run driver, he had not come to fetch her after her stint in the hospital shop. She waited for a quarter of an hour, then telephoned to find out why he was delayed, for he had never been late before, but there was no reply. She waited a while longer and then, after telephoning again and when he had still not arrived, Louise decided to make her own way home, which meant a bus journey and five minutes' walk in the dark from the nearest stop.

As she neared the gate of their small modern house in a quiet estate, where none of the neighbours met Colin's demanding social standards, the lights of a stationary car a short distance ahead suddenly blazed and it was driven straight at her, its engine roaring as it accelerated on to the pavement. At the same moment, startled, perhaps, by the noise and dazzle, a cat, yowling, ran across her path making her instinctively jump away, and this probably saved her life. The car struck her hard on her side, knocking her over and into the hedge which Colin clipped conscientiously twice a year, then roared on up the road, not stopping.

Louise had the strangest feeling that Colin was driving the car, but surely that was impossible? With the headlights on full beam, she could not have made out the driver's features. She told herself that the concussion she had suffered, which had prolonged her stay in hospital, was responsible for this delusion.

Colin could not be traced to be told of her accident, nor was there any sign of his car. Later, she discovered that he had cleared out their joint bank account.

The time since then had been like a dream, and sometimes a nightmare. Louise had been able to tell the police very little, and no witnesses could be found. She had thought the car was dark, but could not be sure, as she had not noticed it until its lights came on and it rushed at her. She did not mention her suspicion that Colin was the hit-and-run driver. It was unreasonable, for why, after years of tormenting her, should he suddenly decide to kill her?

Unless he had discovered her secret: but he could not have done that, for no one knew except her.

Colin had taken all his clothes and personal possessions, so his departure had been planned; he was not listed as a missing person, and, as she had survived and would recover fully, finding him was not a priority. The police concluded that a stolen car, driven by an inexperienced youth, had knocked her down. People did disappear, often for no apparent reason. Sometimes they reappeared, and sometimes not.

When she discovered that he had taken all their money, Louise understood that Colin might have gone for ever. Could it be possible? Leaving no note of explanation? Why should he do such a thing?

She could scarcely believe that she was free.

Louise was not completely destitute. She had a small income from a trust fund left by her mother – money she had always paid into the joint account, until a few years ago when, at last nerving herself to rebel, she had told Colin that the trust had been wound up. She had secretly opened a building society account and had squirrelled away a steadily increasing sum with thoughts of eventual escape, though she feared she would never find the courage.

The solicitor's letter asked her to get in touch, discreetly giving no explanation. Louise instantly feared that what she had told Colin had come true; the trust had ended. She could not explain, even to herself, why she felt obliged to telephone Mr Barnes not from the house, whence the call could be detected on the bill, but from the nearest call box. Now she would never be able to leave the gloomy narrow house, with its darkly varnished floors and ochre wallpaper, which Colin had rented when he retired after his lifetime's work with different companies. He had expected better: Colin had wanted nothing less than a mansion, but whatever had happened to block his promotion in firm after firm had thwarted that ambition.

He had told Louise, each time he left one position for another, that the new job was better than the last but that was not reflected in improved conditions. Almost always the changes meant a house move, and twice there had been periods when he worked abroad, once for a few months and, soon afterwards, for nearly two years, leaving Louise behind each time. It was during the second of these spells that she had had the most profound experience of her life.

'Why can't I live with you, Dad?' Nicky asked his father as the train pulled out of the station.

'We've been through all that, Nicky,' answered Andrew Sherwood. 'School and everything's with Mum. She can look after you better than I can. You know I have to be out at all sorts of unsocial hours.'

'But I'm nearly eleven. I'd be OK,' Nicky insisted. 'Don't you trust me?'

'Of course I do,' said his father. 'It's not that. It's the rules of the country that kids can't be left on their own too long.' Once again, the nag of anxiety pierced him. 'Terry's all right, isn't he? You can get along with him?'

'Oh, sure,' said Nicky, not wanting to worry his father, and in truth there was nothing wrong with Terry, except that he shouldn't be there, taking Dad's place in bed with Mum and everything, in their same house, while Dad was living in a crummy flat. And now Dad had got a girlfriend, Val, so that if Mum did get sick of Terry, he wouldn't want to come back home. It was because of Terry that he'd left, after a big row. Mum had simply gone off loving him. Nicky had worried that she might go off him, too, but she'd hugged him and said that wouldn't happen. All the same, Nicky knew that she and Terry liked being on their own – especially Terry. Terry thought he could have made the train trip to London on his own, but both Mum and Dad said not yet. At first Dad had picked him up by car and brought him back, but then he'd lost his licence. He'd exceeded the speed limit once too often and got too many points, he said, though Terry thought it was being over the limit for alcohol that had been the trouble. Mum hadn't agreed. Andrew didn't drink and drive, she'd said, and as for speeding, some got caught and some didn't.

'Like adulterers,' she'd added, and given a funny sort of laugh, more like a sob.

Nicky wasn't sure what an adulterer was, so he'd looked it up in a dictionary at school. He'd had to read on quite a bit to find the answer. Even then, it wasn't all that straightforward. Lots of people had sexual intercourse, as the dictionary called it, without being married; everyone knew that. Miss Finch at school and her friend Mr Weaver, who was an artist, lived together, and presumably did it, like Mum and Terry. Sex, it meant. They must all be adulterers, and so must Val and Dad. They didn't keep it secret, though Mum and Terry must have tried to, before Dad left. It was very confusing.

At Reading, they got a taxi to the house. Nicky sat close to Andrew on the journey. It took over a quarter of an hour because there was so much traffic. Andrew almost had to push the boy out of the cab when they arrived, but as he did so the front door opened and Hazel stood there, waiting. Silently, slowly, Nicky walked to her and was embraced. Andrew saw him hug her, too.

So that was all right. He was driven back to the station where, in a bar, he proceeded to get rather drunk. Then he realised that he was carrying Nicky's weekend bag. Coaxing Nicky out of the cab, he had forgotten it; careless, but at least he hadn't left it in the taxi. He wouldn't take it back to London with him, for it contained Fred, a threadbare stuffed donkey much beloved by Nicky who found it difficult to go to sleep unless the precious toy was with him.

He caught another taxi out to the house, but when he rang the doorbell, no one answered. He rang again and knocked, then walked round to the back door. He hadn't seen the garden for months. On this wintry day it looked bleak; the lawn could have done with a final cut and the beds were overgrown. Hazel had quite liked gardening till she went back to work when Nicky was five. After that, beyond scattering a few annual seeds around, she left it to him, and he'd enjoyed keeping it tidy and growing vegetables. Hazel had become a sales promoter, displaying gadgets and demonstrating cooking aids such as mixers and knives in shops and at exhibitions. That was how she met Terry, who was a television salesman in one of the stores where she had worked.

She had had an earlier affair, which Andrew had discovered because of Nicky. Hazel had begun going out in the evenings, saying she was working overtime on demonstrations in people's houses, and Andrew had believed her. He was happy enough to stay at home with Nicky when it fitted in with his own work, glad of some peace, for he and Hazel had been snapping at one another for months. At the time, he was a reporter on a local paper and he sometimes covered events taking place at night; when any of these clashed with Hazel's plans, they used a babysitter, a schoolgirl who lived nearby. On one of these occasions, Nicky had been making hot chocolate for the two of them, and had picked up the kettle awkwardly. It was too heavy and too full for him to handle easily and he had dropped it, scalding his leg severely. The frightened girl, unable to locate Hazel, had called an ambulance. Andrew had come home from a council meeting to find the house empty and a scrawled note from the babysitter. He had dashed to the hospital, where the tearful girl, blaming herself for the accident – Nicky was only seven – explained that there had been no reply from the telephone number Hazel had left. The girl had not brought the number with her to the hospital; however, Andrew had found Hazel's note.

Nicky's injury was not serious enough to keep him in hospital overnight, and he and Andrew were home before Hazel. Andrew settled Nicky into bed, then rang the number Hazel had left. After ten rings, a male voice answered. Andrew knew at once from the tone that the speaker was in bed, and not alone.

When Hazel returned, he was sitting in a high-backed chair like a Victorian father awaiting the return of an errant daughter, and she made only a half-hearted attempt to defend herself, for the earlier call had not been answered.

'Well, I had left the number,' she protested angrily. 'The right one.'

It had belonged to Leo, in whose flat she had spent many previous hours; he was a customer, an insurance salesman to whom she had sold a special non-stick wok. Of course he didn't want her permanently, a woman with a kid. After this crisis the marriage creaked on, with increasingly frequent rows and arguments. Things grew very bitter, and then Hazel met Terry. This, she said, was serious, and eventually Andrew moved out. Divorce negotiations were still in progress, and the house would probably be sold when they were settled, but meanwhile Andrew was offered a job, based in London, on a newspaper's weekly supplement. Leaving the district had seemed a good idea at the time; it was a career move upwards, with a higher salary, but now he wasn't so sure. He could have seen much more of Nicky if he had stayed in the area.

But he and Hazel would never get back together. That was a fantasy which he feared Nicky still cherished, but which Andrew no longer desired. Love could die. Neglected, it perished.

All this ran through Andrew's mind as he stood in what had been his garden. The New Dawn rose he had planted to mask the side of the shed had grown and twined itself round the supporting wires he had put in place. Maybe Terry used the tools he had left behind, though not often, judging by the garden's unkempt state. There was a basketball net attached to a wall at the rear of the house: that was new, and Nicky hadn't mentioned it.

Andrew no longer had a key, for Hazel had changed the locks, though technically the house was still half his. He opened the garden shed and put Nicky's case inside, then scribbled a note which he pushed through the letterbox, telling him where it was.

Hazel hadn't wasted much time in taking Nicky out. He wondered where they had gone. Returning to his taxi, he hoped they were having fun.

He might go to the newspaper offices, he thought, see his old mates, have a jar. That would keep him near Nicky a while longer.

2

Louise had learned of Richard's death from the obituary column of *The Times*. She had been reading it at the library, a refuge acceptable to Colin, when the announcement caught her eye. It gave his naval rank, so there was no mistake. During the Falklands conflict she had seen him in a television newsclip before Colin switched channels; it had given her an enormous shock. He did not seem much changed. *Brother of*, the paper said, and named two sisters and a brother. She hadn't known that he had siblings. There was no mention of a wife or children. Had he never married? Was he divorced?

Louise had felt a surge of sadness wash over her. She had not seen him for so many years, more than half her lifetime; all that passion and emotion had faded, but not the memories. She had often thought of him, wondering if they would ever meet again. Now it could not happen. They would never have any of the conversations she had occasionally imagined.

They had known very little about each other. There had not been time, and both were living for the moment. She was married, but Colin was overseas on his second foreign contract. In those days most young women's goal was early marriage, and she had felt a need to escape as soon as possible into this esteemed and respectable state when her widowed mother had remarried. After Louise's father was killed in the war, her mother had earned a living and put a roof over their heads by working as a secretary at a school, where a flat went with the position. The school amalgamated with another, the job went, and Louise's mother found a post as housekeeper to Paul, an estate manager whose first wife, bored by rural life, had run off with an American food-processing magnate, abandoning him and their son and daughter.

Paul and her mother's relationship developed slowly from their roles as employer and employee, but as a deep affection grew between them, her mother bloomed. For Louise, though, it was not so easy. Paul's son and daughter, much younger than she was, were demanding; they missed their own mother and at first resented the two newcomers. However, Louise's mother was used to children and she gradually won them round. Their own mother was a volatile, pretty woman who was easily bored, hence her flight. Louise's mother was patient and efficient; the children's clothes were washed and mended, their dinner money was ready and their school trips planned and organised. Three years passed before she and Paul married, and his son and daughter took it calmly. It did not change their lives, merely secured the situation.

By this time Louise was doing a secretarial course. Paul's house was large and she had a lovely room, but somehow she had never felt it was really her home. Perhaps it was a form of jealousy, she thought, shocked at herself; she had been her mother's sole consideration ever since she was a small girl and now there were other people of importance in her mother's life. Even the memory of her father, whom she remembered vaguely as a large and comforting presence smelling of fresh soap, had been displaced. She welcomed her mother's patent happiness and the security the marriage gave her, and was ashamed of her own discontent. She needed to escape, and when, aged eighteen, she met Colin, she was vulnerable. She was still more vulnerable when, several years later, Richard entered her life.

And now he was dead.

Richard was the father of the child she had given away at birth, the child of whose existence she had told no one.

She was in good time for her appointment with Mr Barnes, the solicitor. The offices of Barnes and Locock occupied two floors of a house in North Oxford overlooking the canal. Louise had never been to Oxford. A city map in her hand, she walked through busy streets, past Worcester College, the Oxford University Press, and the rear of the Radcliffe Infirmary. She found the place at last, rang the bell, and was admitted.

Mr Barnes stood up as she entered his office, came round from behind his desk and held out his hand, a warm, comforting palm.

'Ah – Mrs Widdows,' he said. 'How are you? I'm so glad you were able to make the journey.'

For a moment, nervous, Louise wanted to retort that she was not yet quite decrepit, as Colin would have done – he would have snarled – but she pulled herself up. Mr Barnes knew she had had an accident; it was the reason for her delay in responding to his letter. His remark was a normal civilised greeting under the circumstances. Surely she was not starting to develop Colin's antagonistic response to the most innocent observation?

'I'm much better, thank you,' she said.

'Do sit down,' Mr Barnes urged her, indicating a chair.

He was like a kindly doctor. Louise sat, as bidden, and waited for him to disclose the reason for his summons.

'Well now, as you know, I have some news for you which I was instructed to deliver personally,' he said.

Louise waited. Her expression was impassive.

Mr Barnes cleared his throat and continued.

'My father used to look after this particular matter, but he has now retired and I have taken it over. I have been a partner with the firm for some years,' he added. 'I am familiar with the details.'

'I suppose the trust has run out. The money has gone,' said Louise. This was what she had been expecting. Colin had been bitter about the restrictions placed on her small income, saying that if only they could acquire the capital, they could start a business, but Louise, by now mistrustful of his judgment and resenting the steady decline in their living standards, declared that under no circumstances would the trustees release it. In fact, she had not asked them, thankful that something was out of Colin's control, and when she had made out that it had ceased, the wonder was that he had not insisted on investigating the circumstances.

'No, no! It's nothing like that. It's good news,' Mr Barnes assured her. He had not wanted to put anything definite in writing. The terms of the trust dictated that, as far as was possible, Louise's interests were to be protected and Colin Widdows was to be denied any information he might seek; following from this, it must also be withheld from Louise, and delivered to her personally only when, in the opinion of the trustees, the time was right. The moment had now come.

Mr Barnes decided to go straight to the point.

'Well, the position is that your mother owned Lilac Cottage, a small house in Croxbury – that's a village about fourteen miles from here. She inherited it from her godmother and chose not to sell it. By that time, of course, your mother had remarried and was financially secure. She let the house and took the income. When she died, there were sitting tenants who had rights, and she had said that they were to remain there for their lifetimes or until they wished to move away. The wife died two years ago, and the husband has moved to Cambridge, near his family. The house is yours. Now you may take possession. Would you like to go and see it?'

Mr Barnes steepled his hands in front of him on his desk while his client, such a small, fragile-looking woman, stared at him.

'Your mother never mentioned the house?' he prompted gently, after she failed to reply. Her thin face remained expressionless.

'No. Not a word. But I remember her godmother – Priscilla Jordan – and the house. We stayed there occasionally, before she married my stepfather.'

'Miss Jordan's will was made after the war, when she bought the house. She had no close relatives, and she never revised her will. Your mother was a widow and she was worried about her future security.'

'Why didn't my mother tell me?' Louise wondered, more to herself than to Mr Barnes.

'She thought you needed the limited independence the income from it would provide,' he said. He coughed, and added, in grave tones, 'She knew your husband had had several career changes and she was not confident that he would prosper. She wished to protect your interests.'

This was a watered down account of what Mr Barnes's father had revealed.

'The mother thinks the husband is a bully,' he had said. 'She doesn't want him getting his hands on what belongs to her daughter, and she wants her to have something to fall back on if she needs it.'

'But hadn't I a right to know about it?' Louise asked.

Mr Barnes had been worried about this. He thought she had, and feared his firm had failed in their duties, but the mother was their client. A scheme which his father had drawn up, in conjunction with the bank, referred only to 'certain securities' which were held in trust by nominees, from which her small income had derived.

'She might have changed her mind if she had outlived your stepfather,' he said gently. 'As I understand it, under the terms of his will she would have had an income for life but his estate would have gone directly to his own children. She died suddenly, didn't she?'

'Yes. She had a heart attack. She was pruning the roses,' said Louise.

'It must have been a shock,' said Mr Barnes.

'It was,' said Louise. 'A lovely way to die, but it was too soon. She had been so active all her life. There was no warning.'

The days that followed her mother's death remained a blur. Her stepfather had been grief-stricken; he had said that Susan had seemed perfectly well, and they were planning their annual holiday in Provence, where they owned a small house. Eventually her stepfather had moved there permanently, and had died five years later.

Mr Barnes felt curious about his new client, who had at last shown some emotion.

'How is your arm?' he asked her.

'Oh – mending,' she said.

'It was a road accident, you said, and you had other injuries. Have the police found the driver?'

'No. I don't suppose they will. They often fail to, don't they?' she said. 'After all, I wasn't killed.'

She had not mentioned her husband. Mr Barnes decided not to, either, or not yet.

'Shall we go?' he said, getting up.

They walked together to his car, parked on hard standing outside the building. Louise winced as she got into it; the movement caught her fractured ribs. She was trying to absorb what Mr Barnes had told her. It was miraculous. She had a house. She could live in it, maybe very soon, and if Colin did return, he'd find her gone. Thoughts about how she would manage for money crowded into her head.

'You will be free to sell Lilac Cottage,' Mr Barnes was saying, after he had reversed out into the road and set off northwards. 'Or let it,' he went on. 'There's no need to hurry about a decision.' If it was re-let, the rent could be increased.

'What would it be worth, if I were to sell it?'

'About a hundred and twenty thousand, at a low estimate,' replied Mr Barnes, who had anticipated this question.

'So much?' She was astounded.

'It's in a sought-after village,' Mr Barnes said. And it had potential for improvement and extension. She did not need to know that at the moment.

Louise was reflecting that she could sell it and buy a maisonette or flat for much less, anywhere she chose, needing no mortgage, invest the rest and live off the income. She was silent, her mind whirling around. They had reached the ring road and were travelling round it in a clockwise direction. Louise tried to remember Croxbury. There had been a winding main street of old timbered cottages, some thatched, all very picturesque. There was a school, and there had been a post office which sold sweets, and a few shops – a butcher and a grocer, she recalled.

'You'll find the village much changed,' said Mr Barnes. 'There's been a lot of building. People commute to London from there now, and, of course, to other towns.'

The roads along which they were travelling were totally unfamiliar to Louise.

'Goodness,' she said, as they turned off and passed roadworks near the junction for the M40.

'This is all a bit different, too,' he said. 'Even those of us who live around here find it difficult to keep up with what's happening.'

'Do you live out this way?' she asked.

'Yes – a few miles beyond Croxbury,' he said. 'I drive through Croxbury most days.'

'Oh.'

'Not past your house,' he said. 'It's not on the main road, if you remember.'

'Isn't it near the church?'

'Yes, it's in Church Street. There are active bell-ringers,' Mr Barnes told her. 'When they do prolonged peals, some neighbours find it tiresome.'

'I rather like the sound of distant bells,' said Louise.

'These are not so distant,' he warned.

They were travelling along a busy major road, in a line of cars whose pace was being dictated by two lorries at the head of the procession.

'There's an industrial area on the fringe of the village,' said Mr Barnes. 'But you can still get held up by tractors.'

'It's very different from where I live,' said Louise. 'Kenston's a town.' And an unattractive one, a sprawling overspill from Greater London.

Her moves had been charted by Barnes and Locock, for first her mother, and then Louise herself had always sent the trustees her new address. Mr Barnes decided not to ask why Mr and Mrs Widdows had led such a roving life.

'We're nearly there,' he said.

As they entered the village, they passed a row of modern houses each no bigger than the one which Louise had left that morning, but around these were established trees, shrubs and greenery. She felt her tired heart beat a little faster as she looked out of the window for something familiar.

'We'll have a drive around after you've seen the house,' he said. 'If you'd like to. The village has almost doubled its population in the last twenty years or so. Old houses have been pulled down and replaced by several smaller ones and people have sold off orchards and bits of garden for development, but most of the shops have gone, apart from the post office and the newsagent, who sells sweets and some groceries. There's a new supermarket in Durbridge, and another one about six miles in a different direction. People who leave the village to work find them so convenient that the small shops have gradually been driven out of business. The school has survived, though, and there's a library now.'

'The Red Lion's still there, I see,' said Louise. 'I went there once for supper with my mother and Priscilla.' She was thirteen at the time and there had been a discussion as to whether she was old enough to be admitted. 'They did mixed grills,' she added. Two years later her mother had married Paul.

Mr Barnes was encouraged by this short speech.

'They'll still do a steak,' he said. 'But they go in for rather more elaborate things now.' The pub was making a bid to attract an upmarket clientele after a previous landlord had pursued, with some success, the local youth.

He turned off the main road into a narrower one, driving slowly now. Louise was peering out of the car.

'I'm sure it's on the left,' she murmured.

'Yes. It's a little further on,' he said. 'Past where the forge used to be.'

Louise had a sudden memory of seeing horses going past Priscilla's house, and of watching the blacksmith at work; she remembered the strange burning smell as the hot shoes were fitted to the hoof. It would be silly and sentimental to mention this to Mr Barnes.

She did not recognise the former forge, though later she learned that it was now called Forge Cottage.

'Here we are,' said Mr Barnes briskly, braking, pulling in against the kerb.

Louise's recollection was of a square stone-built house standing in a large garden. Now she saw a smaller building than she had expected, with a rim of garden at each side and, in front, a short lawn, split by a concrete path and fenced off with iron railings. The grass was straggly but a few timid crocuses were pushing through near the gate.

Mr Barnes came round to open the car door for her. She swung her legs round and took his proffered hand, letting him help her to her feet.

'Ah – that's a better way of doing it,' she said. 'It is awkward when I move. I broke some ribs as well as my arm.'

'I sympathise. That's very painful. I cracked a couple playing rugger as a boy,' said Mr Barnes, who still looked quite boylike to Louise, but she supposed he must be getting on for forty. 'It must have been a very nasty accident.'

'It was,' she said. She remembered nothing after the impact until she woke in hospital.

'Come along,' said Mr Barnes. 'I'll lead the way.'

He opened the front door of Lilac Cottage. There was a name plate on the gate.

'There were some lilacs, but I believe they died,' said Mr Barnes.

'I could plant more,' said Louise, entering the house behind him. 'If I decided to live here, that is,' she added.

'Certainly,' said Mr Barnes, still wondering at what point to mention Mr Widdows. Perhaps it would not prove necessary.

The front door opened into a small hall. A flight of stairs rose straight up to the landing above. Mr Barnes opened a door on the left, which led into a square room with windows at the front and side, and though the day was grey, it seemed bright. The walls were painted white. There was a shelved alcove beside the fireplace, and a faded green carpet covered the floor. Flowered curtains with a green background hung at the windows.

'The tenant left the carpets and curtains,' said Mr Barnes. 'And the fridge, the cooker and the washing-machine – all rather old, but in working order. He didn't need them. His maisonette is new and fully equipped.'

'It was good of him to leave them, all the same,' said Louise. 'He could have sold them.' She was looking around her, mesmerised. In all the years with Colin, she had never had a home like this. 'He – they – kept it very well. You could move straight in.'

'Yes,' agreed Mr Barnes. 'Come and see the rest of it.'

It was a total contrast to the drab, dingy house in Moor Street, Kenston. The structure was solid, and, on this chilly day, it was warm. Mr Barnes explained that although no rent was coming in, he had kept the heating on.

'It was prudent to keep it warm and dry, rather than risk burst pipes and damp,' he said. 'If you decide to sell, you'll get a better price for a warm dry house.'

'Yes. If I decide to sell,' said Louise, who was feeling slightly dizzy.

Mr Barnes showed her the dining room, which had a door opening into the kitchen. There was a cloakroom, with a row of hooks beside the washbasin. Upstairs there were two fair-sized bedrooms, a third small one, and a bathroom. She had slept in that small room on her few visits. There had been a serviceable iron bedstead with a lumpy mattress.

'It's got everything. I could have a lodger,' she said, rather wildly.

The house was completely bare, without even a chair, but the larger downstairs room had a recessed window seat, and there they sat while she and Mr Barnes discussed what she might do.

3

Andrew Sherwood had spent that afternoon with his former colleagues and had absorbed a good deal of liquid solace, which they found easier to supply than verbal sympathy. On the way to the station, he'd been tempted to return to Hazel's house to see if she and Nicky were back and extract a last farewell, but that would mean further upset for Nicky. Filled with self-pity and too much alcohol, he boarded the train and, blundering along it, found a seat into which he subsided.

It was dark outside now. Shortly after the train moved off, three youths and a girl, all holding open beer cans, the girl waving a lighted cigarette, lurched along the aisle past him, flapping their arms and shouting. The seated passengers shrank into their seats, leaning towards the windows, already apprehensive.

'Bloody yobs,' said a man three seats further down the coach, and one of the youths halted.

'You fucking say that again, shithead,' he said, standing over the man, swaying.

'I said bloody yobs,' said the man, and added, to the girl, 'Put that cigarette out. Smoking's not allowed.'

'What're you going to do about it, then?' said the girl, and puffed smoke, not at the speaker but into the face of a woman sitting beside him.

Andrew, half-asleep, woke at the disturbance, relieved that he was in the wake of the youths' passage; the commotion was several seats ahead. He saw a youth deliberately spit in the face of the man who had berated him, and one of his friends doused the woman. No one else in the carriage moved as the four proceeded to utter a string of taunts laced with obscenities at the seated passengers.

'Hurt your arm, dearie, have you?' one of the youths jeered. 'Does he knock you about, then? Shame on you,' he mocked.

Other passengers near the fracas studiously read their papers or looked out of the windows. No one tried to deal with the youths or the girl, but, Andrew thought, making no attempt himself, what could anyone do, unless four or five strong men collectively tried to grab them?

'Oh, leave her, the silly old bag,' said the girl, waltzing away from the youths and moving on down the coach, puffing aggressively at her cigarette.

This was an InterCity train. There must be a guard – or a conductor, he who welcomed you aboard and bade you keep control of your baggage. Andrew contemplated summoning this person, who would be there fast enough, if you lacked a ticket. If he pulled the cord to stop the train, the vandal group could soon disappear into other coaches and assume innocence. They were moving off now, marking their progress with further jeers and comments, but their message had been received and no one challenged them. The journalist in him was stirring, and then the man who had originally provoked the youths by his remark stood up, muttering, to allow the woman they had drenched with beer to leave her seat. She came stumbling towards Andrew, her piled-up greying hair and her white face wet, and he recognised the woman with her arm in a sling to whom Nicky had yielded his seat that morning.

Nicky had been chivalrous. Still somewhat drunk though he was, Andrew strove to follow his son's example. He pursued her down the coach and caught up with her at the door of the lavatory.

'Can I help? Did they hurt you?' he asked, as she struggled awkwardly to open the door.

Louise, who had been in a trance-like state of euphoria as she sat in the train on her homeward journey, glanced round, terror on her face.

'I'm quite all right,' she said. She was almost, but not quite, crying.

She had not recognised him.

Andrew said, 'We were on the train together this morning. My son Nicky and I. Do you remember?' He spoke gently.

'Oh – oh—' Sudden relief filled Louise. 'Oh yes,' she said, and then, more calmly, 'They didn't hurt my arm, but look at me. They poured beer over me.' As she spoke, she began to tremble.

At this point, a man approached from the other end of the train.

'Are you going to argue all evening or are you going into the toilet?' he demanded.

'Excuse me,' said Andrew, managing not to use cruder words. 'This lady has just been assaulted by some vandals. You can wait your turn or try elsewhere,' and with heavy dignity he opened the door for Louise. 'I'll wait outside for you,' he promised. 'Take as long as you like.'

She wouldn't be able to do much to improve her condition; she could hardly wash her hair in the train toilet compartment, even if she had the use of both hands.

The other man muttered something and pushed his way past Andrew, heading for the next coach. Hope he meets the vandals, thought Andrew uncharitably, shaking his fuddled head, trying to clear it. He wondered where the woman lived.

She remained in the lavatory for some time, during which interval Andrew realised he needed it himself; it was all that beer he had drunk, after the whiskies. Eventually, however, she reappeared, after he had seen off several more people who wanted to use the facilities. The original man had not returned. Perhaps the yobs had beaten him senseless, thought Andrew, with mean satisfaction. When she did emerge, she had done something about her hair, which she wore drawn back from her pale face and piled into a heavy French pleat. It looked sodden, and the front of the serviceable grey raincoat she had on was also very wet, but even so, fumes of beer rose from her. She managed a weak smile.

'Thank you for waiting,' she said. 'I'm all right now.'

'They won't come back,' said Andrew confidently, though he was far from certain. 'Hang on while I pop in there. We must report what happened to the railway police when we reach Paddington.'

He slipped into the compartment and closed the door. Inside, he rinsed his face well, hoping to sober himself up a bit, but when he came out, she had gone.

She couldn't have moved far. He walked back along the coach to where she had been sitting. The seat beside the man who had provoked the youths and the girl was empty, and the man himself was gazing into space. At least the gang hadn't been muggers.

'Did she come back here?' Andrew asked him. 'The woman those louts attacked?'

'No,' said the man. 'How could I know they'd turn on

her?' he demanded, as if Andrew had accused him of causing the assault.

'It's done now,' said Andrew. 'And I'm not getting at you. Are you prepared to make a statement to the police?'

'No,' said the man.

Andrew sighed.

'They'll do it again, to someone else,' he said.

'She wasn't hurt,' said the man.

'She already had a broken arm,' said Andrew.

'I know,' said the man, who had felt obliged to explain to the occupants of the facing seats and those on the far side of the aisle, that she was a total stranger. Andrew, however, disarmed him with his next remark.

'They'd have gone for someone. They were bent on causing trouble,' he said.

He turned away and began walking towards the front of the train. It would be easier to intercept her there when they arrived in London. He must make sure she was all right to travel onwards.

Two coaches along, he found her standing near the door.

'Hi,' he said. 'You didn't wait.'

Louise turned to face him. She was still ashen, but she looked more composed. 'I'm all right. I'm grateful to you, thank you, but I can manage.'

'How much further have you got to go?' he asked.

'Across to Waterloo. Then on to Kenston, but there are plenty of trains,' she said.

'I go that way, too,' he said. 'We'll go together. But we ought to report what happened,' he repeated. This was a through train, so those yobs would be getting off when they did; they were probably bound for a night out in town.

'No,' said Louise. 'I don't want trouble. If that man had

not spoken, they would have gone on up the train and left us alone.'

Andrew thought they'd probably been harassing other passengers, unless they'd collapsed in some vacant seats to drink their beer. One of the youths had been carrying a supermarket bag which rattled as if it held several cans. However, it was pointless to say this to the poor woman.

'Look, my name is Andrew Sherwood,' he said. 'What's yours?'

'Louise Widdows,' she told him. 'You're very kind,' she added. 'And you are right not to let Nicky travel alone until he's older and bigger.'

'We'll get a taxi to Waterloo,' he said. 'I go that way. My treat.'

But she wouldn't agree.

'I'm perfectly all right. I just smell dreadful. Once I get home and have a bath and wash my hair, I'll be myself again,' she insisted. A taxi would cost a fortune and this man, Andrew Sherwood, must need every penny he earned from whatever work he did to pay for Nicky and his mother, not to mention himself.

She set off in a determined way for the Underground entrance. It was usually quicker than a taxi, he conceded, especially in the evening like this when the traffic was dense, but he could see she was not familiar with the station by the way she was looking about for the entrance to the tube. He stayed close to her, and cast a wary glance around in case the youths reappeared, though if they had any sense they'd keep away from a former victim. But they had none: that was part of the problem; that, and no discipline in their lives.

The Underground train was very crowded but Louise found a seat and he stood close to her, watchfully. So might her son have stood protectively beside her, she thought, closing her eyes for a moment, admitting the fantasy. He'd be much the age of this kind Andrew Sherwood and by now he, too, might have a son like Nicky.

Richard had been a naval lieutenant when she knew him; the obituary notice referred to him as Captain, so he had done well, risen to senior rank. There was no mistake; there was his full name, with D.S.O. after it. He'd probably won the decoration in the Falklands. And what had he done after he retired?

Colin had been away on his second assignment in the Middle East when they met. Louise was living alone in the flat they had rented after his first overseas posting. It was on the outskirts of Portsmouth, and she was working as a cook at a local school. She was already a good cook, having helped her mother while she was growing up, and she had begun a catering course during Colin's first absence abroad. She completed it after his return, reminding him that not to do so would waste the fee already paid. At that time, and after his absence, she still retained some spirit though he could crush her with a word. Louise's mother, uneasy about her daughter, whom she seldom saw, had approved her seeking this further qualification and had paid for the catering course, which, state-run and subsidised, was not impossibly expensive. To Louise's surprise, Colin did not object. He said it would improve the standard of meals she prepared for him.

In their first years, he had not allowed her to work outside the home when he was there, and only rarely later, if an extra wage was essential. It was her job to provide sex when he required it, whether he could complete the act or not; cook, clean, and do the washing; and undertake most of the gardening when they had a plot, which was not always the case. He wanted to know where she was every minute of the day, and though he permitted her to do some voluntary work, he required her to be dependent on and accountable to him. However, with her husband again working abroad, things were different; she was required to fend for herself and he was not there to cross-examine her.

One Sunday, after taking a bus into the country, as she often did at fine weekends, Louise was enjoying a solitary walk. She had never had the knack of making friends, and spent most of her leisure time alone. She had crossed a stile and had almost immediately been knocked over by a large and friendly golden retriever which had bounded up as she stepped down. As she tried to save her balance she had twisted her ankle, and the group in charge of the dog – two men and a woman – had rushed over. One of the men had helped her up; the other had apologised – it was his dog. The woman had said Louise must come back with them for some reviving tea and allow them to look at her ankle. The two men agreed, and offered to carry her, both of them laughing, but she said she could manage. One of the men gave her the stick he carried and the other – Richard – offered his arm, which she took, for the ankle was extremely painful.

In the house, which was not far away – a red brick former farmhouse tucked in a fold of the hills – they ministered to her, one of the men making tea, the other finding ice while the woman helped her take off her boot and thick sock. The ankle was already quite swollen.

'You've probably sprained it,' said the woman. 'We should take you to a doctor.'

'Oh no,' said Louise. 'I'm sure it will soon be all right. Please don't worry.' She felt awkward and embarrassed, yet their solicitude seemed genuine and was difficult to resist as the woman made her comfortable on a sofa. 'You'll need a cold compress on this,' she said, and went to fetch cold water and a cloth.

Richard appeared with tea. He, it turned out, was spending the weekend with the couple; they owned this house and the husband was doing a course in Portsmouth with Richard. Both were in the navy.

Richard drove her home after they had all had tea, and Louise's ankle, soothed by the compress, had been bound with a crêpe bandage. He insisted on helping her upstairs and left her at the door of her flat.

During tea, they had learned her name and that her husband was in the Middle East on business.

'Will you really be all right?' he asked. 'All on your own?'

'Yes,' she said. She was better alone than with Colin. She had discovered that, and already dreaded his return.

'When is your husband due back?'

'I'm not sure, exactly,' she replied. 'Not for a while.'

'Then you must let me cheer you up in his absence,' said Richard. 'I'll come and see how you are tomorrow.'

And he did.

In the Kenston train, rescued once again, this time by Andrew Sherwood, it all came back to Louise.

The incident with the youths and the girl had shaken her badly. As the train travelled on through the darkness, she felt anxious in case other drunken youths or girls came roistering down the coach, but her fellow passengers were quiet, most of them late commuters going home. A few women had been on shopping trips, as was proved by the carrier bags on the overhead racks – Marks and Spencer, Harrods, John Lewis. A mobile phone sounded, and a man sitting behind Louise began an earnest conversation. Another man, not to be outdone, took his out and punched in a number. How convenient if you wanted to tell someone you would be late home, she thought. If there was someone there who cared.

She had a bench seat to herself, which was a relief, for she was deeply conscious of the strong smell of beer wafting from her coat; anyone sitting next to her would have been aware of it. Taking it to the cleaners would be embarrassing; she might risk washing it.

Andrew had asked if she was being met at Kenston: was there someone he could ring on her behalf? What about her husband?

'He – I—' she thought briefly of saying she was a widow, but discarded the idea. 'He's gone away,' she ended.

'Oh. So you'll be alone with your bad arm and a smelly coat,' Andrew stated.

'I can manage,' she assured him.

'A neighbour, perhaps,' he suggested. 'If you need help.'

'Yes,' she agreed. That was no lie; there were Sally and Bob Smith next door at number 35. Colin had a feud with the man on the other side, whose wild cherry tree overhung their garden, shedding pale pink petals in the spring and large, russet-coloured leaves in the autumn. It made a mess, he said. Louise, though, loved the tree, one of very few in their area; she watched for its first flowering, the fragile blossom so soon dispelled when there was a wind, and the fading of the leaves into their glorious shades, signalling the ending of another year.

Their garden was only a small patch, with a lawn and several beds in which Louise sowed seeds, raising various hardy flowers, and vegetables to help the budget. She acknowledged that it was disappointing for Colin to have reached retirement age without achieving professional distinction. For some unexplained reason he had failed to qualify as an accountant, but this had not stopped him finding those early overseas jobs. He told her he knew as much as anyone with rows of letters following their names. Colin was old enough to have done National Service; he had been in the paymaster's department in the army. That was all behind him when they met.

Now she wondered, anxiously, what if Colin had returned while she was away?

As the train drew in to Kenston station, this was her uppermost thought. If he were there, what could she say about where she had been? She could try pretending she had had a medical appointment and been delayed. It did not occur to her that, in such circumstances, she would be due an explanation of his absence. She felt exhausted and the strained muscles around her fractured ribs ached, but there were no taxis at the station. With her new affluence she could have justified the expense of one, but she was obliged to trudge up the road to the bus stop, where she had to wait for ten minutes before one came which connected with another to her nearest stop. This final stage of her journey took almost as long as the one from London. She sat in her beery aura, but at that hour others on the bus had sunk a pint or two, and Louise gazed straight ahead, her face impassive, determined to ignore any mockery there might be. The bus passengers, however, were not in party mood and her trip was uneventful. She descended awkwardly; once, there had been conductors who, if in a good mood, would give you a friendly helping hand, but now it was everyone for themselves as the central doors clanged open. She felt sorry for the drivers, who had to sell tickets as well as drive. She, at least, had a bus pass, which she had only to display.

It had started to rain. She was glad of it. It would rinse her hair and coat. She walked along, starting nervously when she heard a car, reminded of the night when she was hit, but she reached number 37 safely.

There were no lights on, and she couldn't see the car outside, but Colin could have parked it round the corner, and he might be waiting for her in the darkness. It had happened in the past, on the few occasions when she was out without his knowledge or consent.

4

If Colin's absence overseas had not been so long, Louise might have passed the baby off as his. Throughout history, women had successfully managed such deceptions, and over many generations illicit parentage had been a natural remedy for infertility. She wanted to have the child; it was Richard's, and she loved him. But he didn't love her. Not really. He had never said so.

'You're like a little orphan in the storm,' he had said, gathering her to him the first time it had happened. Within his arms, she had felt cherished and protected, and when he kissed her, gently to begin with and then more searchingly, she was quite unable to resist. Her sexual experience till now had been only with Colin, and it had never been like this; at last she understood what it meant to be swept away by passion.

Louise's ankle had recovered quickly, but Richard had made it an excuse to visit her, and had soon persuaded her to have dinner with him. For nearly two months their brief romance endured, and then his course was over and he went to sea, joining his new ship in Scotland. She never heard from him again, and if he ever returned to Portsmouth, by that time she had moved. To him, it had been a happy diversion; to her, a revelation.

Her pregnancy came as a shock. Before their marriage, she and Colin had not discussed having children, but she had expected a family as a natural consequence. Colin, however, soon told her that he did not want children and he sent her to a family planning clinic. She disliked using the diaphragm they gave her and was careless about it; also, Colin, even in the early years, was sometimes impotent, a fact he blamed on her. Louise would have welcomed a contraceptive failure; a child would have given her life some meaning. With Richard, she never thought about precautions until they had made love several times; when she remembered, it was too late.

After the first realisation of what had happened, Louise indulged a fleeting fantasy of a future with Richard, and, briefly, was ecstatic. She would leave Colin, get a divorce and marry Richard. Then she came down to earth. She could not divorce Colin; as the laws were at the time, there were no grounds. Colin was away; cruelty was difficult to prove unless there was evidence of violence; and desertion, as a reason, meant a three year separation. If Colin found out about the baby, he might, in anger, sue her for adultery, and if the father's identity were discovered, the scandal would destroy Richard's career. Louise knew he was ambitious. He must never learn the truth. So, though she could not protect herself, she protected him.

Unless Colin came on leave during his tour, which he had told her was unlikely, he would be away until after the baby was born. What was she to do? Like many another girl at that time, before abortion became legal and simple to obtain, Louise was frantic with worry. And she wanted the child. It was Richard's; she loved him and would always remember him with tenderness, even though he had already, it appeared, forgotten her. The baby would be special.

In later years, when single motherhood became accepted, even commonplace, Louise bitterly regretted that she had not managed, somehow, to walk out of her marriage and keep her son, but without money, it had seemed impossible. Her own mother, a respectable widow, had had a hard enough time. For the baby's own sake, it must be adopted.

Louise confided in no one. She went on working for as long as possible, wearing ever looser overalls; her morning sickness was soon over and she managed to endure the smell of the food she prepared. She was permanently tired, and her evenings were spent alone, listening to the radio or reading. She went to the public library several times a week. Louise had never socialised with the other catering staff at the school; they were older married women who had families to whom they hurried back after work. Towards the end of her pregnancy a few of them recognised her condition and assumed her husband, whom they knew to be overseas, had been home on leave. Louise did not deny it. She gave up her job at the end of the summer term, and, when the baby was born, surrendered him immediately for adoption. If anyone – a neighbour, or a former colleague – asked questions, she would say that he was stillborn; that would soon shut them up.

It worked out smoothly, except for her despair and misery at parting from her child. Her only other plan was to move from the area and, desperate, for once taking charge, she wrote to Colin, care of the company address he had given her, to say that as his return date was still uncertain, she had left the flat and moved to a cheaper one in Dover, where she had found work as a shop assistant. The deed was already done; if he objected, it was too late. Besides, he sent her only occasional short notes and had ceased to forward any money; she could no longer afford the rent in Portsmouth, where he had paid for three months in advance, leaving her to pay thereafter.

It was many years before she questioned these unusual arrangements. Had he really been abroad? If not, where was he?

During this time, while she was visibly pregnant, she had made excuses to avoid a meeting with her mother who had so staunchly brought her up single-handed, but who had expressed doubts about her marriage because it had happened so quickly after she met Colin.

'Wait a bit,' she had said. 'Get to know him better.' Wise advice, as Louise had belatedly realised.

Before their engagement, Colin was working for a building supplier. Louise, on temporary assignment from her secretarial school, had been sent to gain work experience in their offices. Typing invoices, very bored, she had met the new accounts manager, as he had styled himself, though in fact he was the accounts manager's assistant, literally a clerk.

He had asked her out almost at once, and Louise, who, unlike most of her fellow students, had never had a serious boyfriend, was easily flattered. She was still living with her mother and stepfather, and Colin, taking her home one evening after they had been to a cinema, was impressed when he saw the large, comfortable house where they were living. He had called for her the following Sunday and taken her on a river trip; that day, he had met her mother, and she impressed him, too.

Louise had told him Paul was her stepfather, but that had not stopped him from believing that she had a wealthy background. This, she later realised, had been her chief, perhaps her only attraction.

Louise refused her mother and Paul's invitation to go there

for Christmas after the baby, whom she had called David, was born. She made the excuse of the shop being open on Christmas Eve and the day after Boxing Day, but she had more genuine reasons. If she were to go there, she would find it too difficult to leave again when the visit had to end, and her mother would be worried by her pallor and her obvious exhaustion. At that time, post-natal depression was barely recognised but Louise knew that her constant fatigue and sense of desolation were due to giving up her infant. At times she felt suicidal, but she cherished the fantasy that one day she might see Richard again.

She thought about her baby constantly, and most particularly on his birthday. Since his birth, new regulations had made it possible for adopted children to seek out their parents, but it did not work the other way. Parents could, however, express their willingness to be traced, and now, with his father dead, Louise was at last free to take this step. She had put her name on the register immediately.

Louise walked up to the door of her unlit, rented house, and turned the key.

Andrew wrote up the story of the train journey as a feature for his magazine, emphasising his own cowardice in not tackling the vandals but stating, also, that even if a group of burly male passengers had joined in, the results might have been serious. His theme was the need for guards on trains, and he stressed that while more and better public transport was required, people would not use it if they felt unsafe or threatened. In this instance, the hooligans had picked on a woman they could see had already been injured for her arm was in a sling.

While he was with her, he had briefly forgotten his fears about Nicky and his sadness at their separation. He didn't really think Terry was unkind to the boy, but he did not love him, might not even like him, although he was his mother's lover. Love the mother, not the child – though, for her sake, Terry might do his best.

Val, who worked in advertising, had found Andrew remote and silent when they met that night; he had also had too much to drink, but that was not unusual after he had taken Nicky home. It was all rather difficult and she was glad she had not moved in with him, though she often stayed over. Her own flat in Streatham, which he sometimes visited, was larger and more comfortable but tonight they were at Andrew's, which was in a grey, featureless block. Val was not too sure where this relationship was going. The trouble was that any interesting man she met carried baggage from, if not a marriage either in progress or collapsed, a series of liaisons; but she also had a history, though she had never married and had no children in tow. She wanted them, however, and was it wise to encumber them with a much older stepbrother? Not that she and Andrew were anywhere near such a commitment; theirs was a comparatively recent pairing. But if she moved on from him, when or where would she find another unattached man of the right age, to whom she might be drawn? She sighed, poured him a glass of wine to add to what he had already consumed, and asked him to tell her all about his day.

He did not mention his return to the house to deliver Nicky's forgotten weekend bag, and his donkey Fred, nor the temptation he had felt to break in and trash the place, resisted because it would put him in line for a charge of breaking and entering, or at least a court injunction to stay away, and Nicky would be the loser. Instead, he confessed that he had met some of his old mates, and then he told her about the fracas on the train. Val, though disgusted, was not surprised; she had witnessed several unpleasant incidents on trains and avoided eye contact with other passengers herself.

'What was she like?' asked Val. 'Was she old?'

'Not young. Sixty-ish, perhaps,' said Andrew. 'She was quiet, respectable. Very small and thin. By coincidence, she was on the same tube train in the morning as we were, going to Paddington. Nicky gave her his seat. You could tell she was astonished.'

'I bet she was,' said Val.

'She had her arm in a sling,' Andrew explained.

'That makes the assault even worse,' said Val. 'But I expect it gave the kids a real high. There's nothing like bashing up the weak and vulnerable. Makes you feel really great.'

The house was empty. Louise searched every room, to make sure Colin was not hiding somewhere, waiting to pounce.

He had never actually hit her; if he had, she thought she really might have found the courage to leave. There could have been marks to prove she had been struck, and nowadays the police were obliged to take heed of domestic violence. However, he had often stood over her menacingly and had gripped her arm and raised his fist, glowering into her terrified face, threatening her with actions when he had run out of angry words. He would crowd her at the sink, coming up behind her and breathing into the back of her neck, calling her a useless cow. He would push his plate aside when she had taken extra pains over a meal, saying it was not fit to eat; he would throw a freshly ironed shirt at her, complaining that it was creased and unwearable; he would expect her to polish his shoes; he told her she was hideous; and, worst of all, he called her a barren husk. This, she concluded, had become the reason for his hatred.

For now he wanted children, or so he said, quite frequently, when he could not find a new excuse for taunting her.

'A man needs a son,' he declared.

'You've changed your mind.' The first time he took this line, she found the courage to challenge him.

'Since my travels, yes. Sons mean a lot to the men who have been my colleagues,' he said.

Louise, too, began to yearn for a child. If she had another, she might be able to forget the one she had given away and so she was helped to endure Colin's sexual onslaughts. For years his efforts, however frequently attempted, were unsuccessful, and whenever the failure was patently his, he blamed her for being plain and unappealing. Then, at last, she did become pregnant, only to miscarry at nine weeks, and there were four more miscarriages, spread over eleven years. They had moved from rented house to rented house three times during this period, and only once had they remained in the same area. Finally the doctor attending her advised her to accept her situation and go on the pill. She was nearly forty, tired, anaemic, and depressed. Further disappointment would only be more debilitating. Find work with children, the doctor suggested; that would channel her maternal instincts in a positive direction.

It was good advice, and she took it, answering an advertisement for someone to meet two children from school, take them home and look after them until their mother returned from work. After she was happily settled in the job, with the children used to her and she to them, affection developing among them and Louise with a little money of her own, Colin decided that they had to move again.

She did not protest. He said then, as he had before, and was to repeat, that he was going to a better position in yet another new area.

Each move kept her busy. The former house must be surrendered, spotless, to the landlord after the removal van had loaded their possessions, the unloading supervised, and the new house rendered comfortable and clean. Each move meant a demanding few weeks which occupied such energy as she managed to muster, and each move gave her the hope that a fresh start would bring improvement, but it did not happen. At intervals Louise contemplated leaving Colin, but where would she go, and how would she manage? She couldn't run back to her mother, upsetting her and Paul, who had no obligation to help her; after years with Colin, she had absorbed some of his opinions and it never occurred to her that her stepfather might be more than willing to offer support and succour. She couldn't divorce Colin; in law, he had done nothing wrong, whereas she had been unfaithful and had borne another man's child. Her guilt weighed her down; that, and for a long time the hope of another baby, sustained her until acceptance had become a habit, such initiative as she had once possessed had been destroyed, and it was too late to rebel.

But now it seemed that he had gone.

When she was satisfied that Colin was not in the house, Louise put her raincoat, which a label inside declared to be washable, in the washing-machine – this house had one already fitted, so she was spared washing everything by hand, or making trips to a launderette as had often been her lot – and ran a bath, in which she washed her hair, managing to keep her plastered arm out of the water, though it was awkward. Then she filled a hot-water bottle, made herself a mug of Horlicks, and went to bed. She had a lot to think about: the expedition she had undertaken, the extraordinary news which Mr Barnes had given her, and her encounter on the train, both with the hooligans and with kind Andrew Sherwood and his son. And her future.

Louise spent the next day preparing for that future. Mr Barnes had advised her not to decide anything in a hurry; Lilac Cottage would not run away, and meanwhile it would involve her in no cash outlay. He had explained that two years before her mother's death, the property had been conveyed to trustees in an accumulation and maintenance trust. The rent was paid into this, and it was used for the external upkeep of the house, for which the landlord was accountable, while the internal repairs and decoration were the responsibility of the tenant. Mr and Mrs Johnson, her mother's last tenants, who had a long lease but could not sub-let, had been meticulous. The rest of the rent money accumulated interest in the trust, with the income to be paid to Louise after her mother died. Apart from a few pieces of jewellery and some personal possessions of no great worth, this was all her mother left. At the time of her death the value of Lilac Cottage fell below the qualifying amount for inheritance tax and there was none to pay. All this Mr Barnes had revealed, sitting on the window seat with Louise after they had toured the house. He had privately regretted that there were no tea-making facilities in the cottage, for his client looked as if she could do with a cup, but they had had one at the station buffet before they parted. She had promised to get in touch when she had thought things over, but Louise already knew that she would move into Lilac Cottage as soon as she could make whatever arrangements were necessary.

Colin was officially the sole tenant of 37 Moor Street, Kenston, so he, not Louise, was liable for the rent. If it was not paid, they would be evicted, and if he did not return,

Louise would not be spared, though she supposed that the social services would house her somewhere.

She should never have gone back to him after his return from overseas. She had known it then, but guilt and her own misery had denied her the strength and determination to stand alone. In life, you met various crossroads and you might take a path which could set you astray for ever; sometimes there was a chance to divert, to step aside and find a way to pass hazards, but you needed to have a goal. She had never had one; she had entered marriage because, after working for a while at some routine job, that was what girls did then, and she had stayed in it, because however it turned out, you did that too, and you acquired the habit, seeing no alternative. Now, however, at this late stage in her life, she had a chance to make a new start, and if Colin had not left home, it might not have been possible, for he would have found out about Lilac Cottage and claimed it as his.

Where had he gone? What had made him leave?

In just a few hours her perception of their long years together had been reversed, for, until today, she had been wondering what she had done to drive him off. But would he come back? If he did, he might trace her and decide to move into Lilac Cottage too. It wouldn't be impossible for him to find her, despite use of the public telephone to prevent him tracing calls.

There must be a way to keep him out. She would have to confide her fears to Mr Barnes. After all, he was a solicitor; it was his job to know about such things.

Sitting with a cup of coffee at the kitchen table – not in the tiny dining room where Colin insisted they eat every meal: no lowered standards for him – Louise looked sadly back over the long wasted years.

Why had they moved so often? Her mother had asked that

question, and Louise, obstinately loyal and believing what Colin told her, had replied that he had the chance of a better job in the new area; he had not been appreciated in the former post but now his abilities would be recognised at last.

'And they are?' Paul, her stepfather, had been unable to hold back the question any longer.

'Well, he's highly skilled at accounting,' Louise had retorted. 'A stickler for accuracy.' This was true; her own expenditure was examined minutely and she had to record every transaction in the tiniest detail.

'Too skilled, perhaps,' Paul had muttered. 'Got to move on.'

But what he implied couldn't be true. Colin couldn't have been falsifying accounts and leaving before he was detected, for if that were so, they would have more money. As it was, they seemed to be worse off with every change, and they never owned a house but always rented.

'So that he can do a flit,' Paul had later said to Louise's mother, Susan, in the privacy of their bedroom. It had been his idea that she should make the arrangement about Lilac Cottage; he had neither liked nor trusted Colin, and regretted that Louise had never felt herself to be truly part of his family, hence her early rush into marriage. Susan's own future was secure because she would receive a pension, and he had left her the house for her lifetime, after which it reverted to his own children. As it was, she had died first, and he, though intending to keep in touch with Louise, had failed to do so when he moved to France, and she, apart from a stiff little note at Christmas and his birthday, had kept her silence. He had left Louise a thousand pounds in his will; Colin had insisted that they use the money to buy a new car, their old one having become expensive to maintain.

Long ago, seeds of doubt had been sown in Louise's mind.

Maybe he was a gambler, betting on horses or dogs and borrowing company funds to indulge his habit. You read about such cases in the paper. But she didn't really believe that this was the truth. Something, however, had caused him to leave home in a hurry, and to run her over, for the car had been deliberately driven at her and she was now convinced it was Colin at the wheel. He had meant to kill her. If he found her, he might try again.

What could be behind it all? She had accepted his more recent explanations about staff cuts or that, through unfairness, someone else had got promotion and he had felt obliged to resign. Now that he had reached retirement age, paid work was hard to find. In Kenston, he kept the books for a local newsagent, rewarded with what he called a pittance, and, unpaid, those of the British Legion, a local heritage society, and the community centre. He volunteered Louise's services as a tea-maker, cook, and washer-up at functions, often held for charity, in the centre, and on these occasions he would pace round the hall, nodding regally at those participating. Had he gone off with their money? She knew no more now about how his mind worked than when they first married; he would discuss nothing with her, merely tell her what he expected her to do, spelling out her role. She was cook, cleaner, and failed mother, and she was more accountable in these years than ever before, because he had more time to supervise her actions.

During earlier years she was sure he did go to an office when he left the house each day, but was he employed as an accountant? For all she knew, and for the amount he seemed to be paid, he could have been making the tea or sweeping floors. Meanwhile, her own apathy and her restricted domestic life, with the need to guard her tragic secret, inhibited her from intimacy with anyone she met when she was working herself. Louise, driven by necessity, found occasional part-time jobs, sometimes as a shop assistant, and once she had been a waitress, but Colin, recognising that her wages were, at the time, essential, nevertheless made it plain that such menial employment was beneath their social status.

Which was what? She never challenged him, aware that he saw himself as a professional man, on a level with doctors, lawyers, architects and the like, but he was merely an accounts clerk, which was not the same as being qualified, and they had never owned their own house.

'It leaves us free,' he'd said. 'I can move if I wish and the rise and fall of house prices and mortgage rates are immaterial.'

She had not pressed it. Each time they moved, she tried to be optimistic about the fresh location, Colin's new position, and the chance offered by a fresh beginning, but nothing changed and every rented house was a little lower down the scale than the last.

She should have left him before she was too old to make a future for herself. Instead, she had existed from day to day in a grey fog of despair.

Why had he tried to kill her? What would he achieve by her death except his freedom? He could have gained that by a divorce; she would not have opposed it. She had nothing of value which he could expect to inherit; he had not known about Lilac Cottage. Mr Barnes had hinted that it might be wise for her to make a will, now that she had property.

'You probably already have a solicitor,' he had tactfully suggested. 'If not, we, at Barnes and Locock, would be happy to act for you.'

He was right, but who should be her beneficiary? It ought to be her own son, but how could he be found? It was up to the adopted child to find his mother. After she moved, she must make sure her address was altered on the register. David would already have access to his file and birth details, but why would he want to get in contact with her? He would not have forgiven her for abandoning him, for he would view it in that light.

She had committed several wrongs at that time, but no criminal acts. Perhaps Colin also had something to conceal, something illegal. Had he broken the law, and she, unwittingly, had information that could prove it? It seemed impossible, but Louise had never asked questions. When she was puzzled about decisions Colin made, arbitrarily, without consulting her at all, she had sometimes felt like protesting, but to do so would provoke an argument, and she soon adopted an attitude of passive acceptance.

She went through each room of the sombre little house, looking in every drawer and cupboard for any evidence there might be as to Colin's activities, and, indeed, his whereabouts, but he had left nothing behind. He must have worked fast, doing all this in the few hours while she was at the hospital shop. He had acted to a careful, cold and calculated plan.

She'd do the same, and quickly, lest, knowing she had not died, he returned to complete the job.

But did he know? He had been gone for over a fortnight. Her accident had not made headline news, merely attracting a paragraph in the local paper. If she had died, it might have been more widely reported, but probably not: she was not important. One of her colleagues from the shop had driven her home from hospital, an act of kindness that had almost overwhelmed her, and after reading Mr Barnes's letter, Louise had arranged to see him without delay. Mr Barnes had given her no details on the telephone. In the few days which elapsed between this conversation and today's visit, she had grown stronger, but she was very tired after her long excursion. Nervous energy, however, drove her on, for she was terrified that Colin would return before she could escape. She would not let her broken arm or her fractured ribs delay her. Used to moving house, she now arranged her own removal.

At Oxford station, over their cups of tea while waiting for her train, she had at last found the courage to tell Mr Barnes that Colin had left home on the day of her accident and she did not know his whereabouts.

'I suppose my mother was uneasy about him – I know my stepfather was,' she said. 'That was why she kept the cottage a secret.'

'You may be right. I never met your mother,' Mr Barnes diplomatically replied. 'No doubt she wished to protect your interests.'

'A mother would, wouldn't she? Probably,' said Louise.

'Yes,' agreed Mr Barnes. 'It's natural.'

When Louise rang him the following day, the swiftness of her decision to move into the cottage was not altogether a surprise.

Louise notified the police. She telephoned, and eventually managed to speak to one of the officers who had interviewed her in the hospital. WPC Rogers said she would come and see her that afternoon.

'How's your arm?' asked Wendy Rogers, entering the house. The interior was stark and depressing. She had been one of the officers deputed to tell Colin about his wife's accident, only to find he was not at home, and though Sally Smith at number 35 knew Louise slightly, no one knew much about Mr Widdows.

'Much better, thank you,' said Louise.

Because she had already managed to admit an element of marital disharmony to Mr Barnes, she found it easier, now, to do the same to the police officer, adding that as Colin had departed without a word of explanation, she intended to do the same.

'I must tell you my plans, though,' she said. 'I don't want you thinking I'm missing.'

'We may need you if we find whoever ran you down,' said Wendy Rogers, who had not forgotten the incident. Louise had been able to say that the car had driven directly at her, turning its lights on as she approached.

'Perhaps the driver didn't see me,' she had said. 'But he did go on to the pavement.'

'I want to catch him,' Wendy said now. 'You could have been killed.' Although the general police view was that it had been a joyrider, and that Louise had simply happened to be in the way, Wendy Rogers was less certain; she did not share her colleagues' opinion that the husband's disappearance was a coincidence.

Assuring her that under no circumstances would the police give Colin her address, Wendy Rogers told Louise that if Colin reported her missing, all the police had to do was to tell him that she was safe; they were not bound to tell him where she was. With this promise, Louise gave her Barnes and Locock's address. Mr Barnes would know where to find her.

After the police officer had gone, Louise went to the call box and rang a furniture dealer who specialised in house clearances. He came round that afternoon and offered her a price for the contents, apart from the few things she wished to keep which had been her mother's. She bargained with him briefly, managing to extract an extra sixty pounds, and he agreed to remove everything the following day, paying cash.

5

Andrew Sherwood had not told Val the whole story of the incident with the vandals. Before he and Louise Widdows had parted – he had insisted on seeing her into the train for Kenston and finding her a compartment where her fellow passengers appeared to be normal, law-abiding people – she had suddenly said to him, 'I shall be leaving Kenston. I've inherited a house – I saw it today – isn't it wonderful?'

Andrew had called after her, 'Congratulations,' watched her settle in a seat, waved, and walked away, but he could not dismiss the encounter from his mind. Mrs Widdows was a conventionally respectable woman, rather diffident, whose husband had gone away. Where to? There might be a story behind her inheritance of a house, he mused. It lay somewhere to the west of Reading, for she had remained on the train after he and Nicky had left, and she was already on the London-bound train when he returned. That left a selection of stations – Didcot, Oxford, Swindon: the train had stopped at all of them. He'd have no opportunity to look out for her on the train again, for when Nicky's next visit was due, his licence would have been restored and he would be back on the road.

Meanwhile, he had decided to search for Mrs Widdows. He

knew that she lived in Kenston. He would look in the telephone directory for anyone of that name, and ring them all until he found her.

His early efforts met with no success. There were two people listed with that name and with addresses in the town. The first one he tried, C. D. Widdows, at 37 Moor Street, did not reply. A woman answered the other call, and when he said he was trying to find Mrs Louise Widdows, she told him that her name was Joan. He asked her if, by any chance, she knew the other Mrs Widdows but she did not. He tried the first number again, several times over twenty-four hours, but there was still no reply. Whoever lived there must be away. If it was Louise's house, had she joined her absent husband?

For a few days, busy with other stories and researching a piece about a politician who was in the news for unpolitical reasons, Andrew put the matter to the back of his mind. At the weekend, without Nicky, he went to a health club he had joined and did a thorough work-out, then met Val and they decided to have dinner at a Greek restaurant across the river. Val had just taken on a new account and was fired with enthusiasm, keen to find an original slant to promote the product, a herbal soap. Natural ingredients were attractive to the discriminating purchaser, said Val, and the makers believed they were on to something special which would benefit those with allergies, even eczema. They discussed this for some time before returning to his flat. On Sunday morning, while Val was having a shower, Andrew tried C. D. Widdows again, with still no reply.

They went shopping in the afternoon. Andrew bought an electric sandwich maker, and Val bought some clothes. The next day she was going to a conference in Manchester and would be away for most of the week. Andrew had an appointment on Monday morning to interview a bright new actress who was attracting good notices, and after that he had some desk work to do. He could write the interview up at home, any time, as with Val away, his evenings would be free unless some work arose. Working on a magazine was more predictable than the paper, but he had always enjoyed the buzz of a sudden story. He decided to go to Kenston on Tuesday. There might be nothing special about Louise Widdows and her house, but in that case he could forget about the woman.

He mentioned it to Val.

'I expect her aunt left it to her, something like that,' said Val. 'Forget it.' She had noticed before that he worried over things and events she would long since have forgotten, writing scenarios about people they saw in the street, wondering where a certain man might live or where an old woman was going. He had too much imagination for his own good, she often thought, aware that he fretted about Nicky's relationship with Terry and the effect of the marriage break-up on the boy.

'I'll try,' he answered. 'After all, she was just a woman with a broken arm.' But when he spoke to her outside the lavatory compartment in the train she had looked terrified, flinching away. Why? Wouldn't any other woman have done the same?

Since one was with him, he asked her.

'You surprised her, I suppose,' she said slowly. 'If I'd been surprised by some man at the door, I might have turned round sharply – I might have thought it was a try-on, I suppose. I could have told him to get lost – unless I fancied him, of course,' she added, slyly.

'I thought it showed that she was in a highly nervous state,' he said. Her levity, which at another time he would have found amusing, seemed inappropriate now.

'Well, she'd just had beer poured over her and listened to a string of abuse, so I'm not surprised she was startled,' said Val.

But Louise's fear was not simply a reaction to her unpleasant experience with the yobs. She was a frightened woman.

Val had heard enough about the woman on the train. Andrew's speculations, if over-indulged, could become exasperating. She wondered, idly, if Hazel's Terry were more pragmatic.

Andrew drove to Kenston on Tuesday morning. It was good to drive the car again. The day was damp and cold but he didn't notice the weather in town as much as he used to when he lived on the edge of Reading. You were aware of wet or dry, wipers on, wipers off. Today there was a bit of both. When he reached Kenston, his first call would be the public library, for there he could study the voters' list and search for Mrs Louise Widdows. He had a feeling that the not-answering C. D.Widdows at 37 Moor Street might prove to be his target, but it would be easier to check that at the library and, if it were the right address, ask for directions, rather than seek out the street first. Libraries could usually be found without much difficulty. He discovered this one after driving around a number of streets between rows of unprepossessing shops and eventually asking for directions from a traffic warden. Kenston was an agglomeration of drab residential estates and sprawling industrial areas; today, it seemed singularly uninviting, with no relieving patches of green, and without even a building that pleased the eye, or not that he could see from the car. The library however was in an imposing Victorian gothic pile that had once housed the council, until it moved to custom-built modern premises on the site of a former hospital. Andrew learned all this when he went inside and found a librarian with time to chat. He liked libraries; he had spent hours in them in the course of his work. He also liked most librarians. This one was young, with curly red hair and freckles, and steel-framed glasses; he wondered if she really needed the spectacles or if they were a prop to help her conform to the received image of the studious librarian. She had large amber eyes, into which he gazed, through her lenses, as he asked for the voters' list. After a short search he found Moor Street, and there, at number 37, dwelt Colin D. Widdows and Louise M. Widdows.

'Bingo,' he said aloud, attracting very little notice; public libraries, though not noisy, were no longer the silent places of his childhood.

Andrew returned the list. Then he had a thought.

'Do you know Louise Widdows?' he asked the librarian. He had already produced his press card to give his mission credence. 'I met her recently, and she gave me her address, but I've lost it,' he added artlessly.

'Oh yes, I know Mrs Widdows,' said the girl. 'How is she?'

'How is she? Oh, you mean after breaking her arm,' he said.

'Breaking her arm? She broke some ribs as well,' said the girl. 'And she had concussion. She was in hospital for quite a while. I don't think they've got whoever did it.'

'Was she attacked?' That could account for her terror in the train.

'No. It wasn't like that. It was a road accident. A hit and run,' said the librarian. 'Didn't she tell you?'

'No.' But he hadn't asked her.

'She never says a lot,' said the girl. 'She brought some books back when she came out of hospital, but she didn't take any more out, which was unusual. She's quite a reader.'

'Maybe she's moved,' said Andrew, but would she have, so soon?

'She didn't say she planned to, or not to me,' said the librarian. She looked put out. 'We always chatted. She liked me to suggest books she might enjoy. I broadened her range a bit, got her interested in some good modern authors.' At this point the librarian indicated that she had other duties. 'I'm always being told off for chatting, but it's interesting,' she said.

'Yes, it is,' he agreed with warmth. 'What's your name?'

'Clare Fairweather,' she said. 'Awful, isn't it?' and went away, hiding her mirth.

Andrew, too, was laughing as he returned to his car. He was going to Moor Street now, to see if Mrs Widdows was at home.

Before arriving, he tried telephoning from his mobile; it would be more civil than simply turning up, but there was still no answer.

As he was legitimately parked at a meter with time in hand, he went back into the library to ask Clare Fairweather where Moor Street was, but she was nowhere to be seen, having been sent off to the stacks by one of her superiors. However, another librarian was able to answer his question and told him where he could buy a street map.

Andrew drove slowly along Moor Street, studying the numbers on the houses; the even ones were on one side, the odd on the other, and they did not match their opposites, so that 37 was opposite 56, which must confuse the postman. It was a quiet area; there were only a few cars in the road. On a weekday morning, most people were at work. If Mrs Widdows had a job, her injured arm might prevent her from carrying out her duties.

He stopped the car outside the small detached house. It was

identical to its neighbours, built of a yellowy brick which must have been glaringly ugly when it was new, but it had weathered to a dull, bilious colour, darkened today by the rain. Andrew studied it from the pavement before he walked up the short path between narrow flowerbeds, bare of growth, to the front door, where he rang the bell. He heard it echo inside, but no one answered as he waited on the step. He rang again, with no result, so he stepped on to the apology for a lawn and, shading his eyes with his hand, he peered in through the ground-floor window. The room appeared to be empty; there was nothing to be seen, just bare floorboards with a dark stained edging round the central square. Andrew went to the back of the house and looked into the kitchen. It was fitted out with lime-green units, worn and shabby, but there was not an article of furniture, nor a utensil visible. He glanced at the small rear garden. It had been tidied up before the winter. A climbing rose was tethered to the fence at one side; the branches of a tree from the neighbouring house hung over the other side, and in the damp earth beneath it Andrew could see the fragile pale green tips of daffodils tentatively showing.

Andrew had been seeking Louise Widdows on little more than a whim; now his suspicion that there was a story here grew stronger. He went to the house in whose garden the tree was growing, and rang the bell. No one answered, so he tried the other side, where someone was at home; he heard a distant sound that might be a radio, and just before he rang again, the door was opened. A woman in jeans and a green sweatshirt with a hedgehog appliquéd to its front stood there. She held a small baby in her arms.

'I'm sorry to bother you, but I'm looking for Mrs Widdows. Louise Widdows,' he said. 'She seems to have moved. Do you know where I can find her?'

'No, I don't,' said the woman.

She saw a dark-haired man in his mid-thirties, wearing an anorak and brown cord trousers. He did not look like a rapist or a burglar, but you could never be sure.

'I'm a reporter,' said Andrew, reading her mind and taking a chance. He produced his press card again.

'Oh – is it about her accident?' said the woman. 'You'd better come in,' and she stood back to admit him. He followed her past a scatter of toys – small cars and bricks – to the kitchen. 'Sorry about the mess,' she said. 'I've got a three-year-old as well as this one. He's at nursery school. I'll have to go and fetch him soon.'

'I won't hold you up,' Andrew promised. 'Tell me about the accident.'

'I don't know much. It happened in the evening – around seven o'clock. She'd just come back from the hospital – she helped in the shop there, though I didn't know that till after-wards, when the police came looking for her husband.'

'Oh?' Andrew prompted.

'To tell him she'd been hurt,' said the woman. 'He wasn't there, though.'

'Did you see the accident?'

'No. Bob and I were having our meal. The first we knew was when the ambulance came. The people opposite heard a car roar up the road, but no one saw anything. Someone walking down the road from the bus stop, like she was, found her lying on the pavement, unconscious,' said the woman. 'I don't think she'd been there long. Ten minutes, perhaps.'

'And her husband?' asked Andrew.

'He'd gone. Left. No one knows when. The police said that he normally fetched her from the hospital, but he didn't that night.'

'When did you last see him?'

'I can't remember. Ages ago. He – both of them – kept to themselves,' she replied. 'But that suited me and Bob. They weren't our sort.'

'What do you mean?'

'Well, they were older, for one thing. Retired. I think he helped with a charity or something but I don't really know. I never spoke to him. She and I were quite friendly. To tell the truth, I felt sorry for her,' the woman, Sally Smith, admitted.

'Why?'

'Well, she went nowhere – they didn't enjoy themselves like retired people are supposed to. Like my gran and grandad.'

'Hm,' said Andrew. 'Well, the house seems to be empty now. Has it been sold?'

'There's been no board up,' said the woman. 'Could have gone privately, I suppose. Maybe the building society fore-closed,' she added, more grimly. 'Look, sorry, but I've got to go.'

'And you've no idea where Louise Widdows has gone? She didn't leave an address?'

'Not with me,' said Sally. 'I saw a van loading up all the furniture, and that was it. Maybe she's gone to wherever he is. Maybe they owed money round here.'

She was impatient to be off, bundling the baby into a zipped padded nest before stowing him in a pushchair. Andrew's mother had a theory that pushchairs for tiny children sowed the seeds of future belligerence because the mothers used the pushchairs to batter their way through approaching pedestrians. There was something in this, Andrew decided, watching the woman stride down the road, the child in its chariot a trail-blazer before her, but there were few other people about in this residential street. It was different in crowded shops and town centres; it must be frightening to stare out at masses of advancing legs like a forest on the march.

Andrew crossed the road and rang the bell at number 56, and after some delay a man answered. He was much Andrew's age, but unshaven and with unbrushed, greasy hair. He blinked at Andrew, who repeated his apology and explained again that he was looking for Mrs Widdows.

'Who's she?' demanded the man.

'From the house opposite. Thirty-seven,' said Andrew. 'She had a road accident,' he added.

'Oh her – I didn't know the name,' said the man.

'She's moved out,' Andrew persisted.

'Yeah – went off in a transit van full of stuff, a chair and table, boxes and that,' said the man.

'A transit van? Not a furniture van?' Andrew asked.

'No. That was the day before,' said the man. 'She went next morning in the transit.'

This defeated member of the human race had told him more than the brisk, capable mother. Perhaps he had nothing to do except watch the movements in the street.

Andrew thanked him and then tried two more houses on that side of the road, but learned nothing new. No one seemed acquainted with Mr or Mrs Widdows, and he realised that only the fact of the road accident had made them aware of the couple's existence. He decided to return to the library, where Clare Fairweather would give him the voters' list again so that he could check the names of his two informants. He would find their telephone numbers, too, and he would look in the Yellow Pages for removal firms, but even if he rang them all, would they disclose where they had transported Louise Widdows and her furniture?

He could try them.

6

Louise, sitting beside Roy Crampton in the transit van transporting her and her belongings to Croxbury, was elated. She had done it! She had cleared the house and got away without Colin catching her in the act.

It was the taxi firm who had suggested the transit van. Still trying not to leave a trail, Louise, using the call box, had telephoned a firm which often took people to and from the hospital and whose drivers sometimes came into the shop for cups of tea or coffee while they waited for their passengers. She had met Mr Crampton more than once in this way, and on the telephone had explained where she wanted to go and that she would have more baggage than could fit comfortably into a car, as it included some furniture and several boxes. She had kept the kitchen equipment, which she had acquired over the years and which Colin never touched, for he did not cook. It would be expensive to replace and she would need it; cooking was her one skill which might be marketable.

She didn't know how she was going to exist at Lilac Cottage in the long term. Mr Barnes, on the telephone – as before, she used a call box – had assured her that there was enough in the trust fund, now waiting to be wound up, to tide her over for some time, and she had her building society money. She had withdrawn seven hundred pounds from her account in cash because there was nothing in the bank to honour cheques, and she was going to need money to achieve the move, though she had only a vague idea of what it would cost; as soon as she could, she would have the building society balance transferred to a local branch. Her only income would be her state pension, but she told herself she would be able to add to that by finding some sort of work, even at her age, when her broken bones had healed. However, there was always the possibility of a lodger, as she had originally thought, once she had enough furniture in the house. At the back of her mind was the fantasy that she would somehow trace her son. Then he would come and stay. What a dream! She let herself indulge it.

Mr Barnes had agreed that someone from his firm, if not himself, would be at Lilac Cottage at three o'clock on Friday to give her the key. At the earliest opportunity after that they would sort out the paperwork that must be done, but since she was so eager to move in straight away, there was no reason at all why she should not do so. What about her furniture? When would it arrive?

She explained that she would be bringing only the minimum, things that had been her mother's or were incontestably her own. She did not tell him the fate of the rest, lest he advise against such drastic action. Lawyers were cautious people.

Proving the truth of that assumption, he asked her if she was certain she had given her decision enough consideration, and Louise assured him that she had.

The sun shone wanly as Roy Crampton drove her away through the outskirts of Kenston, past rows of houses and small shops and the sprawling industrial area towards the link road leading to the M25. Roy, agreeing with Louise's fear that his taxi would not be large enough to transport what she wanted to move, had said he could borrow a van and do the job quite easily. He would leave Friday's taxi trips to his wife and his son, who were his relief drivers, and he brought a lad along to help, his grandson, who now sat in the back of the transit among Louise's possessions. The two of them had loaded up in no time at all, the lad whistling as he did so and Roy telling her not to worry, they'd soon fix this little lot. Louise had not wasted a moment; it was only three days since she had first seen Lilac Cottage, and already problems which, a week ago, she would have thought insoluble had been resolved as if by the wave of a wand. Mr Crampton seemed eager to help, just like the furniture dealer whose payment would more than meet Mr Crampton's bill, and cover a tip for the lad.

In the hospital shop, Louise and her fellow helpers had worked together as a team; that was one of the things she had liked about the job. Now, to a greater degree, she was experiencing something very rare in her life: support, not hostile opposition. As the van travelled on, she relaxed, leaning her head against the side of the van, and it was not long before, exhausted, she fell asleep, tidily and quietly, strapped into her seat beside Mr Crampton.

Their journey would take three hours, maybe a little more, depending on the traffic, Mr Crampton had said. Louise woke once or twice when they had to stop and start at various roadworks on the motorway, and at last she made an effort to stay awake, apologising to Mr Crampton.

'Tiring work, moving,' was his response. She seemed to be doing some sort of flit with her few bits and pieces, this faded woman whom he had barely noticed at the hospital. He had

seen that the house she was leaving in Moor Street was empty;
after a moment's hesitation, she had posted her key through
the door when the van was loaded and they were ready to
leave. 'The bed's there already, is it?' he asked. 'At your new
address?' She had probably ordered one from a local store.

Louise had not thought further than arriving at the cottage.
Perhaps she should have kept the bed from the spare bedroom,
but, thinking in taxi terms, she had not wanted to take anything
so bulky. Besides, it was in poor condition, with broken springs
in the base.

'No,' she said. 'No. I haven't got a bed. I'll sleep on blankets
at first. Or in the chair.' She had packed up blankets and sheets
which had never been used on her and Colin's bed, some that
had come from her mother and which, at their last move, she
had nearly given to charity, but a prudent instinct had held
her back.

'It's none of my business,' said Mr Crampton, 'but we go
right past a branch of John Lewis, or I could stop off at a
furniture retailer along the way, so that you could get one.
There'd be room in the van. It's just an idea,' he added. 'As it
is, we shall have to make a toilet stop, and eat our sandwiches.'
He couldn't leave her to sleep on the floor or in a chair, not
without suggesting a solution and her with that broken arm.

'Oh! That's a good idea,' said Louise. 'Which would be best?'
And how much would a single bed cost?

'John Lewis is value for money,' he pointed out. And they'd
probably have the type of fast-boiling electric kettle his wife
wanted to replace theirs which was no longer automatic. They'd
been out of stock in Kenston yesterday. 'Going round there
won't cost any extra. I quoted you an all-in rate.' He was
charging her two hundred and fifty pounds, which included
what he was paying for the loan of the van.

Louise briefly contemplated buying a second-hand bed in a sale, but swiftly rejected the idea. It could be some time before she could manage to get one, and then goodness knows what its history would have been.

'We'll go there, then,' she said. 'You're sure there's time? We're due in Croxbury at three o'clock, to collect the key.'

'We're ahead of schedule. We'll be kicking our heels by the wayside at this rate,' said Roy Crampton. 'We can have our lunch in the John Lewis car park.' He realised he had taken charge of his customer, but she needed it; airy-fairy, she was.

They had brought sandwiches and flasks of coffee. The grandson had a can of Coca-Cola. Louise now sat alert, watching for John Lewis's store to appear. She felt a sudden thrill of excitement, as if this were a childhood treat, a surprise outing. Fear of Colin's reappearance had temporarily retreated. At a slip road, Mr Crampton turned off; they crossed a bridge and very soon they were driving down a slope into the premises of John Lewis, close to the motorway.

'You've been here before,' Louise said.

'I have,' said Mr Crampton. 'I come this way from time to time.'

Most of his journeys were local or to one of the airports, but he had some customers who went further afield for various reasons, though they travelled in his Vauxhall saloon, not this utilitarian van. He enjoyed variety, and today was different again.

Louise would have to settle for a bed that was in stock, and Mr Crampton, aware that it might take the store a little time to get it to the collection point, suggested that she should choose one and, while she had transport, do any other shopping which would save her time another day, then meet him and his grandson at the van, where they would eat their sandwiches.

After that, the bed would probably have reached the area from which they could load it.

He was being so kind. Weakness threatened to overcome Louise, but she took hold of herself. A visit to the cloakroom, food, and some coffee would restore her.

'There's a nice restaurant. You could have your lunch there and keep your sandwiches for supper,' said Mr Crampton.

'Oh no,' said Louise. That would be an extravagance. She'd shopped before leaving; she'd brought bread, eggs, and cheese, and the less perishable groceries that were in the house. Colin had not taken any supplies.

The three of them trooped into the store, which was busy. Mr Crampton was familiar with the layout and told her how to find the ladies' cloakroom; then they parted. Soon she was in the furniture department, being advised by a helpful assistant who reminded her that we spend a third of our lives in bed and a careful choice was essential. The deal concluded, the money counted out and handed over, Louise was alighting from the escalator at ground level when Mr Crampton appeared before her and asked if she would mind looking at microwave cookers with him. He was thinking of getting one for his daughter, mother of the grandson travelling with them, and would like her advice.

'I don't know anything about them,' said Louise.

Soon she did, but she was not tempted to buy one as the cooker in the cottage was quite adequate. Mr Crampton, however, chose one which he thought would please his daughter.

It wasn't Mr Crampton's business to ask what had happened to Mr Widdows. He knew, however, about Louise's accident; it had been a local talking point for a few days.

'Did they ever find who ran you down?' he asked as they walked back to the van together.

'No,' she replied. 'And I don't suppose they ever will.' Then she added, 'Mr Crampton, while your grandson's out of earshot, I don't want anyone to know where I'm living. Please keep it to yourself.'

'Certainly, Mrs Widdows,' he said promptly. 'It's no one's business, is it?'

Elsie, his wife, already knew their destination, but he'd pass on this request to her.

It was Mr Barnes himself who arrived at Lilac Cottage, promptly at three o'clock, shortly after Roy Crampton had parked the van outside. Louise was an unusual client and he wanted to see her installed, make sure she was all right for the immediate future, and then, as it would be scarcely worth returning to the office, he would go straight home, early for once as he was already nearly there. He had a pile of papers in the car to work on in his study.

A wintry sun was shining as he drew up. Louise was strolling round her small garden; Roy Crampton was speaking to his wife on his mobile telephone to tell her they had arrived and would soon be on their way home; his grandson was reading the *Express*.

Mr Barnes greeted Louise, opened the front door and then handed her the bunch of keys. The telephone was still connected; the meters had been read and future bills would go direct to her. Gas was laid on in Croxbury; the trust had shared the cost of the installation with the tenants. While they were discussing all this, Mr Crampton and his grandson were unloading the van. They managed to get the single divan bed upstairs, though turning on the small landing at the top was a challenge.

'It's so kind of them. Mr Crampton is really a taxi-driver

but he borrowed the van,' Louise told Mr Barnes. 'I only brought a few things from Kenston. We stopped at John Lewis on the way and got a bed. He quoted me an all-in fee,' she added hastily.

'Wise,' said Mr Barnes.

He had brought a list of addresses for her: the doctor who looked after most people in the village, and whom she should soon see because of her arm; the milkman; a bus timetable – there was an infrequent service to Durbridge, four miles away – the police, the Neighbourhood Watch contact. The vicar, Judith Bright, was new, said Mr Barnes.

Louise thanked him.

'You mentioned a will. If I were to die, I suppose my husband would get the house,' she said.

'Yes,' agreed Mr Barnes. 'He would be the next of kin.' He knew there were no children.

'That ought not to happen,' she said, speaking more firmly than he had heard her yet. 'I would like to talk to you about it,' she continued. 'I must ask your advice.'

'I'll come and see you on my way home on Monday evening,' said Mr Barnes. 'And now I've got something for you.' He turned away and went to his car, returning with a florist's package which contained several bunches of daffodils just breaking into bloom. 'To welcome you to Lilac Cottage,' he said. 'I hope you'll be happy here.'

To his horror, tears spilled from her eyes as she took the bundle.

'Thank you,' she managed to say, blinking hard, as he left her to the care of Mr Crampton and his grandson.

He couldn't think what had made him get them for her; after all, she was just a client. He'd seen them outside a shop as he passed and had bought some to take home, then thought of her;

pcoplc were sent flowers when they moved. Louise Widdows' mother had thought the marriage was a disaster; it looked as if her daughter had seized her sudden chance to flee away from it at last, with just her clothes and a few other possessions. The flowers might briefly cheer her, but he doubted if she had shed all her problems.

Mr Crampton and his grandson had soon unloaded the various boxes from the van. They stacked most of the cartons, which were full of pots and pans, china and glassware, in the kitchen. They had assembled the bed in the large main bedroom.

'Now, you must make sure we've put everything in the right rooms,' said Mr Crampton. 'You can't go carrying things around with that arm of yours. Just check there's nothing more we can do for you before we go.'

They had connected the television set to the existing lead and aerial. For an old place, the house was in fair shape, Mr Crampton conceded.

They all had tea together in the kitchen. Louise had unpacked some of the china and the kettle, and she had brought an unopened carton of milk in one of the boxes. Then they departed, Louise paying in cash, as she had done at John Lewis. She gave the grandson ten pounds.

He had been reading the sports section in his *Express* while he drank his tea; no other items interested him, and he left the newspaper behind. Later that evening, sitting in her one chair, a Victorian button-back that had been in her mother's bedroom, drinking a mug of coffee, Louise glanced at it. She hadn't heard any news for several days. On an inside page there was a report about a woman's body discovered in a house in Kenston. She had been battered to death. It was thought that she had been dead for about three weeks.

What a dreadful way to die! No wonder the police were too busy to worry about a mere road accident which wasn't fatal. Louise spent a moment pitying the unknown victim and then forgot about her, intent as she was on savouring her first hours of independence. Nothing could hurt her here in Croxbury: only Colin, if he tracked her down, but she would ask Mr Barnes what her rights were. She must be able to obtain some sort of order keeping him away. In this English village, life would be gentler. People would be friendly and greet her in the street; she would soon know her neighbours and when her arm and ribs had mended, she would gradually enter village life, help with bazaars, become involved.

She had arranged the daffodils in mugs, one in the kitchen and one on the little table in the sitting room. It was very kind of Mr Barnes to give them to her: tomorrow their buds would have opened fully. Louise pottered round, the curtains drawn against the dark night outside, unpacking what she could, using the piled boxes as shelves to store her clothes. She would have to buy some furniture, second-hand, perhaps, or she could get self-assembly items by mail order; you saw them advertised. After her outlay on the bed, she must not be tempted into buying anything elaborate, unnecessary, or costly; she must cater for only basic needs.

At last she lay in bed. She had salvaged a bedside lamp, one that had been in the spare bedroom, although they had never had guests, apart from once in Kenston when her stepbrother had come for a night. He had made use of them for a free bed, Colin, who thought her foolish to keep passing on each new address, had said. Her stepbrother was now in Singapore and her stepsister was in Canada.

Pure and unsullied, the new bed was very comfortable. Propped up on pillows, tired but too wound up to sleep, she read for a while, a battered paperback edition of an Anita Brookner novel: in elegant, measured prose the soul of a sad, solitary woman was skilfully exposed. The red-haired girl in Kenston library had suggested that Louise might enjoy this author's books; she was right, and Louise had bought two of them at a bazaar in the community centre. By the time she had read them, she would have joined the local library. Finishing a chapter, Louise laid the book down and tried to get into a comfortable sleeping position, sparing her injured ribs and arm. There was no Colin by her side and that was wonderful. She would never sleep with him again. Tomorrow she would tackle various things that must be dealt with, but on the other hand, if it should turn out to be a fine day, she need not rush to accomplish everything at once. She could go slowly, recover from the flurry of the past week, settle in.

With this reflection, Louise was just drifting into sleep when sudden panic hit her and she was wide awake in seconds. What had she done? She was alone in a strange place where she knew no one, with very little money, no future plans, no fall-back, and Colin might find her. If he did, he would extract a dreadful punishment. She lay shaking with terror, icy cold, unable to remind herself that she had been just as alone in Kenston even with Colin there, or to reason herself out of her fear. She must have been mad to move away from her familiar, if hostile surroundings, where at least she knew her doctor, was superficially acquainted with a few individuals, and had a hospital appointment soon. Eventually, she summoned enough strength to get out of bed and go downstairs, checking once again the doors and windows to make sure that they were secure. Then she made some tea. For a long time she sat in the bare sitting room, not consoled even by the daffodils, and to help herself grow calmer, she thought about her son, that tiny infant who would now be a man in his prime, thirty-five years old, nearly thirty-six, older than his father at the time of his conception. By now he could be married, divorced, have several children, be a captain of industry. She yearned to know what had become of him. After a long time, she went back upstairs and levered herself painfully into bed, where at last she fell asleep over Anita Brookner's lonely heroine.

7

Louise had anticipated rural silence in the morning, and when she woke, it was quiet, but it was Saturday. Last night a surprising amount of traffic had gone past after she had drawn the curtains, and she had seen a line of cars parked in the road; few houses had garages.

Getting out of bed was difficult; she had to push herself up with her sound arm to spare her ribs, but they were slowly becoming less acutely painful. She had found that lowering her feet to the floor and rolling over was the best method to adopt.

She went to the window and drew back the curtains. They were yellow, printed with a sprawling design of cornflowers, and very cheerful. She wondered what the tenants – Mr and Mrs Johnson – had been like: happy, she thought, because the curtains they had chosen were bright and all the paintwork was white. The house, particularly with so little furniture, was very light. With her limited mobility, dressing was a slow business, but eventually she was ready, her hair dragged back into its pleat, secured by a large comb which she had been given while she was in hospital by one of her colleagues from the shop who said it would be easier for her than pinning it. It had straggled loose on her shoulders while she was in bed. Years ago, when Colin had pretended to love her, he had said he liked her hair. Richard had, too, but he had meant it. It was dark and silky in those days; now it was grey.

She went downstairs and made coffee. Colin always insisted on fresh coffee; the pack, opened weeks ago, would be stale by his standards but it tasted good to her. While she drank it, she looked out of the window again and saw one car drive past; there were four people in it, a family: parents and two children, going somewhere for the day, or shopping, she supposed. Then she saw a woman walking by. She wore a tweed hat, trousers, and a padded jacket and she had a stick; she had no accompanying dog. Opposite Lilac Cottage, she stopped and scrutinised it, and Louise, anxious not to be seen at the window, shrank back and went into the kitchen to rinse her cup. Uncertain what to do next, she decided to go out. She felt tired; the elation which had sustained her for the past few days had departed. Reaction had set in, and she was adrift again, as she had felt herself to be when she met Colin and saw him as a saviour. Looking back, she knew she had been hypersensitive over feeling herself a cuckoo in the nest in Paul's house; he had done his best but she was difficult and prickly; and, older than his children, she could have made more effort to get on with them. Alone in Portsmouth, however, she really was adrift, and then she had met Richard: he was not a saviour either, and she would not find one here, in Croxbury, but she had the chance to save herself at last, and perhaps to find her son.

If he had begun to look for her, as adopted children, curious about their roots, often did, David could have claimed his adoption papers and discovered her address in Portsmouth. He would have had quite a trail to follow after that as their various removals would have created obstacles in the search; they never left forwarding addresses, not even with the post office. Sometimes Louise had regretted parting from work acquaintances, and particularly, after their last move, a neighbour to whom, in Colin's opinion, she'd got too close when the woman's child was very ill. Louise had shopped for her, and had spent time with the child while Colin was at work. After the little boy had recovered, Louise pretended to Colin that she had distanced herself from the family, but she had not done so; one of her few acts of defiance.

She had sometimes wondered what would happen if her son were to find her: what if he had turned up one day and confronted her and Colin?

It hadn't happened. Perhaps David felt bitterly about the mother who had abandoned him.

There were things which she must do. Her pension was a priority; she believed she could obtain it at any post office. She wouldn't starve, and she had no mortgage to pay, but what would light and heating cost? She would have to work out a very careful budget, for she must conserve her capital and she had no other resources until she could find work. Once her broken bones had mended, she should be as good as before – not as good as new; there was no chance of that, but good enough.

She had just put on her coat when the telephone rang.

It startled her. The call couldn't be for her, unless it was Mr Barnes, but surely not on a Saturday morning? Nervously, she detached the handset from its fixture on the kitchen wall.

'Hallo?' she said tentatively.

A crisp female voice responded sharply.

'Is that Louise? I don't know what your surname is now, but I remember you as a little girl. We met when you and your mother came to stay with Priscilla Jordan. My name is Dorothy Kershaw.'

'Oh,' said Louise faintly. Her heart was thumping. Somehow she had expected to hear Colin's cold, disapproving voice. She took a deep breath to calm herself. She remembered no one in Croxbury except Priscilla and the blacksmith.

'You'll wonder how I knew you had moved in,' said Dorothy Kershaw. 'You were seen yesterday, and a few enquiries were made.' Mrs Kershaw did not say by whom: herself, presumably, but how did anyone know who she was? Perhaps Mr Barnes had mentioned it, though solicitors were supposed to be discreet. 'I knew the Johnsons. Your tenants,' Mrs Kershaw added, but explained no further.

Louise was too startled to ask questions.

'Oh,' she said again.

'I propose to come and see you this morning, at eleven o'clock, if that will be convenient,' Mrs Kershaw continued.

'Oh – oh, yes! How very kind of you,' Louise managed to reply.

'Till then,' said her caller. 'Goodbye.'

'Goodbye,' said Louise, and was plunged into instant panic, aware of the inadequacies of her house for entertaining. Still, there was one chair. Her visitor could have it and Louise would sit on the window seat.

There was plenty of time to go to the post office first. She would ask about her pension, and she would buy a paper. She must pay some attention to what was happening in the world; apart from major events, there was that woman's body found in Kenston. The thought of it made her feel uneasy. There might be something about it on the news. Mr Crampton's grandson had tuned the television set; she was glad of that. In Kenston, having it on in the evening, no matter what the programme – always Colin's choice – had meant, not domestic harmony, for that had never existed between her and Colin, but absence of strife, and when he went out at night, which he did from time to time, never saying where he was going, she could please herself. Now, it would be company. She had had no qualms about its appropriation.

It was cold and damp, though not raining, so she tied a scarf over her head, then set forth. There seemed to be no one about. Last night there had been no sounds from the houses on either side of Louise; all were detached, separated by a few yards of garden. Leaving Lilac Cottage, she turned to her right and set off. This is my home now, she thought, my new neighbourhood; soon it will be as familiar to me as Moor Street was. Louise knew from experience that one could adjust, and often very rapidly.

She had never known anything about Colin's youth nor met his parents, and when, in the early years, she had asked about them, he had said that he had been betrayed. He wouldn't explain any further. More than a decade later, one Christmas, over their roast chicken and emboldened by the modest claret he had provided, she had asked him about Christmas in his childhood, but he had refused to discuss it. Her mother had always made theirs festive; often they had joined other families from among the school staff. After Susan became Paul's housekeeper, things had been difficult for Louise because of her own inhibitions, but there had been laughter, games, excellent food. She had begun to wonder if Colin had been adopted or had been brought up in an orphanage, for whatever the truth, he had never learned to relate warmly to other people.

There were two people in the post office ahead of her. One, a woman, bought some stamps, and the other, a man, posted a small package. Neither took any notice of Louise, who stood back while they were served. When it was her turn, she produced her pension book and said she had just moved to Croxbury; could she cash her pension here in future?

'That's easy,' said the man behind the counter. He was about fifty-five, and wore his dark hair, which had receded from his forehead, drawn sleekly back into a pony tail. He took her book. 'What's your address?' he asked her.

'Lilac Cottage, in Church Street,' said Louise.

'Ah – the Johnsons' house,' said the postmaster.

'Mine, in fact,' said Louise firmly. 'They were my tenants.' For, although she had not known about them, that was what they had been, and she, as a householder in her own right, had status. She felt suddenly confident.

'Is that so?' said the postmaster, crossing out the Kenston address in her book and writing down her new one in a bold hand. 'You'll need to fill out a form, and then your new book will be sent straight here,' he told her, and reached round to get it for her. 'Bring it next time you come in,' he suggested. He had large brown eyes and a rather florid face. 'You've got four weeks' money due,' he added. 'Would you like that now?'

'Yes – thank you,' said Louise. She had a vague idea that because she had been in hospital, she was supposed to inform the social services and would lose some benefit, but perhaps not for such a short stay.

'Have you broken your arm?' asked the postmaster, taking some notes from a drawer.

'Yes,' said Louise.

'You'll find Dr Gibbons is very sympathetic,' he told her.

'Good,' said Louise, and thanked him as she left. She felt heady with success after this encounter as she went on towards the newsagent's, where she bought a paper. On the other side of the road was another shop, beneath a green awning. A sign above it said *Yolande*. Louise looked at it in astonishment: it was a hairdresser's. Who would have expected to find one in a country village?

It was ridiculous to have long hair just because she had always worn it like that, and she could never meet Richard again, so sentiment did not matter.

On impulse, Louise, who for most of her life had cut her own hair, chopping off the ends when they began to split, crossed the road and went in.

There had been a cancellation in *Yolande*'s, and half an hour later Louise emerged with her thick, straight hair newly washed and shorn into a neat, tapered style framing her thin face. Yolande, if it was she, was delighted by the transformation wrought so swiftly with her scissors.

'It will be easy for you to manage,' she had said, snipping away. 'It'll just need regular cutting to keep it in shape. It's taken years off you, Mrs Widdows. Welcome to Croxbury.' She gave Louise a small bottle of gardenia-scented toilet water as a celebration, putting it into Louise's pocket for her. It did her good to see the poor lady looking so much brighter when she left than when she had arrived.

Louise really did feel light-headed now, as, her scarf protecting her new coiffure, she walked home to make coffee for Mrs Kershaw. Already it had been an eventful day, and nothing bad had happened. On the way back she met a woman pushing a baby in a small pram and two other women walking along together. She smiled at the one with the baby and received a smile in return; the other women did not seem to see her. A man carrying a newspaper, walking faster, overtook her, glancing at her, and a father with a child on a tiny bicycle came towards her. Louise stepped out of the child's way, and the father thanked her, smiling. There was a steady stream of traffic on the main road, but when she turned off it was quieter. Back at Lilac Cottage, she put her purse in a drawer in the kitchen. The surplus from the building society was in a tin that had once held assorted biscuits, hidden under sheets in the airing cupboard. She had learned to hide her few secrets from Colin and, at Moor Street, had dug a hiding-place underneath a tub in the garden. Her building society book had been safely concealed there when she returned from hospital, though extracting it, wounded as she was, had not been easy.

She was slow arranging two cups and saucers on a tray, with a plate of biscuits, and taking it to the table in the sitting room, but she was ready, with the kettle on the boil, when the doorbell rang.

On the doorstep stood the woman she had seen walking past the house earlier that morning, still in her trousers, hat and padded jacket, with her stick.

8

Dorothy Kershaw walked steadily back to her house after her visit to Louise Widdows. She had hesitated about telephoning her so soon after her arrival in Croxbury. Could she be bothered with this newcomer? She had the time – except that everything she did took much longer now than it had even five years ago, and she grew tired after an hour's weeding in the garden, instead of being able to work there all day without weariness, but she had been fond of Priscilla Jordan, and she had liked Susan, whom she had met several times. She had no very clear memories of Louise, except that she was a quiet, self-contained child, and docile; not much spirit there, Dorothy's husband had remarked after the trio from Lilac Cottage had been to lunch at The Grey House, where the Kershaws had lived then. In later years, after the widowed Dorothy had moved into Jackdaws, a smaller house near the centre of the village, she had learned from Priscilla that Susan was anxious about Louise whose marriage was, in Susan's opinion, a disaster. Susan herself had found happiness and security with her second husband; she was a contented woman, almost smug, Dorothy had thought, and had wondered why she did nothing to help Louise if she was so concerned about her.

'Marriage sacred,' the unmarried Priscilla had said, with a shrug and a skyward look. 'And no money,' she had added.

'What's so bad about the husband?' Dorothy had wanted to know.

'He's a rolling stone. Stays in no job more than a few years, then they're off, on the move, to another area. He has to go where the work is, Susan says.'

Dorothy knew that Priscilla had left Susan the cottage because she had no living relatives with a better claim than her goddaughter, and now, as Priscilla's friend, she had a duty to Louise.

Every morning, unless the weather was very bad, Dorothy walked round part of the village, a route which took in Church Street, passing Lilac Cottage and the modern vicarage, until she arrived home some fifteen minutes later. Her timing varied, depending on whether or not she had slept well, and in the winter she waited until it was light. Once she had had a dog, a Labrador, which had walked with her, but he had died of old age and she had not replaced him, for there was no denying that he was a tie, forcing her out in bad weather and on the rare occasions when she was unwell, but she missed him. She walked to keep herself active; it was so easy to slump in a chair, reading, or watching racing on television.

When she and her husband first came to Croxbury, the village was still mainly agricultural with many of the inhabitants employed on local farms, though some worked in factories in neighbouring towns. This trend developed in the years that followed. Before the war, Fergus, an architect, had been a partner in a London practice. He went into the navy and survived the sinking of two ships. Ultimately he commanded a destroyer. He and Dorothy had married in 1939; when the war began and Fergus joined up, she did the same. Thereafter they met occasionally on leave, and during the last months of the war their first child was born; Dorothy and the baby stayed with her parents, who lived in Somerset, until Fergus was demobilised.

Adjusting to civilian life was not easy for Fergus, and though by now they had been married for seven years, they had spent very little time together. At first they rented a house in Rickmansworth, where their second child was born, but then Fergus decided to set up his own practice in the country. In Croxbury, he found The Grey House, which needed modernising, and fell in love with it. Over the next years, while he became established, his main interest was its renovation. Gradually they settled down, getting to know one another again, both affected, but in different ways, by the war years.

Some of this was in Dorothy's mind as she walked past Lilac Cottage early on Saturday morning and remembered Susan Henderson, a young war widow with a child; Dorothy might so easily have been widowed too.

She was aware that Susan's daughter had moved in. Dorothy missed the Johnsons. She knew that they had paid their rent direct to the trustees and had never met their anonymous landlady, but they had assumed she was Susan's daughter. The previous afternoon, when the van was seen unloading, a telephone call from a curious passer-by to the Neighbourhood Watch coordinator, whom Mr Barnes had earlier asked to keep an eye on the empty cottage, had soon established the identity of the new occupant.

The curtains were already drawn back in Lilac Cottage when Dorothy took her walk. On some days, she had to force herself to set out, but she knew it did her good, getting her circulation going so that she was ready for her breakfast – coffee and toast, and with any luck the paper would have come; sometimes on Saturdays the schoolboy who delivered it was late, and in the school holidays it could arrive at any time. So Susan's daughter was an early riser: she must have a lot to do, unpacking and getting straight. Perhaps it would be best to let her settle in before making contact; on the other hand, she might be feeling lonely, though she must be middle-aged at least by now. Age and experience did not prevent one from feeling lost, as Dorothy knew, and the deaths of contemporaries brought not only sorrow but also increasing loneliness.

Preferring to err by commission, not omission, Dorothy telephoned; after all, Louise could always say she was too busy to receive a visitor and, in that case, a more convenient time could be arranged. Or Dorothy could ask her to lunch tomorrow, Sunday. She might be glad of such an invitation.

With these possibilities in mind, Dorothy had made her call.

She felt diffident, approaching Lilac Cottage later. Louise was an unknown quantity. Though Susan had occasionally come to see Priscilla after her happy second marriage, more frequently the visits went the other way, with Priscilla staying with her and Paul in their comfortable house in Warwickshire. Dorothy remembered that news of Louise was always sketchy. Louise had stayed alone in Portsmouth when Colin had a job abroad, and Susan had seen very little of her for some time. Paul had had misgivings about Colin from the beginning, but there had been no stopping Louise from marrying him; Priscilla had guessed that the girl had wanted to get away from home and this was the obvious way. Susan had been disappointed that there were no children, and concerned about her daughter's health; though never estranged, their relationship had, over the years, become more distant and the mother had known that the daughter was not happy. Presumably things had settled down as time went on, and perhaps by now Colin was dead; he must be in his mid-sixties, at least. No doubt she would discover some of this, if not today, on a future meeting with Louise.

Jackdaws, her own house, was at the end of a terraced block dating from the eighteenth century. The row had roofs of mellow tiles, but their fronts were far from uniform, having been renovated and altered before the area was protected by a conservation order; since Dorothy moved in, many of them, though not all, had become listed buildings. Now, nothing could be changed without consent, not even returned to what it was before that rule came into force. After selling The Grey House, Dorothy had passed on some of the profit to her children, but only after she had done Jackdaws up thoroughly, with rewiring throughout, and when gas had come to the village, she had had this installed. She had grown fond of the small, compact house, which was large enough for visits from her family in segments, but not for all of them at once. The Grey House would have been too big for her on her own, and, at the end of the village, approached by a narrow lane, was isolated. Since she moved, several large houses had been built between it and the rest of the village. She did not know any of the people who lived there; wealthy commuters, she supposed, though Lavinia, her cleaner, said some ran businesses from home. She cleaned for two of them.

Dorothy pushed open the iron gate, walked up the short path and rang the bell at Lilac Cottage. The door was opened promptly, and she saw a small, thin woman with a cropped haircut and her left arm in a plaster.

'Oh dear,' said Dorothy. 'You've hurt yourself.'

'Yes,' said Louise. 'Unfortunately. Please come in, Mrs Kershaw.'

She had arranged cups and saucers on the small rosewood table. The one chair was drawn up close to it, on the Johnsons' familiar carpet. Their curtains hung at the window. Mrs Kershaw walked purposefully across the room and took the chair, to which Louise was motioning her. Sugar and a jug of milk were on the tray, with four Rich Tea biscuits on a plate.

'Where are you going to sit, Louise?' asked Mrs Kershaw.

'The window seat is fine,' said Louise. 'I'll just fetch the coffee.'

She could do it with one hand. Mrs Kershaw saw that she had planned ahead and did not offer aid. She sat looking round the bare room. Perhaps the rest of the furniture would arrive next week.

Louise, in the kitchen, took a deep breath as she poured boiling water into the cafetière. She gave it a stir, then carried it carefully into the sitting room. She was nearly a pretty woman, Dorothy decided, with her shining, neat grey hair and her pale, thin face with the large blue eyes.

'We'll let it stand a little,' said Louise, setting it down. She smiled a careful smile. 'How very kind of you to call,' she said in formal tones.

'Things postponed sometimes don't get done,' said Mrs Kershaw, and then, as Louise seemed unable to reply, she added, 'Priscilla Jordan and I were great friends.'

'Oh yes,' said Louise. 'I remember her, but not well, I'm afraid. She sometimes came to stay with my mother, when I was a girl.'

'You and your mother once came to lunch with us. You were

a mere child then. That was when we lived at The Grey House, but now I live at Jackdaws, in the village,' said her guest.

'Jackdaws! What an unusual name,' said Louise. She pushed the plunger down and began to pour the coffee, concentrating hard.

Dorothy noticed the concentration. She decided not to offer help.

'The house had previously been called The Nest,' she said. 'Presumably because jackdaws nested in the chimney – they did – and obviously I had to change it.' Priscilla had maintained that the couple who lived there were perpetually billing and cooing, as she put it, and that this was how it got its name. Dorothy elected not to relate this theory to her hostess. 'As the birds were still resident, Jackdaws seemed appropriate,' she said. 'I got rid of them eventually.'

'I'm glad,' said Louise. 'I hope there aren't any here.'

'I don't think so. Wilfred Johnson would have dealt with them,' said Dorothy. 'How did you break your arm? I presume it is broken?'

'Yes.' Louise explained about the accident, and Mrs Kershaw expressed sympathy and dismay.

'It must have made moving difficult for you,' she said.

'Yes, but I couldn't delay,' said Louise. She had crossed to the window seat and sat perched there, her coffee cup beside her. Cautiously, she took a sip. 'Oh – would you like a biscuit?' she asked.

'No, thank you. Tell me why you had to hurry,' said Mrs Kershaw. 'Had you to leave another house?'

'Yes, but not because someone else was moving in.' Louise knew she would have to tell this sharp old woman some of the truth. 'It will be best to tell you the real reason,' she said. 'When I heard about the house, it was like the waving of a magic wand

– the opening of a cage. I could get away from Colin – but he had already gone. On the day that I was knocked down by a car and broke my arm, he disappeared.'

'Left you, you mean?'

'He didn't leave a letter. He just went. The police wanted to tell him about my accident, but he wasn't at home. They went round with my key, while I was still in hospital, and found he'd packed his clothes and disappeared.'

'How strange,' said Dorothy Kershaw. 'Why should he do that?'

'I don't know,' said Louise. 'But our marriage was a bad one. I don't know why it lasted, since we had no children to consider.'

'It takes courage to leave a bad marriage,' said Mrs Kershaw. She drank some coffee, then set her cup down. 'A wife has status, which incidentally you lose as a widow, though for a while you receive sympathy and pity. And, for a wife – or a husband, come to that – there is someone there, even if neither of you like each other very much. Money, too, must be considered. All those things.' She smiled at Louise, and her lined face softened beneath her tweed hat. 'Does he know that you've left, too? Have you sold your other house?'

Louise told her what she had done, growing more confident when Mrs Kershaw, listening attentively, nodded in approval.

'He may find me, though,' Louise ended. 'The landlord will be after him for the rent, so he'll find out I've gone.' She wasn't sure what would happen when the payments ceased.

'He may not want to, since he went first,' said Mrs Kershaw. 'Do you think he's gone off with another woman?' He wasn't too old to have done this; no one was.

'I hope so,' said Louise. For if that was the case, he would leave her alone.

'Time will provide the answer,' said Mrs Kershaw. 'Meanwhile, I expect you'll tell all this to Jonathan Barnes, won't you? He'll advise you about how to protect yourself and your property.'

'Yes. He knows some of it already,' said Louise. 'He's very kindly coming to see me on Monday on his way home.'

'Good,' said Dorothy. 'Now, I'm going to carry these things out for you and wash them up, and you are coming to lunch with me tomorrow. Don't expect fatted calf; I used to be a good cook, but now I'm rather lazy. I won't allow you to refuse. I want to hear about your mother – I was so sorry to hear she had died.'

And she wanted to learn more about this curious marriage. As their house in Kenston had been rented, she had wondered if Louise would be accountable until the lease expired, but Louise reassured her.

'I'm glad you bought a decent bed,' she remarked, when Louise had said it was a stupid extravagance as she could have got something adequate for much less at a discount warehouse. 'You've got the essentials. I can lend you a comfortable garden chair or two, to tide you over. We'll talk about that tomorrow.' She'd drive Louise and the chair or chairs back after their lunch.

9

Andrew was in Kenston again, trying to track down Louise Widdows. He had spent time telephoning local removal firms, spinning a tale that she had recommended one and he couldn't remember its name but thought it might be theirs, with no success. With the Kenston murder still unsolved, he had sought sanction from his editor to look into the victim's background for human interest. Added to other cases, he might construct an article about the effect of crime on victims' families – not a new idea but one that needed emphasising.

The dead woman, Lesley Timson, was divorced, and although she lived alone, there must be people in her life who cared about her. She was found in a derelict warehouse on land awaiting redevelopment, and after the discovery a reporter on the scene had mentioned a hidden garden tucked away in a corner of waste ground near the area. Andrew's editor agreed that, while researching the one, he should also see if there was something in the other. Andrew had a way of discovering the unexpected angle, which was why he had got the job on the magazine in the first place.

Provided with an official reason to go to Kenston, and able to claim expenses, Andrew had eagerly departed. Before going to the garden, he went to the library to seek out Clare Fairweather. She was shifting books from a trolley on to shelves, and she remembered him at once.

'Hi,' she said. 'Did you find her?'

Andrew was absurdly pleased at this recognition, though only two days had passed since his first visit.

'No,' he said. 'I've tried all the removal firms. No joy.'

'It seems strange that she didn't get everything into a pantechnicon. You'd think she'd have had a bigger one. And why didn't everything go at once?'

'You tell me,' said Andrew. 'Any ideas?'

'Maybe it was junky stuff. Maybe she sold it and took the rest with her, or maybe the first load went to the husband, wherever he is,' said Clare.

'If it did go to the husband, a Kenston removal van didn't take it,' said Andrew.

'What about people who clear houses?' Clare said. 'You could try them. Either they did, or didn't, take her stuff.'

'Good idea,' said Andrew.

'I'll get you the addresses from the Yellow Pages,' Clare said promptly, going off to take the directory to the photocopier.

'Are you on all day?' he asked her, as he handed over payment for several photocopied pages.

'No. I'm off at twelve and on this evening, five to eight,' she said.

'Like to come with me to a mystery garden?' Andrew asked.

Clare looked at him.

'Straight up?' she said.

He nodded.

'My paper's let me come here to find out about that murdered woman and the garden,' he explained. 'It's near where she was found. Louise is a private interest.'

Louise: strange that he should instinctively think of her by her first name, not as the woman on the train, or Mrs Widdows.

'I think I've heard about the garden,' Clare replied. 'It sounds intriguing. All right.'

'Meet you outside at twelve, then,' he said, and wondered at himself. What was he doing, chatting up this cheerful, red-headed librarian – for there was no doubt that this was what he was doing – when he was already in a steady relationship with a clever, witty woman? Wanting to prove that you can still pull them, he answered himself. But that was nonsense; his motive was a desire to question her about Louise Widdows. She might know something about her that could put him on the trail.

But he wouldn't have asked her to go with him to the garden if she'd been boot-faced and unresponsive, and she must like him, or she wouldn't have agreed to come.

Andrew went away to telephone the numbers she had found for him, and with the third try, he traced a firm who said they had bought up the contents of 37 Moor Street. Andrew had a devious story ready. He explained that, by accident, his aunt, Mrs Widdows, had let the dealer take a small oak coffer which she had meant to keep. It had been in her family for years.

'There was no oak coffer,' said the dealer, who knew about such things and picked out any good pieces which came his way, selling them on as the antiques they were. He'd have noticed anything like that. Andrew thanked him and rang off; then he drove round to the address. He found a second-hand furniture shop with a variety of goods on display. Looking through the window, Andrew saw that you could make useful purchases here; there were serviceable desks and chairs, china and glassware: relics of lives. However, not everything, he reminded himself, came from the deceased. People moved on and upwards, selling off what they no longer wanted.

He went inside and met the owner, reminding him of their telephone conversation, wondering if his aunt could have put the coffer inside some larger object – a dresser, for example. While speaking, he picked up a china dish; it was pretty, with a flowered pattern. A sticker marked its price as fifteen pounds.

'This is nice,' Andrew interrupted his flow about his aunt. 'I'll give you twelve pounds for it.' It would do to hold fruit, though Val wouldn't think much of it; he quite liked it, though, and after all, it was his flat.

'Done,' said the dealer, who would have taken less. 'But there was no dresser. The kitchen fitments were in situ.'

'Have you still got her stuff?' asked Andrew.

'Some of it. It's split up now, round the back. You can have a look if you like. See if you can find this coffer. Leather-covered, was it? The old genuine ones were,' said the dealer, leading the way through his premises.

This was news to Andrew, who was picturing a small hinged chest which might hold anything.

'No – it was solid oak,' said Andrew firmly. 'About so big,' and he gestured, then followed the man to the rear of the shop. It was a bit like an auction hall, with furniture stacked according to kind. There were beds and chests of drawers and wardrobes. Some of the stuff looked as if it had been there for years; perhaps it had.

'We get rid of what's useless,' said the man. He indicated a mahogany desk. 'That was your aunt's,' he said. 'It's well kept.'

It was. The old wood gleamed.

'My aunt's very particular,' said Andrew.

The dealer pointed out an oak table and some chairs, all in good condition. These, and the desk, he would put in a sale; that was a way of getting a reasonable return on his investment, but he did not divulge his methods to this man.

'She took very little with her,' Andrew stated, guessing.

'Not a lot,' agreed the man, who had been surprised that she had not put the better pieces in an auction. 'I left her with just a few boxes she'd packed up and rather a nice chair – oh, and there was a small table – rosewood,' he said. 'How's she getting on?' he asked Andrew. 'I was sorry she had to move with her arm not mended yet. That was a bad business about her accident.'

'Yes, it was,' said Andrew.

'And then her husband going off and leaving her,' said the dealer, accepting Andrew's payment for the dish. 'My wife thinks she walked right into the car, on purpose.'

'Why ever would she do that?' asked Andrew, genuinely astonished.

'Because her husband had walked out on her,' said the dealer.

'She's better off without him,' Andrew said abruptly, suddenly convinced that this was so.

'You should know, seeing as she's your aunt,' said the dealer. 'Sorry about the coffer. Maybe the husband took it, as it was valuable.'

'Maybe he did,' said Andrew.

'She gone far? Your aunt?' asked the dealer, who had noticed Andrew's gaze wandering round his wares, and thought some other object might take his fancy.

'Yes – quite a way,' said Andrew, and realised that this man had no knowledge of Louise's destination.

Even so, his call here had not been a waste of time.

The garden was a delight. On a plot of waste ground in a part of Kenston over which several contenders for its development were still arguing with the planning authorities, and bids for the land were on hold, an elderly couple, living in a block of flats where they had no garden, had cleared and cultivated a small plot measuring some eight yards long by five yards wide. They had planted flowering shrubs grown from cuttings rooted in pots on their windowsill, sown seeds, built a rockery using stones from the surrounding area, and laid out a short curving path with a seat made from boulders at the end of it. Now, dwarf daffodils were almost out, and a mahonia and a barebranched pink viburnum were in flower.

'Goodness! How amazing, among these wrecked buildings,' Clare said, looking around her. 'It's rather marvellous.'

'It's still more marvellous that it hasn't been destroyed by vandals,' Andrew said.

Pale sunshine filtered down between the abandoned warehouses, slanting off the viburnum blossom.

'I wonder why it hasn't?' said the girl.

A small man in a donkey jacket was scattering peat around the stems of some of the plants. Andrew approached him.

'Mr Gilbert?' he asked. He had been able to discover the enthusiastic gardener's name.

'That's me,' said the man, glancing up.

'You've done all this?' Andrew waved a hand.

'Me and the wife,' said Mr Gilbert.

'How long has it taken you?'

'Two years,' said Mr Gilbert. 'Nearly three. Stuff's growing well now but it takes five years to make a garden.'

'What got you into it?' asked Andrew.

'I've been a gardener all my life. Worked in parks and that,' said Mr Gilbert, straightening up. He had a fluffy white beard. Replace his worn tweed cap with a woolly hat and he would look quite like a gnome, thought Andrew.

'And so?' he encouraged.

'Then I retired and me and the wife were rehoused. We have to grow things or we'd die ourselves,' he said. 'We were just wandering around one day and we came this way. I said as how it would make a fine park if they pulled down those old buildings, which they'll do one day, and as we kept on coming here, we saw some willow-herb pushing up among the rubble and we thought, why not try and clear a bit? So we did.'

'And no one tried to stop you? No nosy official?' Clare said.

'Nary a one,' said Mr Gilbert. 'We come here most days, even when it's wet.'

'I'd have thought young lads might have wrecked it,' Andrew said.

'Them hooligans don't come this way a lot,' said Mr Gilbert. 'It's too far out, and it's in a pocket, see, between the buildings. They do their rollerblading and suchlike round the other side, where there's still some concrete.'

Andrew saw what he meant. The rear walls of the decaying warehouses bordered this small oasis; broken windows and entrances with no doors were on the further sides, and it was in one of these enclosed places that the dead woman had been found.

'Where's your wife now?' asked Andrew.

'She'll be here any minute, with our lunch,' said Mr Gilbert. 'We eat it outside, when the weather's good enough. It's quite sheltered from the wind.'

As he spoke, a tall, thin woman, carrying a basket, came towards them. She wore trousers tucked into shabby rubber boots, a thick parka jacket and a red woollen hat pulled down over her ears.

'Couple's been admiring our garden, Jessie,' said Mr Gilbert, taking his cap off and scratching his head. He had a fine crop of snow-white hair. 'Wonders why we don't get vandals.'

'We wonder, too,' said Jessie. She glanced towards the end of the plot, and as she did so, a robin came swooping across the open space and landed beside them, looking at her enquiringly. 'Yes, Robbie,' she addressed it. 'We're here.' She turned to Andrew and Clare. 'He always comes for his dinner when he sees me arriving.'

Andrew looked at Clare.

'We won't disturb you any more,' he said. 'I think this is just wonderful. Good luck,' and, taking Clare's arm, he led her away, back to the car, where he said, 'I'm supposed to be a hard-headed journalist, ever ready for a story, but I'm not going to do this one. If they get noticed, more than they have already, their little haven will be discovered and lose its peace, if not its plants. That murdered woman was found just round the corner. We'll drive past on our way to find some lunch.'

Outside the warehouse where Lesley Timson's body had been discovered there was, as Mr Gilbert had explained, a concrete section, which was no longer cordoned off by the police; they had finished the scientific examination of the site, a bleak repository with a corrugated iron roof, cement-block walls and wooden doors, bolted now and padlocked.

'Could be a place where junkies go to shoot up,' said Andrew. 'Maybe it was a drugs-related crime. No one seems to know.'

'Was she raped?' asked Clare.

'I don't know. Maybe. Beaten up until she died,' said Andrew. 'Inexplicable. Rage, perhaps.' He shrugged. 'People can do dreadful things to one another. Let's find a pub near where she lived and see what we can learn.'

'How can you use what you find out – if you do discover anything?' asked Clare. 'You're not a crime reporter, are you?'

'No. I write features. Some are commissioned and some are my own ideas which I try to get my editor to publish. Failing that, I may be able to place them on my own. I have contacts,' he said, putting on a deep, mock-sinister tone. 'The police don't seem at all close to making an arrest in this case; in fact, it would seem they haven't a clue. The identity of the victim might be significant, or it may be a random killing.'

'Is it part of a pattern? There hasn't been another murder of that kind in Kenston, but maybe there have in other towns,' suggested Clare.

'It's possible,' said Andrew. 'I think there's a pub somewhere around here.'

They found The Golden Horn in a cluster of shops and houses not far from the victim's home, and Clare asked for a lager. Andrew ordered a beer for himself, and they both studied the menu chalked up on a board, eventually choosing sausage and mash.

'Have they found out who killed Lesley Timson?' he asked the barmaid, when she brought their plates across. 'She worked here, didn't she?' Andrew, saying this, ignored the startled glance which Clare gave him.

'Yes – poor thing,' said the barmaid.

'Did you know her?'

'Slightly,' said the barmaid. 'She hadn't been here long. She was a nice person. She didn't deserve to die like that.'

'Who does?' asked Andrew.

'I can think of a few,' said the barmaid. 'Like whoever did that to her.'

'Divorced, wasn't she? Does her husband come from round here?' asked Andrew.

'No. I don't know where he lives,' said the barmaid. 'I'm not sure if she really was divorced. Separated, though.'

'Any children?'

'Adult ones, at college,' said the barmaid. 'The daughter's in a bad way, poor kid. They're going to do it on one of those crime programmes on telly. See if anyone out there can help. We had them in the other day, the crews and all, filming.'

'Oh,' said Andrew. 'Let's hope it does some good.'

'It was probably the husband,' said the barmaid. 'It usually is, isn't it?'

'Unless it's Mr Bad, a stranger with a grudge against all women, and she got across him in some way,' said Andrew. 'In the bar, maybe,' he added to Clare, after the woman had gone.

'You're a devil yourself,' said Clare. 'You knew all that about her already.'

Andrew did not deny it.

'This crime will be solved, or not, whatever I do. I'm really interested in Louise Widdows,' he said.

'But why?' asked Clare. 'What's so fascinating?'

'The way we met was weird, and she had that horrible experience in the train,' said Andrew. 'Then she flitted. And her husband. Separately, according to the neighbours, but it may have been arranged in advance and her accident forced a change of plan.'

'What experience in the train?' asked Clare.

He told her about it, and about Nicky, but he did not mention Val.

10

While Andrew was trying to trace her in Kenston, Louise was adapting to life in Croxbury, and she felt as though she had been reborn. Nothing was familiar, not even Lilac Cottage, because her childhood memories of it were so hazy and were lost in the past, superseded by all that had happened since, and her recollection of the village was vague, so that it was quite a shock when she recognised particular groups of buildings.

The terraced row in which Dorothy Kershaw lived was one of them. Here, the street must have looked nearly the same for centuries. Dorothy had told her that television companies sometimes used it for filming, but that usually it appeared so fleetingly, and was often so heavily embellished with temporary trees and shrubs, false façades for houses, and additional climbing roses, that it was not easy to identify one's own dwelling.

Louise had walked there to lunch on her first Sunday in the village, the day after their meeting. She had found her hostess, again in trousers, busy in the warm kitchen at the back of the house, where the table was laid for their meal. There was a chicken casserole in the oven; the smell immediately stimulated Louise's fragile appetite. A beautiful cut glass half full of sherry was on the dresser, and Dorothy, after helping

Louise shed her coat, poured one for her and topped up her own.

'Sit down while I finish off,' she instructed, energetically mashing potato in a blue enamelled pan. 'You can't help. Just enjoy, as our American cousins would say.'

Louise obediently sank into a chair on the far side of the table. That morning, she had again seen the old lady walk past, and behind her, in ones and twos, came a straggle of what she had realised were churchgoers, bound for the eight o'clock service. Louise wondered if Mrs Kershaw was heading for the same destination; would she wear trousers in church? Unable to think of a conversational opening, she took a sip of the pale dry sherry.

'I always have sherry before Sunday lunch,' Mrs Kershaw said. 'But only rarely on weekdays.' Her elder daughter, visiting unexpectedly, had caught her having a mid-week nip and had declared this decadent, but Mrs Kershaw had pointed out that it was merely civilised. This daughter, once a pretty, bright girl who played the flute, was now a marriage counsellor and magistrate and had become rather a prig, Dorothy feared.

Here was a woman who, biologically, could almost have been her daughter and who was at a crossroads in her life. Aware that lending a helping hand could lead to its being clutched as though by someone drowning who would not release it and might also drag down the rescuer, Dorothy felt, nevertheless, that she must at least tide Louise over the period in which her arm healed. Besides, she had time to spare, if limited energy, and, with her own contemporaries dying off, she was lonely.

Over their meal – she had thawed frozen chicken portions to make the casserole – she told Louise about various village facilities and suggested she should make an appointment with the doctor the next day. He might be able to fit her in, even though it was Monday, when often he was extra busy.

'They'll need your notes from your previous doctor,' she said. 'Maybe they send them across by computer now. I don't know. Tell me, why did you move so often? I remember your mother saying that you were like a service family, always upsticking. It must have been restless.'

'It was,' said Louise. 'Colin kept changing his job and the new one was usually in another part of the country where he thought there would be better opportunities.'

'But they didn't materialise?'

'No.'

'And now he's disappeared?'

'Yes.'

'He must have been running either away from something, or towards a specific goal,' said Mrs Kershaw.

Louise thought of the murdered woman who had just been found in a derelict building in Kenston; she had been missed at much the same time as Colin had taken off. How could there possibly be a connection? How could she even think of such a thing? It was simply coincidence. Colin was selfish and cruel, but he had never hit her, never actually been violent.

Hadn't he tried to run her over?

'How can you know about anyone, even if you've lived with them for years?' she said.

It was true. And lack of communication, as Barbara never tired of saying, was the major cause of misunderstandings and marital breakdowns.

'You can't,' said Dorothy. 'I expect you had secrets from him. Why not?'

If you only knew, thought Louise.

Mrs Kershaw had two daughters and a son; she also had

seven grandchildren. One family, the younger daughter's, lived in Scotland where they ran a hotel; the other daughter, Barbara, whose husband was a merchant banker, lived in Wiltshire; and the son was a civil servant attached to the European Parliament in Brussels. The older grandchildren were already adult, or at university, but there were still three young ones up in Scotland.

'Teenagers,' Mrs Kershaw had said. 'Horrible word. Don't you agree? It must have been invented to describe that awkward stage after childhood and before one is fully adult. Adolescent is more appropriate.'

'It's a marketing concept,' said Louise. 'There's money in it, aiming at young people who are beginning to assert themselves.'

She surprised herself by coming out with this remark; she had ventured so few opinions in recent years that she wasn't sure she had any, but Mrs Kershaw was looking at her with attention.

'You're right,' she said. Louise was turning out to be more interesting than she had expected.

After lunch, Dorothy showed Louise two folding chairs, with loose padded cushions, which she could borrow, already loaded into her car. Then she drove her home.

'Let me know how you get on with the doctor,' she said, as she carried the chairs into the sitting room and put them up. 'And if you have to be X-rayed, as I'm sure you will, I will take you.' Tiring now, Dorothy wanted to go home and settle down with the Sunday papers.

Louise was so overwhelmed by her kindness that she was barely able to express her gratitude, and after Dorothy had driven away, she sat down immediately to write her a letter of thanks which she delivered later that afternoon, just as dusk was falling, walking once more to the house, Jackdaws, and pushing it through the flap in the door.

The next morning, as Mrs Kershaw had advised, Louise had telephoned the surgery and had been seen by Dr Gibbons, who was sympathetic and thorough, taking her blood pressure, and checking her damaged ribs, which, she told him, were improving. He had welcomed her to the village. Her records would eventually arrive, probably quite soon, he said, accepting her as his patient. He would make an appointment for her at the fracture clinic; soon she could have a lighter plaster on her arm.

Mr Barnes, calling late that Monday afternoon, had managed to conceal his astonishment at the dramatic change in his client's appearance. Her new, sleek hairstyle had transformed her, and she had a little colour in her cheeks. She made tea, which they drank in the sitting room, and she told him about Dorothy Kershaw lending her the chairs.

'You've met her already, have you?' he said. He knew Mrs Kershaw. 'That's good.'

'She came to see me on Saturday,' said Louise. 'She said she knew Priscilla, and the Johnsons. I went to lunch with her yesterday and she brought the chairs round afterwards. It was so very kind.'

'I'm glad,' said Mr Barnes. 'Now, about your will.'

They spent some time discussing it, and at one point Mr Barnes explained that anything she told him remained con- fidential. She still hesitated, reluctant to admit the futility, as she saw it now, of so many years.

'I don't know why I married Colin,' she admitted, as Mr Barnes, to ease things, suggested she might like more tea and poured it out, for the pot had wavered in her shaky grasp when she did it earlier.

'I've heard that phrase so often,' said Mr Barnes, who no longer handled the partnership's divorce cases; these days, specialists were needed for all aspects of the law. 'I do know your mother was anxious about you,' he added. 'Hence the trust.'

'If Colin hadn't vanished, this would all be much more difficult,' she said.

'Indeed it would,' Mr Barnes agreed. He feared the man would find out about the house eventually, and would cause trouble when he did. All the same, his disappearance, and its timing, were odd, to say the least.

'He can't force me to let him live here, can he?' she asked.

'No. If he tries to, you call the police and we get an injunction,' said Mr Barnes.

'I think he was driving the car that ran me down,' she said, the words almost bursting from her.

'Do you?'

Louise nodded. It was a relief to admit it.

'I couldn't be sure. I didn't really see the driver, but the car was like Colin's, and it was waiting in the road. It pounced at me, with the headlights blazing, and mounted the pavement, but a cat ran in front of me and I moved just in time to avoid a full collision. I fell against a boundary wall and was quite badly concussed.'

'You saw that it was the same make of car as your husband's?'

'Not definitely. Colin's car was a small black Renault. It was the same size and shape, and I thought I saw him in it, only I couldn't have because it was dark. But there was a street lamp just there.'

'Did you tell the police you thought it might be him?'

'No.'

Mr Barnes did not enquire why she had not done so.

'But he had disappeared when they went to tell him about your accident?'

'Yes. And he had emptied our joint bank account earlier that day,' she said.

'The police might have traced his car. There could have been proof that it had struck you, if he was responsible,' said Mr Barnes.

'They thought it was a joyrider,' she said. She related how she had abandoned the house and sold the furniture. 'Can the landlord sue me for the rent?' she asked.

'Not if your husband was the sole tenant,' said Mr Barnes. 'Was he? Or did you also sign the agreement?'

'I never signed. Only Colin. Always, wherever we lived, except when he worked abroad,' said Louise.

'Then you have nothing to worry about. He's liable. Perhaps it was paid a month in advance,' said Mr Barnes.

'I think it was,' said Louise. 'There was a standing order at the bank. It was the only thing we paid like that. I know a lot of people pay things directly through the bank, but we never did. Electricity and so on. Oh dear!' She looked worried. 'Perhaps I should do that.' But she hadn't got a bank account.

'There's no need for you to decide now,' Mr Barnes soothed. 'You can always make adjustments later, when your plans are formed. Take your time.' She had come here on a wing and a prayer, literally in flight from her past. It would probably catch up with her: pasts did. Meanwhile, though, she needed a period of calm in which to accept that now she had control over her life and her affairs. Long-term, she could sell the house, buy something small and cheap, and use the rest for income, but having made one impulsive, huge decision, she should make no more unless they were essential.

'I brought some papers to show you how the trust fund stands,' he said. 'It will keep you going for a while, but it's no longer a source of income. Have you any others?'

'I have some building society money. Colin didn't know about it,' she said. 'I put the trust money into that. Colin thought it had stopped when my mother died.'

So she had managed a minor deception, and she had benefited from wives' incomes being taxed separately from their husbands'. She had also sold furniture to which Colin might have some claim, though, if he reappeared, he had some explaining to do.

Louise had taken a deep breath. She clasped the hand emerging from the plaster with the other, continuing to speak.

'I think I must tell you about my son,' she said. 'I want him to have the house, or, if I have to sell it, anything I may leave, if he's ever found. It can't hurt anyone to tell now, as his father's dead.'

She disclosed the bare facts to the startled Mr Barnes: merely that as a young woman, while her husband was abroad, she had had a child and given him up for adoption because to confess the affair would have damaged his father's career. He had never known that she was pregnant. She had seen his obituary in the paper, quite by chance, some months ago, and then she had registered herself as being willing to be traced. Nothing, so far, had happened; she did not know how she could trace David, as she had named the child.

'His father had no other children, as far as I could tell from the paper. Two sisters and a brother, but no other family. Sad, isn't it?'

It was tragic: a man of some achievement, it seemed, had died unaware that he had had a son.

'It was just an affair to him,' Louise was saying. 'To me, it was the world.'

'I'm so sorry,' Mr Barnes said gently. 'It must have been dreadful for you.'

'I couldn't pass him off as Colin's, you see,' she explained. 'Because it happened while he was away and the dates wouldn't work out. After that, I had quite a lot of miscarriages, so I was punished.'

And how, thought Mr Barnes.

'Your son might trace you,' he said, and Louise heard the words with rare delight. No one had ever referred to him like that to her before, not even when he was born. 'You can leave your estate to him, either on condition that he be found before your death, or, if you wish, afterwards, perhaps within a certain period. People can sometimes be traced. But is there anybody else, in case it proves impossible?' What complications, he thought, foreseeing an estate that might be very difficult to settle, with the surfacing of possible pretenders, but this will could be regarded as a temporary safety measure, to be replaced when time had allowed reflection. Meanwhile, the son might be seeking her. Adopted children sometimes did when, with children of their own, they grew curious about genetic inheritance, or when their adoptive parents died.

'The young man on the train,' she said instantly. 'Andrew Sherwood, and his son Nicky. I'd like them to have it, if my son is never traced.' She knew that Andrew lived in Southwark, but that was all she could tell Mr Barnes as she described their meeting, only six days ago. She didn't mention the vandal attack on her return journey. 'He was a kind man,' Louise expanded. 'And unhappy – so was the little boy – kind and unhappy.

What if he were my son? He was the right age. Wouldn't that be wonderful?'

'Things don't work out like that,' warned Mr Barnes, alarmed.

'It would be nice to see him again,' Louise said. 'I wonder if I could find him?'

Very possibly, thought Mr Barnes, but with difficulty. He did not encourage her to try; the man was simply a stranger who had been civil and she had been impulsive enough already. It must have been impulse that led her into her hasty marriage, not to mention her doomed love affair, but the spontaneous instinct had lain dormant all these years. Now it was like a genie released from a bottle.

He had been making careful notes as they talked.

'I'll get this will drafted and send it to you for you to check, or to sign if you find it satisfactory,' he told her. 'You can always change it later, when you've had time to settle down. It needn't cost a lot,' he added.

He knew that this client and her problems would not disappear. The worst scenario was that the husband might turn up.

'You will be able to divorce your husband, ultimately,' he said. 'Without his consent, after a five-year separation. With his consent, fairly quickly. Your separation can be dated from your accident.'

'Oh,' said Louise. 'We'll do that, then.'

'Will he consent, if he turns up?' asked Mr Barnes.

'I don't know,' Louise replied.

If he got a good lawyer, he might make a claim on Lilac Cottage, Mr Barnes reflected; these days, what was sauce for the goose was also sauce for the gander. He wouldn't tell her that: not yet.

He decided not to comment on her new hairstyle as he left;

despite his gift of daffodils, now blooming in their mugs, theirs was a professional relationship. She must have been a pretty girl; no wonder the mysterious lover had been drawn to her. What a bastard, thought Mr Barnes, getting into his car; compared with modern women, girls in those days, with few rights, didn't have a clue, and abortion wasn't legal. On the other hand, it was not so long ago that a man who broke off an engagement could be sued for breach of promise. Jonathan's mother thought things had gone too far the other way; women were expected to fulfil too many roles, and men were at risk of being sidelined. Equal, but different, was her verdict. Jonathan's wife, a teacher until a few months before their first child was born, had recently returned, part-time, to her profession, and was the happier for it.

During his working life, Mr Barnes had heard many pathetic stories, and his firm had handled various difficult cases, so that he was rarely surprised, but Louise's revelation about her child had astonished him. It was very sad. Even if the man were to find her, it could end in disappointment, if not sorrow, for one or both of them, and perhaps also for the son's adoptive parents. It was probable that he had had a better chance in life than she, in her circumstances, could have given him, but at a terrible emotional cost.

If Louise had told her own mother, Susan would have stood by her, and so would her stepfather, Mr Barnes felt sure, but, making her lonely decision, she had not wanted to put them to the test. It seemed that she had made very few decisions since, but now the chance had come to change things, and she had seized it. Mr Barnes would sew things up for her protection as securely as he could, lest Colin reappear.

Money was going to be tight. There were unavoidable expenses – council tax, mounting annually – heat and light, and her subsistence. Could there be anything in her theory that it was Colin who had tried to run her down? He was, according to her mother, an unpleasant customer; he might be capable of such a thing, if he had a motive.

Why had he moved about so much during his working life? What had he to hide – for there must be something in his past which threatened, every so often, to catch up with him?

Jonathan Barnes, arriving home, was thankful that there were no skeletons in his cupboard, no sinister secrets too terrible to be exposed. At least, he didn't think there were.

11

Louise thought she might be able to trace Andrew Sherwood through the telephone directory. She knew that in Kenston library there had been a full set of directories covering the whole country. There was a library in Croxbury, but was it large enough to stock them? She could go there and see; in any case, she wanted to join it, for her enforced inactivity, when there was so much she wanted to do, was frustrating; reading, which had always been a refuge, would help her now.

From a notice on its door, she had already discovered that the library was closed on Mondays and Wednesdays, and open only for a few hours on Thursday evenings; she had passed it on Sunday on her way to have lunch with Dorothy Kershaw. It was housed in a converted bakery, and the windows had bars across them; even so, a pane of glass was cracked, high up in one corner. Louise sighed. She knew the library in Kenston had suffered from occasional bursts of rowdyism, and some of the staff had been subjected to aggressive and insulting behaviour by drunks and others who had come in only to cause trouble. Croxbury, peaceful on the surface, had problems too, it seemed.

Walking up the road on Tuesday at about midday, she met a

young woman pushing a child in a stroller; both were laughing, the woman, pink-cheeked and looking very young, was bending over the child so that they could communicate, for the chair faced forward. What a pity the child has to have its back to her, thought Louise. The girl spared a glance for her and her smile widened pleasantly, but she didn't speak. Mothers must be getting younger again, thought Louise, who had understood that women were postponing having children until they were in their thirties.

The library was busy. Obviously, it was appreciated. There were several mothers and toddlers in the children's section and a few older people waiting to exchange their books at the counter. Louise waited behind them, and when her turn came, asked if she might join.

The only librarian visible was plump and dark, in early middle age. Louise gave her name and explained that she had come to live in Lilac Cottage. The librarian asked for proof of her identity; Louise produced her pension book, with the altered address on the cover, and that seemed to do. She was enrolled and allowed to take out some books. In her good hand she carried a shopping bag, into which she put them, choosing two from the trolley because those were the latest returns and therefore popular, and *Mansfield Park*.

Jane Austen never failed. Louise did not like thrillers or detective novels; she found them too alarming. Real life was fearful enough for her.

Browsing round the shelves, Louise saw that there were no telephone directories. Tentatively, she asked the librarian if they stocked them and was offered help from their computer, which could search for her, but she took fright at this; she wanted to sit quietly with the relevant volumes, going down the lists herself.

'They have them in Durbridge,' the librarian told her.

'Oh, do they?' Louise had felt sure they would be available in Oxford, but going there meant changing buses and it would be quite an expedition. She could go to Durbridge on the local bus.

She hugged to herself the prospect of tracking Andrew Sherwood down. She did not need to contact him, only to locate him, but to make sure she had the right person, she would telephone, saying she wanted to thank him for his kindness after the vandal attack on the train. Meanwhile, she would lose no time in asking for her changed address to be entered in David's file in case her son was looking for her. Strange to think that the adoption authorities knew who his official parents were and where he had spent his childhood, and she did not.

She still felt as if she were living in a dream and that something would soon happen to shatter it. Each night she went to bed in her bare, chaste room, and though she fell asleep quite quickly, she woke early, unable to believe her life had altered so utterly and so swiftly, and aware that this limbo state, enforced on her by her injuries, would ultimately end. She must not drift.

Dorothy Kershaw, however, was not allowing her to do so. She arrived at Lilac Cottage on Wednesday morning, saying she was a refugee in need of sanctuary.

Humour was not Louise's strong point, and she was startled.

'Don't look so alarmed, Louise,' said Dorothy. 'It's the day Lavinia comes. She's my cleaning woman – housekeeper, she likes to be called. And she's a lady, not a woman. Isn't it strange how those who used to be referred to as ladies now prefer to be described as women, but others consider it an offensive term? Everyone's a lady now.'

'I hadn't thought about it,' said Louise. 'But I have seen police officers, in crime programmes, mention men they want to question and call them gentlemen.'

'So have I,' said Dorothy. 'I enjoy those programmes and they do seem to get results.'

Colin had liked them. He had never missed one, watching, rapt, attentive, recording any which came on if he was out.

'Why do you have to escape from this Lavinia?' asked Louise, shepherding her guest into the sitting room.

'My dear, she's so grand. Regal, almost,' said Dorothy. 'She polishes and dusts to perfection, and then tells me about a house she goes to where they have much better furniture than mine, and mounds of silver which she doesn't clean because she's far too lofty – a man does that.'

'Is it true?' asked Louise.

'I don't know.'

'How often does she work for you?' Louise asked.

'Once a week,' said Dorothy. 'I go out when I can, because I get so cross when she makes me feel that she's doing me a favour and is really far too superior to undertake such work.'

'Presumably you pay her,' said Louise.

'I do, and well, and in many ways she's worth it,' said Dorothy. 'It's not easy to get help round here. But there are several contract firms which come with vans. I might decide to change to one of them.'

'I suppose I'm too old to get a job with them, once I'm better,' said Louise. 'I have done a catering training. I'm qualified as a cook.'

'When did you do that?' asked Dorothy, interested. This strange, lost woman had told her very little about herself so far.

'Oh – over thirty years ago,' said Louise. 'Colin was working overseas and I was in this flat in Portsmouth, and I worked in a school. I expect my qualifications are out of date now. I thought I might take in a lodger, when I've got enough furniture,' she added. 'Would I find one, do you think?'

'I don't know,' said Dorothy. 'What sort of lodger?' She thought of commercial salesmen who, in her youth, boarded out in the week and went home at weekends. Was it like that now?

'A student. A teacher. I haven't thought it through,' said Louise.

'You'd have to be very careful. Insist on references,' said Dorothy. These days, didn't students get together and share flats? Her older grandchildren had done this. And teachers, if unmarried, would be paired off in partnerships in the modern way.

At this point in their conversation the telephone rang. It was the surgery, to tell Louise about her X-ray appointment. She could be seen the next day.

'Excellent,' said Mrs Kershaw, quite surprised that it should be so soon.

Louise's will had arrived by that morning's post, with instructions from Mr Barnes to sign it, if she approved it, in the presence of two witnesses. She had read it, and it seemed straightforward. She understood the implication that no time should be lost if her property were to be protected from Colin's possible acquisition by default. After all, she had had one accident; she might have another. Dorothy could be asked to be one witness, but a second must be found.

She burst out with the request, picking up the large, thick envelope in which the document had arrived.

'I've had to make a will. I've never made one before – I hadn't anything to leave,' she said nervously. 'I need two witnesses to my signature. Would you be one? And where could I find another?'

'The vicar,' said Dorothy promptly. 'I don't go to church, but I like her, and she's safe. I won't suggest Lavinia – we could use her but she'd be so curious. I'll ring Judith and see if she's at home.'

Dorothy was pleased with this idea. Judith Bright, the vicar, might, metaphorically speaking, perceive Louise as a lost lamb and scoop her up.

She just caught Judith, who was expecting a visitation from some diocesan inquisitors and an architect who were going to inspect the church's crumbling walls.

'Come at once,' said the vicar, 'or hold your peace until this afternoon.'

Dorothy relayed this message.

'She's very entertaining,' she said. 'The vicar. She has a dry wit which is often wasted on her flock. Her surname is Bright, and she is. She was a lexicographer until she got the call. Come along, Louise. We mustn't tarry.' She helped Louise on with her coat. 'You need a cape, while this business with your arm lasts,' said Dorothy.

They walked together down Church Street towards the vicarage, a modern brick building with white-painted sash windows. On their way, they met the same girl whom Louise had seen the day before, pushing the toddler in its stroller. The girl smiled at them both and the child waved.

'That's the nanny,' Dorothy told Louise, when they were out of the girl's hearing. 'I couldn't understand it at first, she looks so young and the child's father must be in his early thirties, but now I've seen both parents setting off for work in their separate cars – the husband goes first, then that girl arrives in her Fiat Punto and the mother leaves. There are several other daily nannies here. I notice all this on my village walks,' she added. 'I used to play golf, but my cronies all died off or got too feeble, so I had to alter my routine.' She spoke lightly. 'Here we are.' The door opened as they walked up the short, paved path. A sturdy woman with dark hair cut in a cap shape, not unlike Louise's – perhaps also Yolande's handiwork – stood aside to let them in. She had deep blue eyes and a slight scar on her cheek.

She kissed Dorothy affectionately, then held out her hand to Louise, saying, 'Welcome.'

'Before you suggest it, we won't take our coats off, Judith, as you're going out,' Dorothy stated. 'You know why we're here. Let's get it done.'

Louise felt some alarm at this blunt approach but Judith seemed to take it calmly.

'I understand the urgency,' she said. 'It's all very well to say take no heed for the morrow – one must, or one sows seeds of trouble. Come in here.' She led the way into a study which opened off the hall. Ballpoint pens and a large sheet of blotting paper were ready on a table. 'Cover it up with the blotting paper,' Judith said. 'What your document contains is not our business.'

Louise scarcely needed to speak as the task was completed. Within five minutes they were out of the house, with Judith promising to come and see Louise very soon.

'She means that,' Dorothy said. 'She'd have called anyway, but now she sees you're wounded, she'll come all the sooner. What's more, you can turn to her if you're in trouble and she'll be of some use, unlike our previous incumbent who was never seen and went on to become a bishop's chaplain. An excellent administrator, so it was said, but lacking pastoral ability. Now, I won't come back with you, Louise, but I'll take you to the hospital tomorrow.'

Standing in the road, they fixed the times as Judith drove out of the vicarage in a small red car and sped up the road, giving them a wave.

'Her husband's a scientist,' said Dorothy. 'He works in a laboratory doing research of some obscure variety. It's a second marriage for him; he was a widower and he has two children. One goes to Durbridge Comprehensive and the other is studying music in London.'

She turned then and walked off abruptly. Louise, opening her front door, already knew this was her way; she did not waste time on inessentials. And perhaps the dread Lavinia would have gone by now.

Once indoors, Louise read through the will again. Simple wording covered the fact that the whereabouts of neither potential beneficiary was known. However, she, Louise, was going to find them both. That was her immediate aim; then the details could be inserted.

Enclosing a short covering letter, in which she mentioned that she would get in touch as soon as she had traced either address, Louise sealed the will in the envelope which Barnes and Locock had thoughtfully provided, and that afternoon she posted it on her way to catch the bus to Durbridge, where she headed for the library, asking directions from a traffic warden about to put a ticket on a car parked on a double yellow line.

The library was custom-built, modern, with a lot of glass, and inside it was busy. After every move, Louise had sought out the nearest one as soon as possible and, as well as borrowing books, had used it as a sanctuary, a place where she could be alone without feeling lonely: in company, but not of it. She looked around her in this one, which was smaller than Kenston library but bigger than the Croxbury small branch. On one table, newspapers and magazines were displayed. She went past, searching for the telephone directories, and she eventually tracked down the London ones.

Checking through them, she found several A. Sherwoods, but was not sure which areas they came from; however, she wrote down such details as were given, and the numbers. She could look up the addresses in the *A to Z*. The library might have a copy, and then she would try ringing likely ones when cheap calls began. It was possible that Andrew Sherwood might not yet be listed, if he had moved there after his marriage break-up, however long ago that might have been. If she drew a blank, she could try directory enquiries, who would have up-to-date information.

Before seeking out the *A to Z*, still with the sensation that what was happening, and her surroundings, were not real, she sat down to read the newspaper. There was a report about the woman murdered in Kenston. The police were pursuing their enquiries, but now they were linking this killing to an unsolved murder which had taken place in Redditch three years ago, where a woman had been battered to death in a flat. She was divorced, like the Kenston victim, and she had also been working as a barmaid.

Louise and Colin had lived in Redditch three years ago, before they moved right across the country down to Kenston.

Stunned, Louise read the piece again. It must be another coincidence: they had lived in a town where a woman had been battered to death for no apparent reason; then they had moved to another where, after several years, the same thing had happened, but murders took place all the time, and often the killer was a family member. Colin couldn't have done these dreadful things. Colin had damaged her by cruel words and by neglect, and he had allowed her no life of her own, but he had not been violent until her accident, if it had been Colin who had caused it. If it were, she had every cause to fear him, for he must still wish her dead. But if he had killed those other women, he would also have battered her, surely? Why drive at her?

The answer came. He wanted it to seem an accident; if she were battered to death, he would be the prime suspect even if he were innocent. Louise, ignorant though she was of many matters, but by default a viewer of television crime programmes, was aware of that.

Had she gone mad, to think like this? What possible reason could Colin have for battering to death two unknown women? Had he been having affairs with them and feared discovery? Louise would not have minded if he had had a hundred mistresses through the years; if she had known about even one of them, she could have divorced him.

Why had he wanted to stay married? He often pontifi cated about lax modern morals and the high divorce rate, and within the very small circle – scarcely exalted enough to be called social – in which they moved, he sometimes preened himself on the duration of their marriage. Had he had lovers and killed them if they became demanding? And at his age?

It was very difficult to believe in such a theory. Distracted from the purpose of her visit to the library, Louise's head began to spin. She laid the newspaper aside and picked up, at random, a magazine, leafing through the pages. It was a newspaper's weekly supplement, covering a variety of topics, and as she did so, something caught her eye, making her turn back to find what it was.

It was a small photograph, in black and white, and it was

of Andrew Sherwood. There was his name, beside the heading to an article about buying second-hand cars. It was an amusing piece; Louise read it carefully. Then she wrote down the address of the publication.

12

Andrew had also learned about the body found in Redditch, but, unaware that Colin and Louise Widdows had lived there when the victim had been killed, he attached no significance to the news as he tried to trace her, but it was a sad discovery. Who was the woman?

People could disappear, or die, and not be found for weeks if it was no one's concern to notice them. At least, in his case, Nicky would miss him, and Val might wonder where he was. She had been in an odd mood lately, sometimes preoccupied and quiet, and then, in an abrupt turnaround, would become over-animated and demanding, but not, he realised, with a sudden frisson, affectionate. Feeling a twinge of guilt because he had sought out Clare Fairweather for reasons that were not entirely professional, Andrew did his best to respond to whatever humour Val was in, but he sensed an alteration in her response to him, a distancing. Her career prospects had widened since the recent conference and he knew she had been approached by a firm of headhunters; perhaps, with this opportunity, came the need for a lover who was more dynamic, less obsessed about his son, and more available.

They had not been together long, unless seven months was

long in terms of relationships. Andrew had not had one since his marriage, but Val, before they met, had had a series, which he felt was not his concern and he did not want to know the details. Possibly she liked variety, and he had already become too much of a habit, or she might have met someone more exciting at that conference. Maybe she was just waiting for the right moment to tell him it was over between them. How would he feel if she did?

It would not be a heartbreak, as it was when his marriage fell apart. It would be a sadness and another rejection.

He would be lonely. He was happy when he came home and found her busy in his kitchen; she made delicious pasta dishes and exotic soups. However, since that conference and his second trip to Kenston, this had happened only once. She hadn't been at the flat when he arrived home with Nicky this weekend. There was a message on the answerphone to say she'd had a change of plan.

Nicky had said, 'Sorry, Dad. You'll be upset.'

'No,' said Andrew. 'Not at all. Just a bit surprised. We'd thought you might like a trip to Thorpe Park tomorrow.'

'That's not really her thing, is it?' Nicky said.

'I don't know. What do you think is her thing?' asked Andrew.

Nicky shrugged.

'You,' he said. 'On your own. Like Mum and Terry.'

Andrew's heart sank. Did Nicky feel unwanted by both parents? He was certainly wanted here, by him.

'She's very fond of you,' he said. 'She's enjoyed the trips we've done.'

The Zoo. The Planetarium. The Science Museum. All those expeditions parents undertook in a conscientious attempt to spend leisure time with their children constructively. Val had put a good face on these excursions and had shown what seemed to be genuine interest; was it really for love of him, Andrew, that she had come along, or from a sense of duty? Certainly, she'd tried; he couldn't deny that. He put his arms round Nicky and hugged him.

'What would you like to do?' he said. 'Still go to Thorpe Park? Or football? We could find a match. Or we could kick a ball about in the park.'

'Stay here,' said Nicky. 'Watch motor racing on TV. Or whatever sport's on. Have a pizza.'

They did that, and they went for a walk beside the river. Then they hired a video. They played cards and chess, and altogether spent a very peaceful, undemanding weekend. Nicky was more reluctant than ever to go back to Reading, but at least they went by car, not by train, with strangers all around them.

Before the weekend, Andrew had rung Kenston police station to discover if there was any news about whoever had caused Mrs Widdows' accident. From the response he got, it sounded as though the police there had forgotten all about her, so he asked if her missing husband had turned up, and in what seemed to be a matter of sheer chance because she happened to be present in the room at the time, he was passed on to WPC Wendy Rogers who knew about the incident.

Andrew had not revealed that he was a reporter.

'I'm a friend of Mrs Widdows.' He repeated his earlier question. 'I'm concerned.' Neither statement was untrue.

'I wish I could give you some news, Mr Sherwood,' said WPC Rogers. 'I'm afraid there's none on either count.'

'You don't think her husband's disappearance is significant?' Andrew suggested, keeping his tone light. 'It seems a bit of a coincidence that she was run down and he went missing at the same time.'

'Are you implying that he was responsible for her accident?' Wendy Rogers demanded.

'I'm wondering if you should eliminate him from your enquiry – that is, if there is an enquiry,' said Andrew smoothly.

'I'll look into it,' said WPC Rogers. Her voice had hardened.

Andrew realised that this was a new idea, if not to her, at least to her colleagues who were in charge of the case.

'Thanks,' he said. He wondered about asking for Louise's address, but if he did, it would reveal that he was not a close enough friend to have been given it, and he doubted if, in any case, the police would disclose it without good authority.

He had a name now, however: WPC Rogers. He might go back to Kenston soon and look her up. Then he could see Clare again. The thought cheered him.

Meanwhile he had been compelled by his editor to write a piece on the hidden garden. It was to be slotted into a feature about other such surprising havens in unlikely places. Andrew was obliged to disclose its location, though he kept the details as vague as possible, not mentioning Mr and Mrs Gilbert by name. He had told Nicky about it on Sunday, when his son clocked into the piece while playing with Andrew's computer.

Nicky said he would like to see the garden, and Andrew said he might take him, one weekend.

Nicky had had a little plot when they all lived together. Hitherto his main crop had been radishes and nasturtiums. Andrew had asked about it and was told that Terry, who did not understand the mower, had, while cutting the grass, accidentally mown down the lettuce seedlings Nicky had been cultivating to help his mother with the catering.

'She never has enough money,' he had told his father, not adding that she blamed Andrew for this, saying he was mean. Nicky knew he wasn't.

'If Val doesn't come back, could I live here then?' he had asked, as they set off on Sunday for the return trip to Reading.

'Oh, Nicky, it's got nothing to do with Val,' said Andrew bleakly.

But Nicky was less certain. Two was company, three none; he'd learned that from Mum and Terry.

To distract his mind from this major worry, Andrew, driving back to London, turned his thoughts towards the theory that he had trawled in a somewhat random way across his conversation with WPC Rogers.

Could the missing husband have been responsible for Louise Widdows' accident?

Spouses were prime suspects in murder cases. Even when it was obvious that a third party was responsible, the police investigation sometimes concentrated on finding evidence to demonstrate a case against the preferred scapegoat. Innocent people had been convicted on purely circumstantial evidence. However, this time, what were the grounds for suspecting Mr Widdows of evil intent?

He tried to remember what Louise Widdows had revealed on their way to Waterloo. Nothing, really: she had said her husband had gone away, which the neighbour had confirmed. Still, if they were on reasonable terms, and he were innocently absent on business or a holiday, one would have expected him to have left an address or contact number. However, he had vanished without trace, just as she had done. When Andrew met her, she had looked frail, which was understandable. She had not said where she was going, but it was at least one stop west of Reading. Had she been preparing for her move, which took place a few days later?

There was a mystery here; he knew it. If Colin Widdows had run down his wife, it was a case of attempted murder; taking place right outside their house, it was hardly an accident. If he had tried to kill her, he had failed, and might try again.

Andrew parked the car and wearily climbed the stairs to his flat. Nicky had pulled his duvet up, and he had folded his pyjamas neatly. Andrew bundled his dirty clothes into the washing-machine, then dialled Val's number. They must sort things out between them. If she wanted to call a halt, it would be a blow to his pride, but would it be more than that? He was very fond of her, was used to her, liked their closeness which was a comfort in a lonely life, but he could not truly say he loved her. His heart did not leap when he saw her coming towards him, as once it had leaped for Hazel, but perhaps it was romantic folly to expect that a second time in his life. Val had come along when he needed someone, and probably it was the same for her: she had wanted to fill the blank left by the end of an earlier relationship.

There was nothing wrong with space, a gap, an interregnum. Scurrying from one partner to another to fulfil a sexual need, or demonstrate that one could easily find someone else, betrayed a sad lack of inner resourcefulness. He'd see what Val felt and take his cue from her. A period of celibacy might lie ahead, but so what? What was wrong with that?

Not much, unless it was for ever, Andrew thought, lifting the telephone.

Only Val's answerphone replied. He left no message.

*   *   *

Nicky, like his father, was lonely, though Mum had welcomed him with hugs and kisses. She always did, and when he was with her he was sure she was glad to see him back; soon they would have supper and then he could go to his room saying he had homework. He didn't like seeing Terry in Dad's place at the table. Maybe it would be better when the house was sold and they moved to one where it was all new, but then he would have to stop fooling himself that Mum and Dad would get back together again. Partly, he knew they never would, but partly he hoped for a miracle. They talked to each other when they met, but their manner was curt, though not really rude. Each spoke as though to a stranger, but he could remember when they had said 'Darling' and kissed a lot. Now it was Terry who was in bed with Mum and if Nicky woke in the night with a bad dream, he didn't like to go to her to be comforted. Anyway, he was too big for that now, he told himself; it was only a dream, after all, and he could turn on his light, read for a bit, and then go back to sleep. That usually worked. He'd get used to it, Dad had said.

In his mind, he followed Dad back to London. He hoped Val would be there now, because otherwise Dad would be on his own. On the way back to Reading, he'd talked about the lady with the broken arm who they'd met on the train. He'd met her again that day, going back to London. Some yobs had harassed her, Dad told him. She'd lived in Kenston but now she'd moved, Dad wasn't sure where to, but he might find out when he went back to Kenston to see the magical garden in the middle of broken-down buildings. Dad said that you could find good things in the middle of something bad, and he and Nicky would keep a good thing together even though they didn't meet very often. He could always telephone, Dad had said, then he'd ring back so that Mum didn't have to pay. It had worked all right so far.

Nicky wanted to ring him after supper. He asked Mum if he might and she said Dad would hardly have got home yet. He might well have stopped off at a pub to see his old pals.

Nicky decided not to tell her that Dad now had a mobile phone.

'He wouldn't drive after that,' he said. 'Not if he'd had a few drinks.'

'Don't you believe it,' said Terry. 'He did it before. He can do it again.'

Mum frowned at him and shook her head.

'He got caught speeding,' she said.

She hoped Terry wouldn't go out tonight. Sometimes, after Nicky came home, he did, especially if the boy seemed weepy and unsettled. He couldn't stand whining and tears. But when Terry and she had decided to live together, breaking up her marriage, he had walked out on a previous girlfriend. What he had done once, he could do again, if he met someone else he fancied, with no baggage from the past.

This prospect terrified Hazel. Terry was exciting and at the moment it seemed as if they could not get enough of each other, but she sometimes wondered if, at this intensity, it could last. And she felt guilty about Nicky, though she reminded herself that children were adaptable; her parents had divorced when she was thirteen. That had been difficult, but her mother had not remarried until very recently, and though she had had various boyfriends, none had ever moved in with them. Her father and his new wife had two children, and Hazel had liked them, whilst realising that she had become a convenient unpaid babysitter when she stayed with them. Her half-brother and half-sister had been upset when she and Andrew parted and had tried to bring them back together, but in the end had accepted the situation. The marriage had simply died, Hazel had told them; otherwise, she would not have been drawn to Terry. They did not know about her earlier affair. Her half-sister was staying overnight when they had this discussion, and Nicky, unable to sleep, had got out of bed and come downstairs, seeking consolation, but, hearing his father's name, had halted at the door and listened. You should never listen to other people's conversation, he'd been told, and now he learned there was good reason for such an edict. His mother and father's marriage had died; he had heard his mother say so. What about their love for him, their child? Each had assured him that this was unaffected, but he wondered. His father hadn't changed: that was certain; but what about his mother? Terry was the problem. He had called Nicky a mummy's boy who needed toughening up. If he'd had brothers and sisters, he'd have had his corners rubbed off, Terry had said, when Mum was out one day. Nicky didn't understand what he meant, but he knew Terry would rather it was just him and Mum on their own, just as Nicky would rather Terry wasn't there. Terry was always wanting to go out with Mum to meet their friends in pubs, with Mum all dressed up and looking wonderful, so that Nicky felt proud of her, for she was very pretty. If Terry went out without Mum, which sometimes he did when they couldn't get a babysitter, she was miserable. So really if he were to live with Dad, it would be better for her and Terry. Meanwhile, he'd said he didn't need a sitter now; he was old enough to be left on his own.

'When you're twelve,' his mother had said. So quite often Sandy from two doors away came in with her homework, and he liked that. She was friendly and helped him with his, and then they'd watch television or play card-games and Scrabble, like he played with Dad. Dad hardly helped him now, with Scrabble, except over spelling, and Nicky often got triple-scoring words where Dad failed to see the opportunity.

After he'd had his bath and was ready for bed, Nicky asked his mother again if he could telephone his father, and this time she let him.

'You can ring from upstairs,' she told him.

Nicky, happy, ran to her bedroom to make the call, too quickly to hear Terry tell her that she spoiled him.

'He'll turn into a proper wimp,' said Terry.

'He's still getting used to things,' said Hazel. 'Of course he's torn between us both.'

'Not thinking of going back to Andrew, are you?' asked Terry.

'Of course not,' Hazel said, and doubted, privately, whether, if she were, Andrew would even consider a reconciliation. She set about proving to Terry that she meant what she had said, while upstairs, Nicky, in his chat with Andrew, learned that Val hadn't been able to come round that night and that he'd had the idea, from seeing the Kenston secret garden, of embarking on a major plan on his balcony, with tubs and boxes. There was a veritable forest growing on another balcony at the far end of the block; he'd take a lead from that one, and if necessary call on the owner and ask for advice.

'Can we set it up next time I come?' asked Nicky.

'Sure thing,' said Andrew, and at last persuaded the boy to go to bed and think about it if, at first, he couldn't go to sleep.

Replacing their respective handsets, each thought about the other, picturing what they would be doing now: Nicky pulling the duvet up and nestling under it with Fred, his donkey, and Andrew finishing his reading of the Sunday papers.

What do we do to our children, wondered Andrew sadly, as he studied a rival supplement. Nicky, exhausted but consoled, fell asleep while speculating as to whether runner beans would grow in a pot on his father's balcony. He didn't see why not; they could creep up the posts at the side.

Valerie, in the pleasant flat which she had bought five years ago and filled with objects picked up here and there when pottering round markets and antique shops, knew that it was Andrew who was ringing her on Sunday night, though he left no message. She felt badly, but she told herself she needed time and space to think about where their relationship was going. However, she knew the answer, and it was nowhere. They had shared some happy times; Andrew was a nice man, and kind – kinder and nicer than several she had been involved with before. She felt safe with him, and comfortable, but she was not sure that this was what she wanted from a partner: she liked fireworks and excitement, even if they brought with them arguments and bouts of misery. Very ambitious, Val was not yet ready for a quiet life, and though she liked Nicky, there was no denying that on his weekend visits he was an encumbrance, always there, having to be put first. Such reflections were not creditable; love me, love my child, was the proper sentiment, but she didn't really love Andrew. He had boosted her recovery when her previous affair, which had lasted three years, had ended. Rupert, who was in advertising, had moved in with her and she had expected them to stay together for a long time, if not for ever, but quite suddenly one day he had abruptly told her he was getting married to a girl he had known all his life who wanted to live in the country and have babies.

'A wifey,' she had said bitterly, in tears.

'Exactly,' he had said. 'Sorry.'

He didn't need a high-earning career wife to help pay the

mortgage. He had paid half Val's while they were together, so she couldn't say that he had battened on her, but now he wanted a conventional family. Her pride was hurt, as well as her heart, and Andrew, entering her life a few months later, had brought consolation. They had been good for one another; she had helped him through his first loneliness; but now, with professional horizons opening before her, she would not have time to tend their relationship, and, lacking nurture, it would perish.

She would have to tell him, but not yet. Let him get over his forlorn return from Reading and adjust to work again; then she'd face the inevitable interview and he would have to make the best of things. Someone else would come along; nice, unattached men were rare. Perhaps he needed a wifey, too, but he wouldn't be able to afford one; Andrew would have to find an earner if he wanted to get married and have more children, which was the long-term future he probably needed.

The new job she'd been offered would open up her own future; success was very satisfying.

13

Colin Widdows had sold the car which he had driven at Louise in an attempt to kill her. Though his effort had not succeeded, she couldn't have recognised him; the night was dark and she should have been dazzled by his headlights. After knocking her down he had sped away, northwards, to Manchester, where they had never lived together and where he had rented a room as Adrian Mount, a retired insurance salesman. From there, he had rung Kenston General Hospital, to discover Louise's fate. He had pretended to be a neighbour, and had learned only that she was 'stable'. Not dead. Unfortunately, she was going to recover.

After decades of controlled, planned living, Colin's past was catching up with him.

He had thought that marrying Louise would save him, bring fortune and respectability; perhaps it had brought the latter, but the money he'd expected wasn't there, and he'd been saddled with a milksop of a wife, all repressed gentility, a schoolgirl who'd never grown up and who'd inherited nothing from those grand relations.

In those early years, his security had suddenly been threatened and twice he had fled abroad. He had found work, clerical jobs, not the sort of positions he had implied he was filling, but well paid. He'd returned to Louise because he had always thought there would be money in the end, and he had stayed because he enjoyed being able to keep her down, cow her, be in control. More and more, he relished frightening her, and he'd done it without hitting her once. He'd salted away some money under various names – Widdows wasn't his real name; he'd enjoyed the pun – for he'd been working scams for years, unknown to Louise: milking bank accounts, floating small companies from rented offices, attracting funds, then abandoning the premises – never large sums – but enough to meet expenses while he waited for his wife's inheritance. Louise had said the money was all Paul's, and there wasn't such a lot of it; Colin hadn't believed her but it had turned out to be true.

When she became pregnant, he'd been worried; they'd agreed not to have children, and the first time was a mistake, but after that he'd begun to think it wasn't such a bad idea; a kid would tie her down, distract her, keep her busy, maybe get that woebegone look off her face, only it hadn't worked out, and during those weary years she'd ailed and grown pale and anaemic. She'd been too self-absorbed to be curious about his work, which had involved constant moves to make him difficult to trace. It wasn't just his creditors whom he needed to evade; there was someone else, one of only two people who had known of his past involvement with murder. Over the years, he had bought the silence of the blackmailer, but now the crunch had come. A body had been found. The connection would be made; the case would be reopened. To save himself, he had to get away, and sparing Louise from discovering the truth would be a kindness in the long run. However, he had failed to remove her, so he would have to decide whether to try again.

He imagined she was still in the house in Moor Street,

carrying on with her daily round and probably talking to the neighbours, now that he wasn't there to stop her.

Sooner or later, he would have to find her and finish what he had begun.

14

Louise had started going for daily walks round the village, but not as early as Mrs Kershaw's routine march – for march she did, at a great rate, wielding her stick. Louise saw her pass Lilac Cottage most mornings. Though her timing varied, she usually went by at half past seven, or soon afterwards. She would already have drunk a cup of strong tea; on returning to Jackdaws, she would eat brown toast with butter and honey, and have one cup of strong, freshly ground coffee while she read the paper.

'I give myself small treats,' Dorothy had told Louise, as they returned from the hospital where, after an X-ray, Louise's arm had been put into a blue lightweight plaster. 'An unhurried breakfast is one of them, but on Wednesdays, Lavinia arrives while I'm having it. She knows I get up early, and sees no harm in turning up at her convenience, not mine. Nine o'clock is the time we had agreed at the outset.'

'Can't you ask her not to be so prompt?' asked Louise, who couldn't imagine employing anyone in any role, least of all as cleaner. She'd find herself apologising for any smear or speck of dust.

'I have mentioned it,' said Dorothy Kershaw. 'She goes on

afterwards to that grand household I told you she favours with her services, which is filled with valuable antiques.'

'But you've got some lovely things,' said Louise. She was shocked. Here was tough, resolute Dorothy Kershaw clearly nervous of her cleaning lady. 'Have you asked her to come later?'

'Yes, and the only alternative she has proposed is to come on Thursday afternoons. I don't want that. I want the house to myself in the afternoons.' She gave Louise a wry look and confessed, 'I like watching the racing on television. And golf, when there's a big tournament. Wimbledon, too, in the summer.' And snooker, but that was in the evenings.

'And why shouldn't you?' said Louise. 'It's your house. Couldn't you get rid of her?'

'I've got no excuse to, because she's reliable and a good worker,' said Mrs Kershaw. 'She'd sue me.' She added, 'I need someone. I hate housework.' And if she did sack Lavinia, she'd have to tell her daughter Barbara what she'd done, supplying reasons. Barbara was capable of ordering her to eat humble pie and plead with Lavinia to return, or even arranging it direct with Lavinia. 'It's not easy to get good help.' She had told Louise this before.

An idea was forming in Louise's mind. She could offer to replace Lavinia. It was too soon to suggest it, for her injury would prevent her from working for some weeks yet, and to mention it might create a new problem: she did not want Mrs Kershaw to feel obliged to take her on.

'You might be happier with one of those agency teams,' she said. 'They'd be impersonal, wouldn't they?' Louise had seen a smart blue van, with the sign DustAway painted on its side, parked outside a house near the vicarage.

Mrs Kershaw, too, had been wondering if she could offer

Louise the post as Lavinia's replacement, when she had recovered. Then she could give Lavinia proper notice. But did she want this pale, tired woman to become an employee? It would change the nature of their budding friendship, and she could imagine Barbara's caustic comments.

'I might enquire about them,' Dorothy conceded, and Louise thought she had lost an opportunity which would not come again.

She had written to Andrew Sherwood. There was no need to conceal her address from him, for he was not an enemy. She headed her plain Basildon Bond, bought from the ponytailed postmaster, accordingly.

Dear Mr Sherwood, wrote Louise.

You were so kind on the train. I do hope you and Nicky are well and have seen more of one another. I wanted to thank you for your help but did not know your address, and then I read an article you had written, about buying cars. Your photograph was beside the title and so I knew it had been written by you, not someone else with the same name. I am therefore sending this letter to you at the paper. Being a journalist must be interesting.

I have lost no time in moving into the house I have inherited. I should be very happy to see you and Nicky if you should be coming this way at any time.

She signed it, addressed the envelope and sealed it, then walked up to the post office to mail it. She had bought one first-class stamp, with the stationery.

'Just the one?' the postmaster, Greg Downey, had asked, and she had nodded. Who else would she be writing to?

He had greeted her warmly, asking after her arm, and commenting on the improving weather, even though cold spells must be expected. He told her the library would have a list of societies and activities in the village, some of which might attract her.

'I go to upholstery classes myself,' he told her. 'I'm reviving an old armchair.'

'Oh,' said Louise. 'Perhaps there's painting?' It was the only thing she could think of as a leisure activity.

'Oh yes. There's a thriving art club here,' he replied. 'You could begin any time, if you're right-handed. You wouldn't have to wait to have your plaster off.'

'So I could,' she said, tempted, but to enrol would cost money and there would be the equipment needed. Still, maybe she could take up something else; she'd ask at the library.

She was feeling a great deal better. Although she still thought Colin might find her and threaten her in some way, fear was retreating; she was sleeping well, and with several daily walks, she was taking exercise and getting fresh air. She bought her food needs at the village shop, and Dorothy had taken her into Durbridge to the supermarket, where the fruit and vegetables were very fresh, and there were tempting varieties of bread. There was a happy bustle in the aisles; Dorothy told her that the advent of this good, upmarket store had changed everybody's lives because conditions were so pleasant. There was plenty of parking space provided, and in the store one met one's acquaintances, but at the same time, its arrival had killed several shops in villages around, for whilst in it, people bought things that formerly they would have obtained locally. And it stayed open until late in the evenings, so that shopping could be done after work.

'It's a great convenience,' Dorothy had said. 'But the whole pattern of life in Croxbury has changed in the last ten years or so. People have come here from London; they expect town convenience and what they think of as rural peace, so that if a donkey brays or a cock crows, they demand silence.' She gave a snorting laugh. 'But then, I'm an old reactionary,' she said. 'I like old ways. Courtesy, even,' she added, as a large man stepped backwards, almost knocking her over.

Louise helped her put the shopping in the car.

'We must go to John Lewis one day,' Dorothy said, as they drove out of the car park. 'That's where you got your bed, you told me. You could price some of the things you need and decide if you'd rather get them somewhere else.' She changed gear as they slowed in traffic. 'Londoners who have country cottages often call there on Fridays.' Barbara was one such; she and her husband had had a cottage on the Wiltshire downs before moving out of London permanently to a farmhouse near Salisbury. 'We'll go on a Wednesday.'

Dodging Lavinia, thought Louise.

'That would be nice,' she said.

'I need some towels,' said Dorothy, defensively. 'And if you do decide to get anything bulky, they deliver.'

After the extravagance of her bed, Louise did not think she could afford any more of their furniture; a discount warehouse it would have to be, and she must be content with the minimum. When she went to collect her pension, she asked Greg Downey if he could tell her where to go, reachable by bus.

'I've only got the basics,' she explained. 'I need a few more things – a kitchen table, and some chairs, to start with.'

'You might see something advertised at the shop,' he suggested. 'They've got cards pinned up in the window.'

'Oh! I hadn't noticed,' Louise said, feeling foolish.

'Bit of a dreamer, that one,' Greg Downey told his wife that evening.

And so are you, she thought: he had been a building society

manager until he was made redundant and they moved to Croxbury from Birmingham. He had let his hair grow in what he said was an attempt to live the teenage years he'd never had, and had started keeping bees. She, meanwhile, worked at the checkout in the new supermarket in Durbridge, where she benefited from staff discounts.

Louise studied the cards in the shop window and saw a chair advertised, and a kitchen table, priced at ten pounds each. But what if she went to see them and didn't like them? It would be most embarrassing.

She'd leave that for the time being. A free paper was delivered weekly round the village; it advertised all types of sale, private and otherwise. She'd study it and see if there was one which she could reach easily on a voyage of inspection.

Louise still woke early, and on some mornings panic hit her, as it had the first day, but she forced herself to be calm. Even if Colin found her, he could not enter Lilac Cottage without breaking down the door or smashing a window, and while he did so, she would ring the police. As it was, at the end of each day she asked herself what was the worst thing that had happened, and it was usually a minor nuisance due to having the full use of only one hand.

On her walks, she had begun to notice individual people. Depending on her timing, she might see children walking up to catch the school bus outside *Yolande*, where there was a parking bay. Two boys lived on one side of Lilac Cottage; she had seen very little of them so far but when the weather improved she supposed they would be out on bicycles or playing football in the field on the outskirts of the village where there was a pitch. She had seen them and other boys on rollerblades skating by. She'd seen no girls on blades. Did Nicky Sherwood have them, she wondered, and let herself pretend that Andrew was her adopted son and Nicky her grandson. It did no harm to dream.

Meanwhile, she waited for a reply to her letter, for surely he would answer?

But if he didn't, nothing had altered. And if he did, what was she expecting? How could he respond except to acknowledge her note? He was not likely to accept her invitation. She would bore him.

On days when the library was open, she called there to catch up with the papers. She had been to church, too, finding it peaceful, sitting at the back, not joining in but not apart. Judith had preached briefly about honesty, and afterwards, at the door, had apologised to Louise for not coming round to see her, promising to do so soon.

Louise had not been disappointed; she had not expected a prompt visit from the vicar, if she came at all.

Andrew had received Louise's letter. How extraordinary to have his chase resolved by the quarry!

He dialled directory enquiries to find out her telephone number, but they had no record of it, so he wrote to ask if he might take her up on her invitation and call the following Sunday. He and Nicky would like to take her out to lunch and would arrive at about twelve-thirty unless he heard from her that this was not convenient. He wrote down his telephone number both in the office and at home, and said he had an answerphone at his flat.

Louise was elated. She walked round the house gasping with excitement. The nice young man and that dear boy were coming here, to her very own house, and luckily she had three chairs, though not much else in the way of furniture.

Dorothy was away. With regret, she had abandoned Louise, obliged to house-sit for her daughter Barbara, who, with her husband, was on a skiing holiday – an annual event – and had builders in who, Barbara said, needed supervision.

'I'm still useful sometimes,' Dorothy had told Louise. 'Telephone if you get wretched. One does sometimes. I'll give you the number.'

Louise, after consulting Mr Barnes, had decided that she must keep the telephone for emergency use, but that her own number should be ex-directory. In that way, if Colin should ever trace her, he could not telephone her unawares. She could give her number to anyone who needed it legitimately. She had explained this to Dorothy, who thought it a sensible precaution. It was strange how the man had disappeared; after sitting up in bed at night reading a particularly alarming thriller, Dorothy had wondered if Louise, finally tried beyond bearing, had dealt him a fatal blow and buried him in the garden, but it seemed unlikely, unless she had injured her arm in some struggle at the time and invented the car accident story as a cover.

Relinquishing this intriguing theory, Dorothy had sought sleep, unable to think of a plausible reason for Colin's vanishing trick unless he had taken up with a mistress or committed a crime. Either was possible.

For Louise, however, life had focus. She would accept Andrew's lunch invitation, making it clear that she did so on the understanding that as soon as her arm was out of plaster, he and Nicky would have lunch with her. Meanwhile, she went to the post office to ask Greg Downey, who, in the absence of Dorothy, she counted as her only friend, what sort of food a ten-year-old boy would like for his tea. Greg advised savoury things – sausage and chips, cheese biscuits – and Louise, who was thinking in terms of cakes and sandwiches, felt bewildered. After all, they would have had a proper lunch. However, she went to the shop where she bought Cheddar biscuits and KitKats, remembering that at the hospital shop KitKats were popular with everyone. Then, on Saturday afternoon, she set about making a chocolate sponge cake. It was the first real cooking she had done since her move, and, despite her arm, she managed.

Louise could not remember when she had last had guests of her own to a meal. There had been none since her mother's death, and they had had very few of Colin's; those that came were people he sought to impress, who might assist his work. Louise could be relied on to provide a good meal and to be an adequate and self-effacing hostess. There had been none of these occasions while they lived in Kenston.

She turned her mind away from such reflections, refusing to think of Redditch and that dead woman, and all the evenings when Colin had been out. But she had kept a major secret from him through those years. He might have one also. Or several.

She slept badly on Saturday night, convincing herself that Andrew and his son would not turn up. Weren't young people very casual these days? They made arrangements but did not honour them. She'd heard tales of such behaviour from fellow helpers in the hospital shop, where she had done a lot of listening but very little talking.

Crocuses and early daffodils were out in the garden. Louise picked some and arranged them in a small pot on the rosewood table. She'd put tea things ready on a tray. Now there was nothing to do but wait.

The boys from next door were rollerblading up and down the road. Louise had barely seen their parents, nor the couple on her other side; they left home together very early, in a large white car, and returned late; so far these comings and goings had been in the dark, and at weekends all Louise had noticed was the sound of vacuuming coming from the house, and the rear view of a burly man washing the car. On Friday night they had had a party. A number of cars had parked in the road outside and she had heard voices as people arrived and were admitted; then she was aware of the faint beat of pop music, but she was not troubled by their noise. She was pleased that people were enjoying themselves, whereas Colin, had he been there, would have paced up and down ready to complain as the decibels rose. He had done that, at other times, in other places.

Louise thought, obscurely, that intolerance to noise did not go hand in hand with taking pleasure in the company of barmaids, for bars were not quiet places, and how did you get friendly with a barmaid unless you met her in her place of work? Colin did not drink excessively. She had never seen him drunk, unless his cold, black moods were due to alcohol; she could not picture him at ease in public bars. She had seldom been in one herself.

She was completely ready for her visitors by ten o'clock, and as she had not yet had a walk, she set out for a quick turn round the circuit along the main street, past Jackdaws, and home.

The vicar was riding up Church Street on her bike. She braked and dismounted, and, without preliminary, invited Louise to supper next Tuesday evening. Louise, flustered, accepted instantly, and they parted, Judith clearly in a hurry, rushing off to see someone before the morning service. Walking on, she recognised that, after an interval, she would have to ask the vicar back. Could she do it? Could she manage a dinner for the vicar and her husband – for he must be included – on her own?

Of course you can, she told herself. You're a trained cook and you've kept in practice, and there won't be Colin to complain and criticise if anything goes wrong. What's more, it can't happen until your arm is completely better, and you have a table and four chairs, for you will ask Dorothy as well, and she will help by talking to the guests. In fact, it might be rather pleasant.

Pursuing this line of thought, she approached Jackdaws, and, to her surprise, saw a figure move past the front window. Dorothy hadn't come back early, surely? Lavinia would be going in on Wednesdays, but Louise did not know if anyone else had a key.

She hesitated, then took a deep breath, walked up the path and rang the bell.

There was a pause before the door was opened. A tall woman with hennaed hair, wearing black trousers and an expensive white sweater, faced Louise.

'Yes?' she said.

'Is Mrs Kershaw back?' Louise asked. She used a firm voice, modelling herself on Dorothy.

'No,' said the woman.

'I see,' said Louise, and stood her ground. 'And you are?'

'Her housekeeper. Mrs Nisbet,' said the woman.

Louise did not know Lavinia's surname, but the air of condescension exuded by the woman was in line with Dorothy's description.

'Naturally I come in from time to time, while Mrs Kershaw is away, to pick up the post and see that things are in order,' added the woman.

'Of course you do,' said Louise.

'And you will be?' said the woman.

'Mrs Widdows, of Lilac Cottage,' said Louise, paying Lavinia back in the same coin.

'I'll mention that you called,' Lavinia said.

'Thank you,' said Louise, and turned away.

As the woman closed the door, she thought she heard a man's voice in the background, but decided that she must have been mistaken.

15

The church bells pealed before the morning service, and as time wore on, Louise prepared herself for disappointment, but at twelve o'clock she was sitting by the window, watching for Andrew and Nicky. They might be early, but then again, they might not come at all. At twelve twenty-five a black car went slowly past, and then, a few moments later, it reappeared and drew up outside the gate.

Louise felt almost giddy with joy. They had arrived. She saw them getting out of the car – the man, dark haired and sturdy, and the boy who was so like him, turning to talk to him, laughing, not the sad child she had met in the train. He would be living in the present, Louise thought, as she had learned to do in tranquil intervals. Now they were round at the back of the car and opening the boot. Out of it they took a bunch of flowers. Her eyes filled. In less than a month, she had been given flowers twice. Mr Barnes's daffodils had lasted for two weeks, and before they withered she had broken some branches from a forsythia in her garden and brought them indoors. In the warmth, they would soon break into bloom; there had been a forsythia at the house in Redditch, and at another in Nottingham, and she had done the same there, a tip she had learned long ago from her mother.

Too eager to wait until they rang the bell, she opened the door and stood beaming on the step.

She was so small. Andrew had noticed this before, and it had made her all the more vulnerable to the bullies on the train, but now she looked different: animated, and younger. She'd had a haircut. Gone was the dignified coil of heavy grey hair, too weighty for her height.

He stooped and kissed her cheek. Somehow it seemed the natural thing to do.

Louise's heart was pounding; feeling his soft mouth on her skin, she was ecstatic.

He's my son, her heart was saying, while her head was telling her not to be ridiculous.

Nicky, after being confined in the car, was jumping around as they entered the house.

'Dad says you live here. It's nice,' he was saying. 'How's your arm?' he remembered to add, and she said the plaster would be coming off soon.

Andrew was smiling down at her.

'You've changed,' he said.

'I know,' she agreed. 'My whole life has been revolutionised.' Then she put her hand to her mouth. 'Oh!' she said. 'I should offer you a drink, but I haven't any in the house.'

'That's all right,' said Andrew. 'I'm driving, and one glass of something is all I dare swallow, which I'll have at lunch. But you can have as much as you like.'

'Dad lost his licence, but he's got it back,' Nicky said. 'He'd been speeding. I won't have to go on the train again.'

'That's good,' said Louise. She looked at the little boy, whose face was pink, his eyes bright.

'I'm spending all my weekends with Dad now,' he said. 'Mum said I could.'

After Terry had failed to come home one night, Hazel had suggested this arrangement, to the astonishment of Andrew and the delight of his son.

'I'm very glad,' said Louise.

'Unless I have to be away on a story,' Andrew said. 'But that doesn't happen very often. Now, I think we'd better be off to have our lunch. When we come back, perhaps you'll show us round your house.'

'Oh yes,' said Louise.

He helped her into her coat, one empty sleeve tucked inside, today, to make it easier.

'Like Nelson,' Andrew said.

She laughed.

'Sort of,' she said. Richard had once taken her into Portsmouth dockyard to see the *Victory*, and unlike modern children, she had received a general education in the history of her country.

Nicky hadn't, and had to be told. In the car, driving to the riverside restaurant at which Andrew had reserved a table, Louise and Andrew filled him in, touching lightly on Lady Hamilton's role in the admiral's story.

'She was like Val. His girlfriend,' Nicky suggested.

'Yes,' said his father.

So Andrew had a girlfriend.

'And like Mum with Terry,' Nicky tried.

'Mm,' said Andrew, with reluctance.

'Val might come back,' said Nicky, in consoling tones.

'Maybe,' said Andrew, changing gear jerkily and earning a pained cry of 'Dad' from the rear seat.

Andrew's romance had gone awry. In a few short minutes, Louise had acquired significant background knowledge about this little family. She sat beside him feeling unusually alert, and yet, conversely, relaxed, as they drove along country roads towards their destination. The day was cold but a thin sun shone through the bare trees and the sky was a pale blue. Not realising she was doing so, Louise sighed with contentment, sitting back in her seat and looking about her.

'I haven't been this far before,' she said, as they twisted their way through a straggling village where there were attractive old houses on both sides of the road. 'I've been to the hospital about my arm, and shopping in Durbridge, but that's all, so far.'

'How did you get to the hospital?' asked Andrew.

'A friend took me. Well, a kind neighbour, really,' she said. It might be presumptuous to call Dorothy a friend so soon.

'It sounds as if he or she is a friend,' said Andrew.

'It's a she. Dorothy Kershaw. She's away at the moment. I stayed in Croxbury when I was a child and met her then. The cottage was owned by my mother's godmother, who left it to my mother, and so it came to me.'

'I see.' Andrew waited for more to be revealed, but Louise, who spoke so seldom and then only briefly because she thought no one would want to hear what she had to say, was silent.

'You lived in Kenston, didn't you?' said Nicky, from the back of the car. 'Dad went there because there's a magic garden in the middle of a lot of ruins. And there's been a murder.'

'I know about the murder. I didn't know about the garden,' said Louise.

'We'll tell you about it at lunch,' said Andrew, who did not want her to discover the lengths he had gone to in trying to find her. What would she think if she heard he'd consulted the voters' lists?

Nicky grew excited when a Ferrari shot past them on the road; he said it was an old model, but it was impressive, a blue bullet whizzing by. They came up to a covey of cyclists in bright helmets and jackets, a cycling club on an expedition, and had to pass them very carefully, the long line of riders spread out, so that when there was a bend, it was difficult to see if it was safe to pass.

'It's a bit different from Kenston, isn't it?' said Andrew.

'That's just what I was thinking,' said Louise.

'Had you lived there long?' asked Andrew.

'In Kenston? No – about three years,' said Louise.

'How did you break your arm?' asked Nicky.

'A car knocked me down,' said Louise.

'Didn't you look when you were crossing the road?'

'It was in the dark. I was on the pavement. The car suddenly put its lights on and rushed towards me,' said Louise. 'It dazzled me and it came right up on to the pavement. The police thought it was a joyrider. Someone who probably couldn't drive properly.'

'Ugh,' said Nicky. 'That's sick. Hitting you.'

'It could have been worse,' said Louise.

'A person could get run over in Croxbury,' said Andrew mildly. 'Anywhere, in fact. Here we are,' he added, slowing down. 'It's just down this road and then you'll see the river bank.'

He turned the car down a narrow lane which brought them to what had once been a popular pub and was now a restaurant, such as Louise had not been to since Richard took her out, so long ago. Colin had never included her when he had a business dinner. She would be no help, he had said; she was too dull and dowdy, and no good at making conversation. Except for an occasional sandwich, and the buffet at a charity bazaar where she had prepared some of the dishes, until she went to hospital, she had not eaten a meal cooked by someone else for longer than she could remember. Now, since moving, she had been out to Sunday lunch once, and here she was, doing it again. And she was going to supper at the vicarage, next Tuesday. She laughed to herself.

'What's the joke?' asked Andrew.

'Oh – nothing,' said Louise, not wanting to confess. 'I'm just having a happy time.'

'Good,' he said, meaning it, as he inserted the car between two others. The Ferrari was also in the restaurant's yard, and Nicky went to look at it as Andrew helped Louise out of the car.

'You should laugh more often,' Andrew told her.

Richard used to say that to her, teasingly, gently twisting a lock of her hair, telling her she was too solemn. His voice was different from Andrew's, though: deeper, a bass rather than a tenor.

'I haven't had a day out like this for a long time,' she said. 'What a lovely place. Have you been here before?'

He had, to dinner once, with Hazel; it wasn't all that far from Reading. Somehow that didn't matter now.

'Yes,' he said. 'I thought Nicky would like the boats, but it's a bit too chilly yet to go out in one. Maybe in the summer.'

'That would be fun for you,' she said.

'I meant all of us,' said Andrew, astonishing himself. 'You, too. If you'd like it.'

'I would,' she said, and he saw a faint flush spread over her pale face.

'I like the hair,' he told her, as Nicky returned to them, saying he was starving.

'It's symbolic,' she said. 'A new beginning.'

'Excellent.'

Nicky was somewhat subdued as they ordered lunch, for, as with Louise, the restaurant was of a type outside his experience.

'He's more used to McDonald's and pizza places,' Andrew explained, as they consulted their menus. 'It'll do you good to move upmarket now and then, Nicky.'

Louise was embarrassed at how expensive it was, but Andrew sensed this and helped her choose her meal.

'I'm going to have the lamb,' he said, so Louise said she would do the same, with soup for the first course while Andrew went for a mushroom dish. Nicky picked prawns, and was guided towards the lamb. Louise looked worried when Andrew suggested ordering wine, and he went hastily on, 'I'd love us to sink a bottle of burgundy between us, but it's not practical, as I'm driving, so what if I have a beer, Nicky has his favourite Coca-Cola, and you have a glass of wine? You can always have a second, later.'

'That would be lovely,' she said. 'One glass, I mean.'

'Mum and Terry like getting tipsy,' Nicky observed, watching out of the window as a cabin cruiser went past, crewed by several people wearing oilskins.

'Do you like football, Nicky?' Louise asked, to divert him. She had an idea most boys were mad about it, but it was a subject of which she knew nothing.

'A bit,' he said. 'Terry does. He watches *Match of the Day* all the time.'

When he wasn't out getting tipsy with Nicky's mother, thought both Andrew and Louise, and she had the further thought that because of Terry's fondness for the game, Nicky might be denying a natural inclination towards it. He seemed determined to reveal Terry in a less than favourable light.

'What else do you like doing?' Louise asked him.

'Gardens and stuff,' said Nicky. 'Terry mowed down all my lettuces. But me and Dad are going to make a garden on our balcony. We've already got some pots and things.'

'That's a lovely idea,' said Louise.

'It'll be like that garden in Kenston. The magic one,' said Nicky.

'It's amazing,' Andrew said. 'It's on waste ground, where there are some derelict buildings due to be developed soon.' There was no need to tell her it was near the murder scene. 'An old couple, Mr and Mrs Gilbert, have made it.' He described them, and said he had wanted to conceal its location when he wrote about it, but that it wasn't possible.

'Why didn't you want anyone to know about it?' Nicky enquired.

'I didn't want shoals of people going and bothering them. It's their special secret,' Andrew said.

'Like the book,' said Louise, and when they both looked blank, she said, '*The Secret Garden*. Surely you know it?'

But neither of them did, though Andrew seemed to think there had been a film.

'Didn't your mother read it to you?' Louise asked him.

'He's adopted,' Nicky said. By now they had reached the pudding course and he was delving into a mountain of varied ice cream. Andrew had chosen zabaglione, which he said he loved, and Louise, who had never tried it, had it too; she soon saw why he favoured it. 'And I haven't got a gran,' Nicky went on. 'His mum's dead.'

'Your adoptive mother?' Louise felt her head begin to spin.

'Yes,' said Andrew. 'They were wonderful parents, but they're both dead now. I had a perfect childhood, with an adopted sister – not a blood one.'

'My other gran took off,' Nicky said. 'To America.'

'She did,' Andrew confirmed. 'Several years ago, into a mature second marriage,' he explained. 'But she's still your gran, Nicky, and she writes.'

'I'll tell you a bit about that book, *The Secret Garden*, since neither of you knows about it,' said Louise, anxious to discuss less personal subjects. She began to relate an outline of the story, and then said perhaps it was the sort of thing that appealed more to girls than boys or men.

'Could be,' said Andrew, and added, when she had brought the tale to an abrupt end, 'I wonder if we should look for a garden centre on our way back, and buy some plants.' The bill had arrived, and he took out his credit card. Louise, embarrassed, looked away.

'It's rather cold for putting them in,' she said. 'It might be better to wait a bit. They probably don't have much ready yet.'

'You know about gardens,' he stated.

'A certain amount, yes,' she said.

Before returning to the car, they took a turn along the river bank. It was a peaceful scene, the water black and very still except when a few boats went past. Nicky ran on ahead.

'Is he all right? He won't fall in?' she said anxiously.

'I think he's safe enough,' said Andrew. 'Have you any children?'

'Colin and I were not so lucky,' she said carefully, then went on, 'Haven't you been curious about your real mother? Have you tried to find her?'

'I wasn't till after my mother – my adoptive mother – died. Then I began to wonder about heredity, because of Nicky,' he said.

'Did you ever think that your real mother might wonder what had happened to you? She might be thinking of you every day,' said Louise. Her voice shook a little.

'Or she might never have given me a thought, after getting rid of me,' he said.

'I'm sure it wasn't like that,' said Louise. 'Giving you up was probably dreadful for her. Things weren't so easy in the days when you were born. People are more tolerant now, and there's family support and so on.' She spoke with passion, astonishing him.

'I know. I don't condemn her, because I don't know her circumstances,' he said.

'She might be very glad to know how well things have turned out for you,' she said. 'You say you had wonderful parents. Your real mother would be proud of you. And of Nicky.'

'Maybe I'll look for her one day,' he said. 'Of course, she might be dead, too.'

'I'm sorry your other mother has died,' said Louise.

It was getting cold, so they called to Nicky and were soon in the car driving back to Croxbury. Louise showed them her small garden, and then round her bare house. Andrew saw her hairbrush and toilet things on her bedroom window sill, and her bedside light balanced on a cardboard carton.

'I've got to get some furniture,' said Louise. 'But it'll have to wait till I'm out of this.' She indicated her sling, leading the way down to the kitchen, where the cake and biscuits were all ready, set out under tea towels on the worktop. She switched the kettle on and Andrew sent Nicky ahead into the sitting room.

'You need help,' said Andrew. 'You left Kenston in a hurry, didn't you?'

She nodded.

'Yes. Since I'd got the cottage, by a miracle.'

'I think you're a fugitive,' said Andrew gravely, and she did not deny it, picking up the cake plate, leaving him to follow with the rest.

Before they left, he gave her his home address, and the telephone number, which he had already given her in his letter.

'I'll come again, if I may,' he said.

'Oh, please,' she said fervently. They'd mentioned the boat trip; would they remember it?

'And me,' said Nicky. 'I'll come too.' He had eaten most of the Cheddar biscuits, and had asked if he could take a KitKat to eat in the car.

Restless after they had gone, Louise put her coat on and went out for another walk. She turned right, so that she would go past Jackdaws.

A light showed faintly behind the closed curtains in the sitting room. Had Dorothy arranged for someone to go in and draw them every evening, putting on a light? It might be a security precaution, but Louise was still uneasy because of the man's voice she had heard when, that morning, Lavinia had opened the front door, though of course it could have been the radio. Back at Lilac Cottage, she dialled the Jackdaws' number.

There was no reply.

Perhaps Lavinia had been asked to go in every night and morning. Louise could telephone Dorothy to find out, but it seemed an unnecessary fuss. Lavinia was, after all, Dorothy's paid help. She let it go.

Driving back to London after leaving Nicky in Reading, Andrew thought about the day. It had been a strange one, and he was more intrigued than ever with Louise. She had become almost emotional when they discussed adoption, and, he remembered now, she had said that she and Colin had had no children, not that she herself had none. Perhaps she had wanted to adopt, and Colin had refused.

Meanwhile, Louise was writing him a careful, unemotional letter of thanks for giving her such a happy day.

16

On Monday morning Louise walked up to the post office, bought two first-class stamps and posted two letters, one to Andrew, and the second to Mr Barnes to tell him she had located Andrew Sherwood. She explained that she had read a magazine article he had written, thus discovering him to be a journalist, and that he and his son had been to visit her. She hoped he would come to see her again soon, and supplied his address and telephone number.

After posting the letters, she walked past Jackdaws, where the curtains were drawn back and the house looked normal. Because Dorothy would be away for a fortnight, she would have wanted someone to go in more frequently than once a week, and obviously that person would be Lavinia, who might find Sunday a convenient day to call. It made sense.

As the library was closed on Monday, she went to the shop and bought a paper; Colin had taken the *Daily Mail* and she had grown used to reading it after he had discarded it. Kenston library took *The Times*, so it made a change.

Inside the paper there was a report of a body discovered in the garden of a house in Sheffield when foundations were being taken out to build an extension. The body had not yet been identified; it had probably been buried at the time the house was built. Reports of people missing at that time would be checked against any details which forensic scientists would be able to uncover after such a period.

Horrible, thought Louise, turning the page to read about something less upsetting.

Later, she settled down to look at furniture advertisements in the local free paper, and saw there were several warehouses in the area, though not in Durbridge. Tomorrow, when she went to supper at the vicarage, Judith Bright might tell her the best way to get to them, or Greg, at the post office. As before, he had greeted her with warmth this morning when she bought the stamps; he spoke cheerily to all his customers, she'd noticed. Consulting him would give her a mission, and afterwards she could make a plan. Having so much spare time felt strange, and, incapacitated as she was, she did not know how to occupy it, though she had been reading a lot, often dropping off to sleep over even an enthralling book. Docile, and not given to introspection except to castigate herself for her inadequacies and failures, she did not realise that after decades of defeat, she was utterly exhausted in both mind and body, and that this was nature's way of helping her to heal.

She walked up the road again to talk to Greg, who was helpful. He told her that when the post office closed on Wednesday afternoons, he often went to Durbridge, and, depending on their plans and his wife's requirements, sometimes on more major shopping expeditions. It so happened that they were going to do up their spare bedroom, and he had to buy some paint. If she liked, he would take her with him this Wednesday to the Do-it-Yourself store where he planned to get it, and other items which were needed. She could have a look around; she might find something which she needed.

B&Q sold furniture and there were other retailers in the same complex.

She was stunned by his kindness, and she managed to thank him warmly, not finding the words as difficult to utter as she would have done even two weeks ago.

'Started painting yet?' he asked her, and she said that no, she hadn't, but she had borrowed a book on sketching from the library.

When she reached home, she took it out and, using precious Basildon Bond because she had no other paper, began to draw the flowers Andrew had brought her. Then she tried, with less success, to draw Andrew and Nicky.

It made the time pass pleasantly enough, until sleep overcame her once again.

On Monday evening, Val went round to see Andrew. She was in the flat when he came home. As part of the research for a joint feature he and other staff writers were preparing he had been interviewing the families of people suffering from a rare illness and it had been a fairly depressing day.

Glancing up at the balconies after he had parked the car, he looked along the block to the verdant effort produced by his neighbours; all through the winter, some foliage had been visible. In the summer it had been full of brilliant colour; doubtless they took their more delicate plants inside in the cold weather. Andrew was a competent general gardener, but he had not been one for tubs and planting out. Growing healthy, uncontaminated vegetables for his family had been his main interest, but now he'd bought a book about gardening in confined spaces using pots and boxes. You took cuttings from your geraniums and put them on the window sills indoors. He'd have to buy some geraniums in order to take the cuttings for the following year.

This was in his mind as he walked up the flights of stairs to the third floor, and it was a surprise to find more lights on in his flat than were controlled by time switches, and to hear sounds of activity from the kitchen. He hadn't thought about Val all day; indeed, he had planned to telephone Clare Fairweather and make a date for lunch, as he intended to nose around in Kenston to see if there was any news about the murder and also to find out if Colin Widdows had turned up. Andrew had learned nothing about the man from Louise herself; her only mention of him was to say, on the day they met, after she had been assaulted, that he was not at home.

Now he had a slight shock as he realised that Val was cooking a meal in her old way, which once had been so welcome.

'Hi,' he said, in an interrogative tone, taking off his raincoat and hanging it up while he wondered what mood he should adopt. He felt dismay. Exposure of emotions lay ahead.

Val came out of the kitchen. Her fair hair stood out from her head like an aureole. He had never learned whether its exuberant corkscrew curls were natural; it sprang back like wire when it was smoothed and stroked, and he had found it fascinating.

'I bought turkey breast,' she said. 'I'm doing it in a special sauce.'

Were they to go on as though there had been no interruption?

'Have you been watching television cookery?' he asked.

'Yeah – funny you should say that,' she replied. 'I have. I went home at the weekend. My mum's hooked on those programmes and she's always taping them to show me.'

She kissed his cheek. That was a sign. Andrew felt sad because he did not want to hold her closer.

'I'll find some wine,' he said.

He set about being helpful in the background. As he laid the table, he found himself resenting the fact that she had just walked back into his life without ceremony after moving out of it so casually, but they had never treated their relationship as one of commitment.

'Did you get that job?' he asked her as, simultaneously, she asked him how Nicky was. Then they both laughed, but awkwardly, and Andrew poured wine into two glasses.

'You go first,' he said.

She was starting her new job in a month's time, and meanwhile was going to take some holiday that was owed to her. She was off to Barbados.

'Want to come with me?' she said.

'I can't. I'm not due any leave yet,' Andrew said. She would know that, and she would know that he would want to spend his holiday with Nicky, so had she really meant her invitation? 'I expect you can find someone to go with,' he said. There'd be a girlfriend, at the least, and two unattached, attractive females would have a good time, floating free.

The meal was almost ready. He wondered what she would have done if he hadn't come home this evening. After all, he might have been away following a story. She'd have eaten her share, put the rest in the fridge and left him a note, he supposed, and as though anticipating what he was thinking, she told him that was what she would have done.

'I really came to say goodbye. Collect my stuff. All that,' she said. She had kept toilet things and a few clothes at the flat. They sat down to eat the turkey. It was very good, the flesh wrapped round a collection of spicy vegetables. 'We've come to the end, Andrew. I'm sorry. We had some good times.'

It was true, and she had helped him through a very wretched

patch. He said so, feeling no urge to try to persuade her to change her mind but, instead, a sense of freedom. This shocked him.

'You'll be all right, you and Nicky,' she assured him.

'Oh yes,' he said. He told her about the new weekend arrangement.

'That's great. Why did Hazel change her mind?'

'It's probably Terry. She may be afraid he'll dump her if he sees too much of Nicky,' Andrew said.

'He's all right with Nicky, isn't he?'

'I think so, in a basic way, but it's unreasonable to expect him to take Nicky to his heart just because he's got something going with his mother,' Andrew said, and didn't add, just as you found him a problem.

'I expect it's easier when there are other children on both sides,' said Val bracingly. 'Then they can all get along together.'

'But why should they? They might hate each other. Why should they like each other just because their parents do?' he demanded. 'Poor kids. It's rotten for them.'

Val, whose parents lived in comfortable retirement in Norfolk, and who wished she would get married and be as happy as they were, nodded in agreement.

'I suppose it could be tough,' she said.

'You know it can be, Val,' he told her. 'You must have friends who've been in that situation, or have put their kids into it.'

'You should do a piece about it,' Val replied.

'Perhaps I will,' he said. 'But it's been done a hundred times already.'

'Well, how was Nicky? You still haven't told me,' she said, determined to treat this last meeting with the gravity it demanded.

He described their weekend. Though she already knew about

his original meeting with Louise, he had not told her about his subsequent search for her. Val, however, showed no surprise; it was just the sort of thing he would do.

'She made a swift decision, moving like that, so fast,' she said.

'Yes, but sometimes things just fall into place,' he answered. 'It may have happened at the right time for her.'

'So she's a puzzling lady,' Val said.

'Yes. Yet she seems rather dull. Quiet. Subdued,' he said.

'Shall you see her again?'

'Oh yes. I promised,' Andrew said.

A surrogate mother for him, Val reflected. She knew he missed his own. Val did not know that he had been adopted.

'It'll be nice for Nicky, visiting in the country,' she commented.

'I suppose it is country,' said Andrew. 'Yes, of course it is, but I doubt if many of the people living there now were born locally. It's old cottages, all prettied up, and a few clumps of newer houses tucked in here and there. It must once have been really rural, but I should think most of the inhabitants commute now.'

'Even where Mum and Dad live, it's getting more like that,' said Val.

'Well, people commute to Paris,' Andrew said.

'And the other way,' said Val. 'Expensive, though.'

They smiled at one another, relieved to have moved the conversation on to impersonal ground, and they managed to prolong their neutral dialogue until the meal was done. Then, while Andrew washed up, Val quietly collected her possessions. Before she left, she gave him back his key.

For an instant each hesitated, on the brink of an embrace, and then they both drew back.

'Better not,' said Val, kissed him again on the cheek, and left.

WPC Wendy Rogers, driving through the streets of Kenston in a patrol car, wondered if Colin Widdows had, by any chance, come home. Passing near Moor Street, she turned down it and stopped outside number 37. There was no sign of life: the windows were shut, the curtains open. She got out of her car, walked up the path, and rang the doorbell, but there was no response. The place was deserted.

She did not like unresolved cases, and although she had had reservations about Andrew Sherwood's theory that Mr Widdows might have caused his wife's accident, she had not forgotten it. Brooding on the possibility, she had had further thoughts about Colin Widdows' disappearance.

At their final meeting, she had asked Louise Widdows which letting agent had arranged their lease. Louise could not give its address, but she knew the name; it appeared on their bank statements, and recently she had been reading those when Colin was out of the house. He wrote few cheques, usually withdrawing cash, but there was a monthly standing order to the agent.

Now, back at the police station, Wendy decided to make a few discreet enquiries and she looked up the addresses of the various agencies in the town, seeking the one Louise had mentioned. Wendy did not consult a superior officer. Louise's accident had disappeared from the front of everybody's mind, and the CID had a number of serious crimes to investigate, some of them very nasty. The murder enquiry was more important than a hit-and-run, and, if she sought sanction, Wendy might have been told to forget about it.

She waited until she was officially in the same neighbourhood as the agency, which dealt in lower-priced property sales as well as rentals, then took her opportunity, entering the small front office and telling the woman behind the desk that the police wanted to trace Colin Widdows of 37, Moor Street, whose wife had been hurt in a road accident, since when he could not be found.

The woman consulted her computer. Advance rent, hitherto paid by standing order, was overdue. There had been no previous default. Was Mrs Widdows in hospital, she asked, and was told no, but she had gone away. This information seemed to startle the woman. She checked her register.

'She's not liable. The sole tenant was the husband,' she volunteered, and added, 'That's unusual, these days. Most couples share responsibility.' She said the agency would investigate at once, rather than wait for replies to reminders which, routinely, would be sent. The lease, renewed every six months, would expire at the end of April. A deposit of two months' rent would have been paid when the lease was signed, but the money was held, not against rent default but to cover damage. In this case, any balance left after such damage was assessed would be forfeit to meet the rental.

Later, in the canteen, Wendy relayed this information to Detective Constable Griffiths, who was attached to the murder case.

'Colin Widdows disappeared just about the time that woman from The Golden Horn was killed,' she said. 'Coincidence, maybe, and he's an old guy, but even so, it could be worth finding out if he knew the victim.'

The murder enquiry had been getting nowhere. Any theory was worth considering, but Griffiths, checking, found that Colin Widdows had no record. Wendy muttered about dusting the house in Moor Street for prints, for possible future reference, but Griffiths said what she already knew: without some reason to support such action, costing time and money, it would not be authorised.

'What if we decide he is a suspect and look for evidence to support it?' she asked Griffiths.

'We need a firm connection, not just your hunch,' said Griffiths. 'What you've just said – proof he knew the victim.'

'Look for it, then,' she answered. 'Ask if he was known in the pub where she worked.'

'I could do that,' said Griffiths slowly. 'Have we a photo of him? Do we know what he looks like?'

'No. But we can get a description from the neighbours,' Wendy said.

'Waste of time,' Griffiths, still reluctant, decided.

But when Andrew Sherwood turned up at the police station and came to see Wendy, she, off the record, mentioned this idea to him.

Remembering that she had not been receptive to his earlier theorising, Andrew had begun their interview carefully, asking if there was any news about the hit-and-run driver, or the missing Colin Widdows. However, because he now knew where Louise lived, and moreover, he could truthfully say that they were friends, he felt himself on firmer ground than when they had talked on the telephone, but to his surprise, the policewoman was now much more forthcoming.

'I've been thinking about what you said,' she told him. 'You wondered if Widdows ran his wife down. There was a murder here, about the time he disappeared.'

'Yes. Have you found out who did it?' Andrew asked. She did not know he was a journalist; he wouldn't tell her unless or until it would open doors for him. If she knew, it was likely that they would be firmly closed.

'No.' She hesitated. Would he think of it himself, or must she prompt him?

Until that moment, Andrew hadn't, but suddenly it made sense of Louise's flight and her nervous state.

'Colin Widdows – suspect,' he tried out.

'You said it. I didn't. It's too much of a wild card,' Wendy said. 'He's an old man.'

'Was it a sexual crime? Old men have sexual urges,' Andrew said.

'Yes, they do,' she replied, not giving him an answer.

'Did he go to the pub where she worked?' asked Andrew.

'We're not pursuing that line of enquiry at the moment,' Wendy told him.

There was a pause. She looked at him steadily from beneath her short fringe of brown hair. Griffiths wouldn't pick this up, but Andrew Sherwood might. She waited. Had he got the message?

He had.

'I could,' Andrew said. 'I'm in Kenston to see a friend. We could go there for a drink. What's it called?' He'd better not seem to know too much about it though he had already been there.

'The Golden Horn,' Wendy told him. 'You'll know what he looked like, as you were a friend of theirs,' she added. He could provide a description.

'I'm a friend of Louise's. I've never met him,' said Andrew.

'Oh well—' Wendy left it there. If he chose to chase after this idea, it was up to him. He was bright enough to think of asking a neighbour to describe the man.

Andrew did so, finding Sally Smith, the woman with the

baby, at home. She was pleased to see him, gave him coffee, and said that Colin Widdows was thin and spindly, with plentiful grey hair, which was slightly yellow. She'd never spoken to him, so she could not give him any further details.

'Why do you want to know?' she asked. 'Has he done something?'

'Why do you ask?'

'Well, you're a reporter. You might know something about him. And it's those quiet ones you want to watch out for,' she said.

'The answer is, I'm just curious,' said Andrew.

Clare, when later he found her at the library, produced a newspaper photograph taken at a bazaar at Kenston community centre; it showed Colin and Louise, among a group of other helpers. Clare's parents were supporters of the children's charity for whom the bazaar was held, and had been among those manning the stalls. After the event, Clare had recognised Louise in the photograph, and the Widdowses had been discussed. The husband did the books, Clare's parents had reported. Otherwise, they scarcely knew him, and the wife seemed very shy.

Today, Clare was working through the lunch hour. She provided Andrew with a photocopy of the photograph, and he went with it to The Golden Horn, walking in with confidence, as it was his second visit. This time, he revealed his profession but did not say what paper employed him. Several customers, and the landlord, were, as he expected, keen to give their story.

Colin Widdows was not a regular but a visit he had made was remembered. He had been in just before Lesley Timson disappeared, and had met another man. They had sat in a corner talking. Neither had come back after the woman's body had been found.

Andrew debated what to do with this knowledge.

He couldn't keep it to himself and hope, like an inspired fictional sleuth, to solve the crime. It strengthened the possibility that Colin had something to hide and had decided to flee, killing Louise first, either because she knew something damning about him, perhaps without being aware of it, or simply to get her out of the way so that he could leave unhampered. But what a dreadful, drastic thing to do. Why not just take off? Unless the reason for his flight was because he had already killed someone, and another murder made no difference.

Why, though, should he choose the barmaid as a victim? Was he a psychopath? If so, what sort of torment had he put Louise through?

He must give WPC Rogers the information. Andrew drove back to the police station, only to find that Wendy Rogers was out.

He did not want to trust his message to a third party. Instead, he left his home telephone number and asked her to call him. He'd ring her, too, and go on doing it until he reached her.

Then he went to pick up Clare. He told her about his and Nicky's visit to Louise.

'It sounds weird,' Clare said. 'A woman her age all alone in rather a nice cottage, with scarcely any furniture. How did she get there?'

'A taxi-driver took her, in a van. They went to John Lewis on the way and bought a bed.'

Louise had related this while they had tea. Nicky had thought it a great story. Andrew had found it poignant.

'Everyone's been so kind,' Louise had said. 'Ever since that day on the train, when you gave me your seat, Nicky. And now here. Dorothy Kershaw. The postmaster. Everyone.'

Andrew had made no comment, but he had the feeling that she had not received much kindness in her life. On the other hand, remembering her reluctance to accept his help after the assault on the train, had she, by reason of her own personality, made it difficult for others to be friendly?

'She needs more bits and pieces. Furniture,' he told Clare now. 'And she can't really hack it, with that arm out of action. Even when it's better, she'll need some help. I don't want to be too pushy, but Nicky and I could lend a hand. If she wants self-assembly stuff, we could put it together for her.'

'Or try to,' Clare said. 'It isn't always easy.'

'I don't know how much money she's got. Not a lot, I'd guess,' Andrew said. 'She's got a pal in the village, some old duck who knew her mother. She's helped – the old duck has – but she's away just now.'

'You could just turn up,' suggested Clare, who hadn't heard about Nicky until today. She had also learned that Andrew, though not yet divorced, was separated from Nicky's mother. 'Ask her if she wants to go shopping, and take your tool kit so that you can fix what she buys.'

'I could suggest it,' he said doubtfully. 'Just one bedside table, maybe, to begin with. She's got her reading-lamp perched on a biscuit carton.'

'Oh dear,' said Clare.

They looked sadly at one another, and then they began to laugh. Neither of them quite knew why.

'Tell me some more about Nicky,' Clare invited. 'Have you got a photo of him?'

He had, of course, in his wallet: several.

17

When Louise went to supper at the vicarage, she had an interesting evening. Judith had begun by apologising for not inviting her round sooner.

'She couldn't,' said Judith's husband, pouring wine for them before the meal. 'She's been overloaded. Several parishioners with major problems and I've been in South America at a symposium. Then Billy – that's my son – broke his arm, just like you.'

'I hope he wasn't run over,' said Louise.

'No. He did it playing rugby,' said Leonard Bright. 'You'll meet him in a minute. He's upstairs doing his homework. He went back to school today.'

Louise hadn't seen the children going to school that morning. She was always sorry when she missed them.

Billy, aged fifteen, soon appeared, smiled at Louise and said, 'Snap,' indicating their plastered arms. She asked about his fracture; his elbow had been pinned, so it was a more serious injury than hers. Over the meal – fish pie – her hosts discovered that Louise had another hospital appointment on Thursday when she hoped to have her plaster off, and Judith asked her how she planned to get there.

Louise had wondered that herself.

'It must be possible by bus,' she said doubtfully. A taxi would cost a fortune.

'I think Dorothy will still be away.' Judith was thinking aloud.

'Yes,' agreed Louise. 'But I couldn't expect her to take me again.'

'I'll organise something,' said Judith. 'There are volunteers willing to do such trips. Leave it with me.'

'Oh! How kind,' said Louise.

'It's her job,' said Leonard. He was a big man with a neatly trimmed iron-grey beard. 'She's good at the pastoral role.' He was smiling, twinkling at his wife across the table.

'It's very important,' Judith said. 'And neighbourly helpfulness is not what it was, with everyone so busy doing their own thing. People may want to help but simply don't have the time.'

Louise said that she had been overwhelmed by kindness since her move — and even before it, when she came to see the cottage.

'Look at you, being so friendly to me now,' she said. She was enjoying the wine Leonard had poured for her, and as is its way, it had eased some of her inhibitions.

'Have you met your neighbours?' she was asked.

'Not really,' said Louise. 'But I've been here such a short time. I've moved a lot in my life, and I know people aren't always quick to talk to newcomers.' Especially if you've been forbidden to respond.

'I expect they want to let you settle in,' said Judith. 'It's different for me. When we came here, it was up to me to introduce myself around.' She had been delighted at being appointed; Leonard's laboratory was just outside Oxford so it was convenient for him, and had meant minimal upheaval for the family.

During the evening the Brights discovered that Louise had been a professional cook, and they both thought she might do well catering for people entertaining at home.

'So many couples are out all day now, they can't do everything themselves and they can afford to pay for help for parties,' said Judith.

'I thought I might find a job cooking in a restaurant or a pub,' said Louise, who had seen some advertisements for part-time cooks and helpers.

'Yes, you might,' agreed Judith. 'But wait until your arm is really strong again. Give yourself time.'

After Louise had gone home, escorted down the road by Leonard, who waited outside Lilac Cottage till she had found her key and let herself in, Judith asked him what he made of their guest.

'She's very withdrawn,' he said. 'She didn't tell us much about herself.'

'No,' said Judith, who had deliberately shown no curiosity. Dorothy had told her that there was a question mark over Louise's husband, who was no longer on the scene, and that the marriage had not been overtly happy. Judith, who had experience of working with battered women, thought she had just entertained another.

Andrew rang Louise the following evening.

He thanked her for her letter and asked what she had been doing since Sunday. She told him that Greg Downey had taken her to a furniture warehouse that afternoon and she had bought a kitchen table and four chairs.

'Now I can have you and Nicky to lunch,' she said. 'Would you like to come on Sunday week?'

'Are you sure? What about your arm?' he said.

'I'm going to the hospital tomorrow. My plaster should be coming off,' she said.

'But your arm will be weak. You must be careful,' Andrew said.

It was wonderful to hear him saying this. So might her son speak to her, warmly and with kindness.

'I know, but you won't expect too much,' she said. Suddenly she knew that it didn't matter what they had; soup, and bread and cheese would be a feast, because it was the company that mattered. 'I wonder if Nicky likes spaghetti.' That would be easy, with no need to lift heavy pots and dishes.

'Loves it,' Andrew answered.

He felt pleased that they had made this plan, yet puzzled, too. He must really like Louise; it wasn't just that he was intrigued by her situation, and the riddle of her husband.

WPC Wendy Rogers had telephoned while he was out. He hadn't managed to make direct contact with her yet though he rang her several times. He should have given her the number of his mobile phone.

Kenston CID, for want of another idea, had now decided to investigate Colin Widdows. DC Griffiths had decided to adopt Wendy Rogers' theory as his own and had put it forward. Thanks to Wendy, he had provided the name of the letting agency which had rented out 37 Moor Street, and was sent officially to their office where he learned which bank had made the monthly payments, and confirmed what Wendy had already learned, that the next was overdue.

Banks respect their clients' confidentiality, but Louise had told Wendy that the account had been emptied. If required, an order could be obtained insisting that the details be revealed, but at this stage, it was not necessary. Finding Widdows, so that he could answer questions, now became the only sustainable line of enquiry in the murder investigation. When he was found, his DNA could be matched with that of the murderer, who had sexually assaulted the victim, thus eliminating him if he were innocent. Griffiths and another officer were sent to Moor Street to ask if any neighbours knew where he had worked, or could name any of his associates, and their task was difficult; it seemed that the couple had been almost invisible, until the unemployed man living opposite number 37 mentioned that he had seen Widdows in The Golden Horn, the pub at which the murdered barmaid had worked. Sally Smith, at number 35, said that she thought he had worked for various charities and named the British Legion, some of whose members were then traced. Colin had been their treasurer but had not been at a recent meeting where he should have made a statement of accounts.

Griffiths did not want to alarm the Legion about the safety of their funds; nevertheless, he suggested they should check, and to the horror of the secretary, it was soon revealed that the bank account, held in a different branch than the Widdowses' own, had been emptied.

Now the police had a valid reason for questioning Colin Widdows: a possible case of theft. The Legion secretary said that they would certainly have a photograph of their assembled members at a function, and, after some searching, found one. The machinery could be set in motion, and when Andrew, at long last, managed to speak to Wendy Rogers, confirming, as had already been discovered, that Colin had been seen at The

Golden Horn, she was able to disclose that active measures to find him were already in place.

The problem was, where to start the search? Widdows had vanished. He might be dead; he could have left the country; he could be lying low somewhere under another name. A serious effort to trace his car was the first step to take; if there had been any reason to connect him with his wife's accident, it could have been done weeks ago. If she had been killed in the house, he would have been the prime suspect: because she did not die, and her injuries were deemed due to accident, the file about it, though not closed, was no longer urgent.

While Louise was in hospital, she had been asked for the car's registration number because the police wanted to tell Colin what had happened to her: next of kin had to be informed of accidents. She did not drive herself, but she knew it. In any case, as long as it was legitimately registered, it could have been traced on the computer. Police in Kenston had been asked to look for it while on their other duties, but there had been no concerted hunt. It had not been located in the area and as it had not been reported stolen, no national call was put out for it.

The computer showed that its ownership had been transferred from Colin Widdows to a dealer in the Midlands.

Colin Widdows was now known to have absconded with the British Legion's funds. He had cleaned out his own bank account, and, it soon transpired, money belonging to a heritage society he was in charge of had also been removed from the building society account in which it had been lodged. He was proved to be a thief, but not yet a murderer.

Had he a secret passion for barmaids?

There was no reason to suppose that the Kenston murder victim, Lesley Timson, had known him before she came to Kenston. She had moved there from Wales after the break-up of her marriage. Her husband had a solid alibi for the days when she had failed to go to work at The Golden Horn, before the landlord made enquiries and she became officially a missing person. The pathologist's report had established that she was killed at the start of that period. The husband had never left Wales and he had been at work – he was a motor mechanic – throughout that time.

As a mechanic, he would have had access to cars and could have driven back and forth to Kenston easily, but careful checking confirmed that he was where he said he had been at the relevant times, and, distressed at what happened to her, he willingly gave a blood sample for DNA testing.

Lesley herself had no record with the police, but a priggish, psychopathic murderer might have labelled her and all barmaids as sluts, if not prostitutes. Colin Widdows, from the little that the police knew about him so far, seemed to be a buttoned-up, prim individual, strict and controlling with his wife. That much emerged from Sally Smith.

Sally kept quiet about Andrew Sherwood's interest; let him get his story, if there was one, without the police freezing him off. The detective who interviewed her hadn't told her why the police wanted to talk to Colin Widdows.

'Is she all right? Louise Widdows?' asked Sally.

'Why shouldn't she be?'

'She left in a hurry, and he'd gone – I don't know,' said Sally. 'You wonder, don't you?'

'She is safe and well,' Griffiths said.

'That's a relief,' said Sally. Old Misery-Guts, Bob had called him.

At the station, the police soon christened Colin The Invisible Man. They sent a forensic science team into 37 Moor Street to see if there were any traces which might be linked to the murder, and they dusted for prints, finding several sets, including plenty left by police officers who had been to the house while Louise was in the hospital. Sorting through them would take time; Louise's prints would have to be taken and eliminated in order to learn which were likely to be Colin's. Must they ask the Thames Valley police to visit her and see to this?

Cost entered into their deliberations, but there was no doubt that Colin had some explaining to do, apart from answering charges about the missing money. He had chosen to disappear at a time when his wife had had a serious accident. Was that sheer coincidence?

Then the team searching 37 Moor Street had a minor breakthrough. They had to fend off the rental agent while they carried out their investigation, but their efforts were rewarded when they found an old envelope wedged behind a drawer in a kitchen unit. It was inscribed to Louise Widdows at an address in Redditch and contained a recipe cut from a magazine. Her fingerprints should be on it, unless time and the friction of the drawer had erased them.

Though Kenston CID had begun to consider the possibility of a link between the murder on their patch with the discovery of a woman's body, similarly battered, in Redditch, they did not, at this stage, link it with the body recently unearthed in Sheffield, which the police suspected might be that of Rene Driver, a prostitute who had disappeared many years ago, and for whose murder a man had been convicted. The testament of a woman who had been with the missing girl and the accused man, Stan Brown, the last time she was known to be alive, and other circumstantial evidence, had been enough to convince the jury, even without a body. A second man, Bruce Atkins, had been with them after they left a bar in the town; he and Sylvia, the witness, had spent the night together after parting from the other two, but soon afterwards Bruce Atkins had left the area and she had not seen him again.

The police had been unable to locate Bruce. They had, however, found bloodstains on a pair of Stan's shoes; it was impossible to prove that it was Rene's blood, but it was not Stan's, and a jacket of his, described by Sylvia and other witnesses who had seen him in the bar could not be found, the inference being that Stan had got rid of it because it might be bloodstained. After the trial it was revealed that Stan had been convicted of an earlier murder, where again no body had been found, and that he was out on licence at the time of Rene's death. The police, convinced that he was their man, had been anxious to gather enough evidence to send him back to prison. He had received a life sentence for that first killing, but in practice this meant his release at the discretion of the parole board. He had received another life sentence.

The police stepped up the search for Colin. Had he, as seemed possible, ever lived in Redditch? The DSS could track his records and provide the answer. Once they found him, there would be bits of fibre, contact traces, and, proof positive, his DNA.

18

Louise knew that unless her son had shown a wish to find her, it was an almost impossible task for her to trace him.

She had not seen him for more than a few minutes after he was born, sure that if she nursed him the parting would be all the harder. Her work colleagues in the school kitchen had not doubted her when she said she was going to stay with her parents; how easy it was to lie and be believed, and after a while, the lie became accepted truth. Those running the home believed she was unmarried, because she said she was, and most of their expectant mothers were single girls who had 'got themselves into trouble', as it was called then. Aware that it would leave a mark on her finger if she took it off, Louise wore her wedding ring, saying she had bought one to protect herself from hostile comment during her weeks of pregnancy. How different attitudes were these days, she thought: there was no need for shame or concealment. Desperate to try every possible source of information, she wrote to children's homes and charities whose addresses she had acquired from Croxbury library as well as the one through whom he had been adopted, seeking advice about how she might pursue her quest. The librarian did not ask why Louise wanted them; people gave to many children's charities and if this newcomer to the village, a keen reader, was one of those generous donors, that was fine.

On Thursday morning, when Judith Bright herself arrived to drive her to the hospital, Louise took the letters with her.

'I'll have to drop you and fetch you later,' Judith explained, on the way. 'There are two other parishioners of mine I want to visit, both in another hospital. I'm not sure how long I'll be, but we'll arrange a meeting place, and I hope you won't have to hang about too long.'

She thought it more likely that she would be the one who waited. X-ray departments had to deal with emergencies and accidents which took priority over routine cases such as Louise's.

'What a pity you can't combine this trip with one Billy needs,' said Louise.

She had written a note of thanks for Tuesday's dinner and put it through the vicarage door on Wednesday morning, before her shopping trip with Greg. Now she told Judith about their expedition and how grateful she was to him.

'Helpfulness like that used to be quite general in villages like Croxbury where everyone used to know everybody else,' said Judith. 'But there are so many newcomers now, who don't have time to get acquainted or to join in community activities, that it's on the wane, though the elderly hang in together pretty well.' There was a centre where the able-bodied old ministered to their frailer contemporaries, but she did not tell Louise about that. 'The younger ones make friends through their children, which is good.'

Some of these families were second marriages of one or other partner, with new families, and older children who stayed at weekends. Judith had not sorted all of them out yet; a number of them came to church and sent the children to the Sunday

Club. Judith had inherited from her predecessor something called Tinies' Time, a new version Sunday School, which she had re-christened almost instantly, and which was run by two young grandmothers who had volunteered as soon as the name was changed. She had aspirations to resurrect the choir, which had perished during the former incumbency, but she was still moving forward carefully. Greg Downey was a Baptist, which Judith lamented as he would have been such an asset to her; cynically, she hoped he wasn't on a mission to secure Louise's allegiance to this rival flock, though as all were supposed to be servants of the same shepherd, that should not matter. Too often, the various divisions came into conflict, which depressed her. Still, it was her mission to do what she could to bring peace and comfort, and in her car she clearly had a troubled soul. When Dorothy Kershaw returned from her daughter's house, she might throw more light on Louise's past history.

Judith asked Louise when Dorothy would be coming home, and Louise said not for another week or so.

'I thought of telephoning her,' she said, doubtfully. 'She gave me her number.'

'Why don't you? I'm sure she'd like to hear from you,' said Judith.

'I might be a nuisance, interrupting,' said Louise.

'Don't ring her when there's racing on,' advised Judith. 'If she's reading, she can put the book down, and if she's watching some pet television programme, she'll tell you and she'll probably call back later.' She slowed down for some traffic lights. They were nearly at the hospital. 'She's lonely,' Judith said. 'She was very friendly with the Johnsons, who lived in your house, and she misses them. Mrs Johnson had died before I came here, of course. Most of her other friends in the village have died or moved nearer to their families. She thinks playing bridge is a waste of time, so that cuts out what provides social contact for a lot of people. Do you play?'

'No,' said Louise. 'Greg Downey thinks I should take up painting or some other hobby.'

'Well, you could think about it,' Judith said. 'Do you sing?'

'No,' said Louise, then added, 'Well, I suppose I did as a child. Not since. Why?'

Judith did not frighten her off by revealing her plans for a choir. She told her there was a choral society in Durbridge always looking for fresh voices.

"They're doing the St Matthew Passion for Easter,' said Judith. 'But some of them, who call themselves Harmony Hummers, get together to sing more popular stuff and they perform at various local bashes – fêtes and things. Quite fun. Greg's a member. He'd take you along if you were interested.'

Louise had this to think about as she waited in the busy hospital. It was a frightening idea. Learning to paint sounded safer.

The plaster was removed. Her arm was healing well; physiotherapy would be arranged but meanwhile she should do exercises to strengthen the muscles. Judith had said she would meet her near the shop, where there were some chairs. Louise was there first, so she bought some stamps and sat down with her letters, which she had left open; inside each was an envelope addressed to herself, on which she now stuck stamps. She was just sealing the last envelope when Judith arrived to collect her.

'You've been busy,' said Judith. 'We'll post them on the way home.'

She put them in the box for Louise, stopping outside a post office they passed. She did not look at the letters as she mailed them.

Nevertheless, Louise told her what was in them.

*   *   *

'I know you'll treat it as a confidence,' she said. 'I can't tell you how it all happened. It was so long ago – things were different then.'

'Of course they were, and of course it's confidential,' Judith said. 'But isn't it very difficult for the surrendering mother to find her child?'

Louise liked that phrase, the surrendering mother.

'It's supposed to be impossible,' she said.

Thoughts of private detectives and studying adoption certificates rushed through Judith's mind, but such a search would be expensive. When they reached Croxbury, she accepted Louise's hesitant suggestion that she come in for a cup of tea because this conversation was important; Louise might not be in the mood to unburden herself again for weeks, if ever.

Judith hovered in the kitchen as Louise put the kettle on and found cups and saucers; she admitted that her left arm felt strange, her grip weak.

'I'm not rheumatic, which is lucky,' she said.

Judith helped her, not bossily but with firmness. The sooner they were sitting down the better.

Louise explained about the borrowed chairs, manoeuvring her guest towards the button-back.

'Now go on with what you were saying about your son. What is his name?' said Judith.

'David, but his new family may have changed it,' said Louise. 'And they may not have told him he was adopted. In those days, people didn't always tell the child.'

'That's true.' This was new territory for Judith. She knew some people who had been adopted, but they had all been told about their circumstances, as was the modern practice. She must go carefully, advising nothing except prudence.

'He can look for me, and when his father died last year, I registered myself as willing to be found,' said Louise. 'Until then, I wouldn't, because his father didn't know about him. It could have damaged his career. I saw his death announced in the paper, quite by chance,' she added.

'David may be happy as he is and not want to trace you,' Judith felt obliged to point out.

Hearing someone else refer to David by his name made Louise feel a rush of warmth.

'I know, but some adopted children feel curious,' she said. She was not going to tell Judith that she wanted him to have Lilac Cottage, or whatever she had to leave him. 'I was married when he was born,' she said. 'My husband was working abroad when it happened and he didn't know about it.'

'And your mother?' Judith betrayed no shock.

'No.'

What sorrow was here revealed: years of pain and guilt, for Louise had loved the man; why else would she have protected his career?

'I couldn't make it up to Colin,' Louise said. 'I couldn't even have another child.'

'Is this the first time you've talked about it?' Judith asked. She was sure it was. It explained so much about Louise.

'Like this, yes. Mr Barnes – the solicitor – knows I had a child adopted, because of my will. You kindly witnessed it. I had to make one, so that Colin doesn't get the house if I die first.'

She'd left it to the unknown son: it was tragic.

'I see. Poor Louise, you must have felt so wretched,' Judith said. And so lonely, she thought, standing up reluctantly. 'I'm going to have to leave you, as I've got to see someone at the vicarage.' She was late already for a meeting with the sacristan, who would have seen her car outside Lilac Cottage and been curious, if not impatient. 'Look – any time you want a chat, let me know, and also let me know if you get any useful answers to your letters.'

But would she? Judith feared that any replies might be palliative, but not constructive. Writing the letters was a long shot, and could have been therapeutic for Louise. Certainly breaking her silence would be healing, though she might regret revealing such a secret, even though it was her own. Judith would be prepared for that.

It was no good hoping for a delightful, successful man to turn up on Louise's doorstep crying 'Mother!' Life wasn't like that.

Next morning Louise took the bus to Durbridge. All her married life she had lived within walking distance, or a short bus ride, of a group of shops supplying everything essential for existence. Expeditions further afield were rare.

The previous evening, after Judith had gone, old wounds had re-opened and she had sat in her sparsely furnished, peaceful room, brooding on the past. How had she let herself be subsumed again when Colin came back from overseas? Why had she not broken away then and made a life for herself, with or without her son?

Because she was indoctrinated by the conventions of her generation; she was also meek, and lacking in self-confidence. To be married conferred status; today, marriage meant nothing to feminists, who would mock her for what they would see as her unnecessary martyrdom, and which she had regarded as her punishment. Because Colin had never raised a hand to her, she had not thought of herself as battered, like the bruised and beaten women she had read about, who seemed unable to leave their violent husbands, often bound to them because of the financial needs of their children. Colin wasn't a brute; he was a selfish, domineering man who, by marrying her, had acquired her as he might buy a pair of shoes. He had purchased a housekeeper, servant and bedmate; her side of the transaction was respectability, with the provision of her food and a roof over her head.

Her own mother, widowed young, had found work where she could keep her child as well as herself. Louise could have kept her baby, left Colin, and done the same. Why hadn't she? She was not unskilled; she had secretarial training and her catering qualifications.

She lacked her mother's courage, and she was shattered when Richard abandoned her without a word, but she had wasted her entire adult life living with a man who had no soul. Louise had wept, sitting there in the darkness in her mother's old chair, lamenting all the waste and sorrow, and that she had not had more faith in her mother if not herself. Stubbornness had stopped her from admitting that her marriage, which had been a sort of flight, was a dreadful mistake. Her mother would have helped her, and so would Paul. She knew it now. Hadn't her mother, with the legacy of the cottage concealed from Colin, taken prudent care of her?

Her regret was tinged with horror, for now she knew that Colin was more than just a cold and heartless man.

He conducted his life as if he had been programmed, sticking to a self-imposed routine which he did not discuss, each movement calculated and precise. His breakfast tea – two sugars, milk in first – must be meticulously poured, and his toast must be just so. In the days when he had required a boiled egg each morning, it had to be accurately timed, three and a half minutes, or there was trouble. Often, in his working life, he telephoned during the day to ask Louise what she had accomplished so far, and what she was doing when he rang. Her only respite from this scrutiny was when she had a job herself. He constantly demanded a full report of her day's activities, and though she was permitted visits to the library, she was supposed to occupy every other minute on household duties. Time spent in the garden, when she could not hear the telephone, was a means of avoiding this severe supervision. Her physical strength had been slowly sapped, but her initiative had disappeared much earlier.

Perhaps, at last, she was becoming a real person in her own right.

The bus dropped her near the supermarket entrance. She saw cars pouring into the parking lot, Land Rovers and similar large vehicles manoeuvring into narrow spaces, and big saloons, each driven, it appeared, by a youngish woman. What a lot of car for one person, Louise thought, and told herself that probably they were farmers' wives, who needed tough machines to get about in mud, or frost.

But they weren't all farmers' wives. Similar vehicles could be seen in Croxbury, some parked outside quite modest houses, and she had noticed others near Dorothy Kershaw's former home, where there was a group of imposing new houses. She had walked up there once, curious; the development seemed to be a small enclave on its own, not part of the village. What did all these people do?

In Durbridge, Louise bought a few items at the supermarket, extravagantly, for the pleasure of shopping in such an agreeable place. She still felt detached from what was going on around her; her new surroundings were so different from Kenston. Durbridge was a market town which had grown in recent years and sprouted industrial estates on two sides, but the centre was compact, though many former shop premises were now occupied by the offices of estate agents, solicitors and building societies. Everything was clean and bright, though doubtless there were less salubrious areas, but it was a prosperous town; that was the big difference. Kenston had been run-down. Colin had been run-down. She was run-down, but no longer.

Now, without a sling, people did not stare at her and then glance away, as had been happening, but they did not give her the same space, and being so small that other shoppers did not notice her, she was mildly jostled. She soon felt tired. All that crying the night before had been exhausting; she had not wept like that for years. She bought a gardening magazine and then went to the bus stop. No one spoke to her on the bus, and why should they? No one knew her, nor she them; it would take her years to be accepted, if she ever was.

On the way back to Lilac Cottage from the bus, which stopped near the newsagent's, she paused to read the cards in the window, to see whether there were any chairs or beds for sale. If Andrew and Nicky came to stay, as she hoped they would one day, they must have somewhere to sleep. And she would like a dressing-table, or a chest which she could use as one. Several advertisements looked promising, and she set her shopping down to make a note of them.

The supermarket's carrier bag had grown heavy by the time she reached the cottage. She would have a nice meal tonight, for she had bought a small French loaf, a chop, some fresh vegetables and three apples. Now she was not solely dependent on the sliced bread available in the village. The milkman sold fruit juice and eggs. She'd make another trip to Durbridge next week, to prepare for the following weekend when Andrew and Nicky would be coming.

How soon would she get replies to the letters she had posted yesterday?

When she reached home, the telephone was ringing. She flung down her shopping and went to pick it up, but it had stopped before she reached it. Louise, not modernised, did not know about dialling 1471 to obtain the caller's number.

19

Colin, still in Manchester, read about the body found in Sheffield. In those dreadful early years, blackmailed for his part in what had happened though he was innocent of the killing, he had twice fled abroad, only returning when he could pay off his extortioner. But it had not been the end; there were more demands, and with his identity discovered, he would not be safe when Stan was eventually released. He and Louise had moved frequently, staying nowhere long, never settling, but in Kenston he had panicked for it seemed the reckoning had come. He must save himself and disappear, unhampered by his useless, feeble wife. He'd known this would happen in the end, and he'd put some funds by, but that was the easy part.

Marrying Louise – marrying at all – had been a gross mistake, but she had seemed to be the perfect camouflage. She was prudish and respectable, patently above suspicion, and this must rub off on him. When she had arrived in the office where they met, shy and diffident, awkward and gauche, with those conventional, apparently prosperous parents, she had seemed the ideal solution to his problem. He needed to lie low, arouse no suspicion, and, no longer Bruce, strengthen the identity of Colin Widdows which he had recently set up. At that time, criminal investigation, though thorough and painstaking, was not sophisticated; there were no police computers, no DNA profiling, no accurate photo-fits; few of the techniques used now were in existence. He had not needed to vanish permanently, move overseas for good, or so he had thought. Now he would have to do so, but he was not too old to pull it off; he'd learned a trick or two since his youth, and he had money and a passport in yet another new name. He had used the birth-certificate trick, obtaining a copy of one of someone his age already dead. In spite of the popularity of cremation, graveyards still provided information and Colin had acquired several sets of papers over the years. In Kenston, however, his luck had run out, but flight might still save him. He was too old to face exposure, with inevitable trial as an accessory, and imprisonment. Shedding Louise would remove any risk that she might assist in his pursuit; dead, she could reveal no secrets, not that she knew any of them. Besides, she could never manage on her own, not after all these years when he had taken care of her; she'd not take kindly to being housed in a bed and breakfast hostel when the rent ran out. He must return to Kenston and finish the job he had begun when he had impulsively decided to remove her so that she could not report him missing. After he had disposed of her, he would cross the Channel, catching the Eurostar train. He'd head south, and then go on to Spain. He'd pick up a job there, seize an opportunity, and maybe a rich widow. Plenty went there in the winter and he'd need one, or some other source of income, for he had not squirrelled away enough to last him long, even living modestly, as he had always done. He'd never been extravagant.

He packed up his possessions and, with a damp cloth, wiped every surface clean of fingerprints. Though he had no police record, he would have left fingerprints in the Moor Street house. Then, in a Ford he'd bought from a dealer's forecourt, he headed south again.

It was dark when Colin parked at the end of Moor Street and walked along it towards number 37. He wore jeans, trainers, a bomber jacket and a baseball cap and no one would have recognised in this figure the spruce, dapper former resident.

His disappearance must, by this time, be established but there had been no hue and cry for him; he had watched the press, and followed news bulletins on radio and television. People might assume that he was dead. There had been no mention of suspicion that he had been the driver of the car that ran down Louise.

If she'd died, there would have been an extensive search. She'd seemed to move sideways before he hit her, driving straight at her approaching figure. Like a startled rabbit, she'd stopped short, dazzled by the headlights; then, as he roared towards her, she'd swerved, but the car had struck her hard; there was no doubt of that.

This time, he'd surprise her, strangle her from behind, or, if he had to, stab her. He'd brought a knife. Then he'd ransack the place, make it look like a robbery, but clear off fast. He'd dump the car, change his clothes again and make his way to London, using public transport.

He opened the gate and walked quietly up the path of the house where he had lived so recently. She hadn't swept the concrete; it was very muddy. The slut. She was supposed to sweep it weekly.

The place was in darkness, which was surprising, for Colin, not wanting to be caught unawares at any time, had fitted security lights at the front and rear. The bulbs must have blown and Louise had been too idle to replace them, he supposed. But there was no light showing at the windows; even with the curtains drawn, cracks were usually visible. Had the silly cow gone out? If so, where to? Anger rose in him. She'd always made him angry; it was a wonder he hadn't beaten her, but he'd subdued her using words, not violence. He'd brought a torch; it could be useful as a bludgeon, if required, to knock her out, but he did not use it as he inserted his key in the door; after living here so long, he could do it blindfold.

If she was out, he'd lie in wait for her and catch her by surprise. He'd enjoy seeing the terror on her face, the realisation that he, her husband, had come to kill her.

As Colin pushed the door open and silently entered the house, his feet brushed something on the floor. He shone his torch and saw a batch of circulars and some bills, but, slowly, he became aware that there was no furniture. The small table that had held the telephone had gone and the instrument was on the floor. The worn Indian rug was missing, and the single chair that had stood at the foot of the stairs was not in place. He went cautiously around the ground floor. All the rooms were bare; only the curtains still hung at the windows. Colin went upstairs, still using his torch and moving carefully, but he knew that she had gone; though the rent was only just overdue, the bailiffs must have come in and taken everything away. The fiends, to act so soon.

But he'd find Louise. Wherever she was, he'd run her to earth.

Downstairs, he glanced at the mail, gathering it all together. Some was already neatly stacked on a window sill. There were letters from the rental firm and bills from the electricity and gas companies, and the telephone account. After a moment's hesitation, he opened this one. Numbers dialled by Louise after she left hospital – assuming that she had, and was not still occupying a bed that was needed more urgently by someone else – might give a clue to where she was.

But no calls were recorded. It seemed that she'd rung nowhere after her accident.

Perhaps she had died after all.

He tried the telephone. He'd ring the hospital and ask. However, it was dead: cut off, disconnected.

Colin, frustrated and alarmed, became furiously angry. He stormed around the house shaking his fists, banging at the walls, and only fear of discovery lent him some control. In his rage, and using only torchlight, he failed to see the powder marks left by the detectives who had dusted for fingerprints, at last seeking to identify those which could be his.

After a while he calmed down, left the house, closing the door quietly, and returned to his car. He must discover what had happened to Louise. He drove away, stopping at a call box from which he rang Bob and Sally Smith's number.

He put on a false voice, one lower pitched than his own, and told Bob, who answered, that he was Louise's half-brother, just returned at short notice from abroad. He had gone to see her, only to find the house empty. Did Bob know where she was?

'She had an accident,' said Bob. 'Perhaps you didn't know. Badly concussed, broke her arm and some ribs, but she's mending. She's left the area.'

'Oh,' said Colin. 'Where's she gone?'

But Bob didn't know.

Hanging up, he turned to Sally, and reported the exchange. 'He didn't ask about Colin,' he added.

'She didn't have a half-brother,' Sally said instantly. 'She had a stepbrother and a stepsister. The brother came to stay. He wouldn't have called himself her half-brother.'

They looked at one another. Sally had told Bob about the reporter who had called and the police enquiry.

'It was Colin, looking for her,' Sally said. 'He might not have been bothered about the difference. Thank God we don't know where she is.'

After some debate, they decided not to ring the police; it would have meant a lot of hassle and by now Colin, if he were the caller, would be long gone.

In the morning, however, Sally rang Andrew Sherwood.

Colin drove off in a fury. Now where could he search? He had no records – Louise's address book, with its few entries, had gone with her. In it there might have been an acquaintance he could trace, but he had successfully prised her away from any friends she had before they married, and discouraged new ones, and her mother and Paul were both dead. The brother and sister were the only connections, and she was unlikely to have been taken in by one of them since both were overseas and Louise had no passport.

Any clues must be in Kenston. There were those people at the hospital shop, but she had never seen them outside the place unless she'd done it secretly, deceiving him. If so, she could be staying with one of them, but it seemed unlikely for she was seldom disobedient, and she did not know them well. He must be wary as he tried to find her, because by now his appropriation of the funds he had handled would have been discovered.

He was driving down a side road near The Golden Horn when he saw a taxi parked at the kerbside ahead of him.

A taxi. She might have hired a taxi to take her to wherever she had gone. But which taxi?

It wasn't late. He could try telephoning all the local firms, saying he was a police officer attached to the enquiry about her accident, needing to know where she was.

His fifth attempt, when he rang Ray Crampton's number, was successful. Ray and Elsie were both out, but their grandson, spending the night with them, was in the house, minding the telephone while his grandmother was on a station trip, and Ray was meeting someone at the airport.

Neither Ray nor Elsie would have given Colin any information without checking that he was genuinely a police officer, for Louise had asked Ray not to reveal her destination. The grandson, however, unaware of this and anxious to be helpful, supplied the full address.

20

Among the advertisements Louise had seen in the newsagent's window were one for a sofa and another for two small chests of drawers. The advertisers gave their telephone numbers, and she rang them as soon as she had reached home and unpacked her shopping, arranging to see the chests in the morning, but getting no reply from the vendor of the sofa. Whoever it was must be out at work. She tried again in the evening, this time with success. The couple selling it lived nearby, in a close off Church Street developed on the site of a Victorian villa which had been demolished, and the woman who answered the telephone suggested she should come round right away. Louise agreed.

She bought the sofa on sight. The pale cream covers were worn, but if she washed them, they would do. Bright cushions, if she made some later on, would be a help. Twenty pounds was all it cost, but she could not move it. How was this to be done?

'I'll get Fred to pop it down to you first thing tomorrow,' said the woman, whose name, she had already told Louise, was Aileen. 'It's not a bother. We want the space so's we can get our new one in. A bigger one,' she added.

How simple! Louise, so used to obstacles, realised that not everything was difficult.

'You'll be the new lady at Lilac Cottage, then,' said Aileen, as Louise counted out four five pound notes.

'Yes.'

'How're you liking it?'

'Oh, very much,' said Louise.

'Had a bad arm, haven't you?'

'Yes. It's much better now. Just a bit weak,' said Louise, surprised that anything was known about her.

'Fred'll bring the sofa in for you. Don't you worry,' said the pretty, bright young woman. She wore a black skirt and white shirt; a mustard-coloured jacket hung over the back of a chair. She must be just back from an office job. The house was spruce, and something cooking smelled delicious.

The girl was looking closely at Louise.

'Lost your husband, have you?' she asked. 'Sorry – I'm tactless – but it must be difficult, on your own.'

The girl thought she was a recent widow. Louise did not correct her; after all, she had lost Colin. She nodded.

'I'm learning how to do various things,' she said, and added, 'I'm very lucky to have the cottage.'

'Renting it, are you?' She must be hard up, otherwise she wouldn't be buying a worn-out sofa for twenty quid, but she was living in a really nice house, with loads of character.

'It's mine. It was left to me,' said Louise.

'Great!' said Aileen, curious, but anxious to get changed and finish preparing dinner. 'Well, Fred'll be round in the morning.'

And he was, soon after eight o'clock. Single-handed, he carried in the sofa and set it where she asked him, then departed, saying he had to take Aileen shopping now.

Louise managed to get the covers off and into the machine,

which made a curious noise but worked; she was lucky to have inherited this equipment. When they were washed, she draped them round the kitchen. They would never dry if she hung them outside, where there was a clothes line strung between two trees.

After this, it was time to keep her second appointment, and she bought two small pine chests of drawers. Once again the vendor, finding she had no car, delivered them. This time, the sellers were a middle-aged couple in a large house not far from Dorothy Kershaw's former home; they were re-furnishing, they said. They'd moved to Croxbury from Hendon because they liked the country; the wife made costume jewellery – she had some of it hung about her neck and arms, and wore heavy silver rings on almost every finger – and the husband was in hardware. Louise thought this meant ironmongery but when he brought her purchases round, he laughed merrily at this assumption and said no, it was computer hardware.

Louise was not much wiser.

The wife had asked her if she played bridge, and, hearing she did not, said, 'Oh, that's a pity. We're always looking for a four.'

'She plays three nights a week,' the husband said.

'Well, you work so late,' the wife had answered.

They were not as well suited to each other as Fred and Aileen, sellers of the sofa, Louise decided.

'You must come round for a drink some time,' said the husband.

'Thank you,' said Louise, who knew they would not invite her.

She met the husband, Brian, though, on Sunday morning, when she went out walking. It was a dull, grey day, but fresh air and exercise were doing her good and she was not deterred by the weather. She was feeling stronger and she was sleeping better, only occasionally frightening herself by thinking about Colin. She was walking up the road towards the estate near The Grey House when he came towards her, accompanied by a golden retriever.

'Good morning,' he cried. 'We meet again so soon.'

'Yes.' Louise bent to pat the dog; its plumed tail waved to and fro approvingly as it snuffled at her gloved hand.

'Dawn's cooking,' he told her. 'We've got people to lunch and I must be back on time to do the drinks. Meanwhile, it's best to keep out of the way.'

'Oh,' said Louise. 'Well, I just needed exercise.'

'This road goes nowhere, you know,' he said. 'Unless you go over the fields, that is. There's a footpath behind the houses, but it's a long way round.'

'I didn't know about the footpath,' said Louise. 'I've met Dorothy Kershaw, who once lived at The Grey House and I come up here sometimes. I don't really know the best places for walking. I haven't been here long.'

'You'll need boots to go over the fields,' he warned. His brown cord trousers were tucked into green wellingtons. 'It's pretty muddy.' He had turned round as if to walk beside her. 'May I come with you to the end of the road and back?' he asked. 'It's too soon for me to go home. I'll only be in the way, and so will you, won't you, Flora?' he told the dog. 'And I'll be in the doghouse if I go to my study. Sorry, I didn't mean the pun,' he added, laughing.

It took Louise a few seconds to understand what he meant. She was remembering how she had met Richard on a country walk, but today she had not sprained her ankle, and her companion was an overweight middle-aged man with the faint trace of a Yorkshire accent.

'Perhaps you can tell me who lives in all these houses,' Louise said, stepping along beside him. The dog, well trained, stayed at their heels.

'I'm not sure that I can,' said Brian. 'Dawn knows them. She's hawked her jewellery around – she goes from door to door as well as having a stall at various fairs. Does quite well,' he added, with some pride.

He pointed out one house, from which the wife ran a cleaning agency and the husband his accountancy business. That must be the headquarters of DustAway, Louise decided.

'I'm surprised,' she said. 'I thought everyone commuted.'

'Plenty do,' he agreed. 'But it's not difficult to work from home today, with computers, you know.' He smiled down at her. 'You don't know much about them, do you?'

'Not a thing,' said Louise.

'I'll have to teach you some time,' he said. 'You might enjoy the Internet. You could make new friends.'

'By remote control?'

'Yes,' he agreed. 'But it's fun. In that house,' and he nodded towards the one they were passing, built in neo-Georgian style, attractive, but, to Louise's eye, enormous, 'lives a man who was a pop star years ago and now he owns a chain of fish and chip shops – very profitable – in towns across the country.'

'Really?'

'Really. Wise man. He invested his huge earnings while he was still flavour of the month,' said Brian. 'The others aren't so interesting,' he added. 'Bankers and such.'

'And there's The Grey House,' said Louise, as they reached it.

'Yes. What a lovely place. Dorothy Kershaw must have been sad to leave it,' Brian said. 'I'd have loved that house but it wasn't for sale when we came here.'

'Yours is very nice,' said Louise. 'Nicer than all these new ones.'

It was. Theirs was a post-war house built of rendered brick, washed a pale yellow. It had plain, clean lines and, from what she had seen of it, was well planned inside, large, with a wing someone had added recently.

'I agree,' said Brian.

He walked with her till their ways divided.

'I hope your lunch goes well,' Louise said.

'It will,' Brian replied. 'Dawn's good at everything she does.'

No future cooking job there, then, thought Louise.

In Church Street, people were coming up the road towards her and Louise realised that they were churchgoers walking home. She had heard the bells earlier, before she went out. Immediately, the cheerful mood which was so strange to her, yet so delightful, was swept away by the more familiar sense of guilt. She had not repeated her attendance; after Judith's kindness, the least she could have done was to go to the morning service. It didn't matter that she had no religious conviction; just to be there would have been enough.

She was never going to manage this new life. She had been here just over three weeks and money was disappearing – not fast, but steadily – and eventually her savings would be gone. What would she do then? What if she got ill?

She let herself into the house, sank on to the new sofa with its exposed stained calico covering, and she wept.

In all the years with Colin, she had seldom cried. She had schooled herself to feel no emotion, and most of the time she had succeeded. Trained to rebuff any friendliness that came her way, she had learned to react with suspicion to the slightest warmth from anyone, and to question the motive behind any apparent overture. People want something from you all the time, Colin had taught her; no one will like you because you are so dull and plain so why would they want to talk to you without a hidden purpose? Charitable tasks she carried out had been obtained by him; except for those while he was abroad, the few jobs she had held during her marriage had been undertaken only with his consent and even then he required a detailed description of her day. Now, she had to account to no one but herself. At first the liberation had been gloriously intoxicating, but today she felt directionless, unanchored. No one told her what to do and there were no rules.

She could read, as she had always done in her spare time, warding away her misery and fear. Thank goodness for the library; she had a book she had picked at random from the trolley, about the colonisation of Australia. Louise forced herself to sit down with it, forgetting about lunch. It was three o'clock when the doorbell rang and, bringing herself back to Croxbury and the present, Louise got up to open it.

Andrew Sherwood stood on the step.

'Oh – Andrew—' Louise put a hand to her hair and rubbed her cheek. After her bout of tears she'd washed her face, but she hadn't re-applied the pressed powder which was the only make-up she used.

'I'm disturbing you,' he said.

'No – not at all. I'm delighted to see you,' she said. 'Come in.'

'I had to take Nicky back to his mother early – there's a party he's supposed to go to, and it's important for him to keep up with his mates,' he said. 'I thought I'd see if you were in, instead of going straight home.'

'I'm glad you did,' she said. She was pulling herself together, coming back into the present.

'You've done some shopping,' he said, following her into the sitting room and noticing the sofa.

'Oh yes – the sofa. I've washed the covers. They're not dry yet – well, they may be, by now. They're hanging in the kitchen.'

'Let's have a look,' he said. 'I can put them on for you, if they're dry enough.'

'They're not ironed,' she protested.

'My mother never ironed them,' Andrew told her. 'She said putting them on a bit damp stretched them nicely.' Hazel had insisted on having a tumble-drier.

The sofa was improved by the resumption of its covers, but they decided not to sit on the slightly damp result. Andrew sat in one of Dorothy's chairs, and Louise took the button-back.

'How's the arm?' he asked.

She waved it around.

'Not bad, really,' she said. 'A bit feeble. I have to do exercises and it will soon be strong again.'

'Good,' he said.

'Tea. You'd like some tea,' she said.

He followed her out to the kitchen, and after she had put the kettle on, she said she must pop upstairs.

'Right. Leave this to me,' he said, beginning to get out cups and saucers.

Louise brushed her hair – with this new short style it fell into place very easily – and dabbed her nose with powder. She felt more composed when she went downstairs again.

'Tell me what you've been doing since last weekend,' Andrew said.

Louise's spirits had soared. Gone was the gloom of the afternoon and she was back in her euphoric mood of the morning. She told him about dinner at the vicarage, then took him upstairs to admire the chests of drawers in her room.

'The people I bought them from delivered them,' she said. 'Weren't they kind?'

Andrew agreed.

'If you want to do any more bulky shopping, Nicky and I can fetch things for you next Sunday,' he said.

They had settled down with their tea. Louise apologised because there was no cake – she had finished the one she made for them last weekend – but they both ate several biscuits. Andrew had thought she looked very pale and strained when he arrived; perhaps she had been dozing. She seemed brighter now.

He had heard from Sally and Bob Smith about the mystery telephone call, and as the couple had decided not to tell the police, he felt obliged to respect their decision, for unlike the Smiths, he now knew from WPC Rogers that Colin was wanted for embezzlement of charity funds; if he had made the call and was back in Kenston, they'd soon find him. Andrew had intended to telephone Louise tonight, regardless of Nicky's plans. Torn between wishing to go to the party and not wanting to lose time with his father, Nicky had been sheepish about it, but this had simply made it easy for Andrew to call round, although it added miles to his journey. It filled the day.

He told Louise about Nicky's conflicting loyalties. She was sympathetic, but praised his recognition of the child's problem.

'It will take him some time to accept the situation between you and his mother, I suppose,' she said.

'I think he has – or had – a fantasy that we'd get back together,' Andrew replied.

'Is it a fantasy? Couldn't you?'

He shook his head.

'It's gone too far. I bored her,' he said. 'But I'm not sure that Terry is a stayer. I think she may end up on her own, and she won't be able to hack that. She needs someone around.'

'You get used to it,' said Louise slowly, then shook herself sharply. 'I was used to it – being married. Now I'm getting used to being on my own.'

'What happened?' Andrew would like to hear her version of what he already knew.

'Do you really want to know?' she asked.

'Only if you want to tell me,' he said, untruthfully.

'I had this car accident, when I broke my arm. Colin disappeared that night. He wasn't at home when the police went to tell him I'd been injured,' she said.

'Did he leave a note? A message?'

'Nothing. He took all his clothes and just vanished,' she said. She hesitated, then added, 'He emptied our bank account. I sold all our furniture, except a few things, like this chair, which had been my mother's. She left me this cottage but it had been let for a long time.'

Gradually, she told him about Mr Barnes and the trust arrangement.

'I had a stepfather, like Nicky,' she added. 'Mine was kind, but I resisted his benevolence – I didn't recognise it, I resented him because of my father's memory. It was so silly. A sort of jealousy, really. It was a waste of love.'

'Your stepbrother and stepsister – what about them?'

She made a little face.

'They did resent me. I didn't imagine that,' she said. 'They resented my mother, too, but she went slowly with them and she and Paul didn't get married for several years. She was just the housekeeper. We might all have become friends if I hadn't been so prickly.'

'It can't have been all your fault,' he protested.

'No. I can see that now. But it was why I married Colin so soon – I was escaping. I could have escaped another way, through a job somewhere else, but he came along.'

'Like a bus which you hopped aboard,' said Andrew.

'Yes.'

'It might have been all right,' he said. 'But it wasn't.'

It was a statement, not a question.

'No, but I had to pretend it was,' she said. 'I knew Paul never liked Colin, and I couldn't admit that he was right.'

'Why do you think Colin left home that night?' Andrew wanted to pursue his original line; sympathy for her must not deflect him.

'He'd had enough of me, I expect,' she said. 'He'd said so, often enough. Criticised me, I mean,' she explained. She was not going to mention that poor woman's body and her fear that his reason might have been something far more horrifying.

'Another woman?' Andrew hazarded.

She gave a little snort.

'I don't think he had affairs,' she said. 'He might have used prostitutes, though.' She had never spoken the word aloud before and was embarrassed.

Andrew did not want to alarm her by revealing his suspicions.

'He has no idea where you are?' he pressed her.

'No. I made sure that no one did, except the police. I had to tell them, because I didn't want them thinking I was missing, and they might have wanted to talk to me if they caught whoever ran me down. The taxi man who brought me here, Roy Crampton, knew, of course, but I made him promise to tell no one.'

'Who do you think ran you down?' asked Andrew.

She looked at him, weighing up her answer.

'I didn't really see him, but there was a street light near me. I thought it was Colin,' she said. 'Of course it can't have been. That's ridiculous.'

It wasn't, though. Andrew shared this suspicion.

Andrew stayed some time after that revelation, coaxing from her the story of their many moves, Colin's two absences abroad, and her history of miscarriages.

'Why didn't you leave him, after that second long absence?' Andrew asked. 'You were working. You were keeping yourself. You had no children, tying you.'

'I've asked myself that so often, when I'd left it too late to leave,' she said bitterly. 'In those days it was much more difficult to walk away from a marriage, and I suppose I didn't want to have my mother and Paul more or less saying, "I told you so", though they'd never actually spoken against Colin. And I hadn't been well.' She looked at him. 'Andrew, when and where were you born?' she asked.

He was startled.

'May the third, nineteen-sixty-two,' he said. 'In London. Why?'

'That's your proper date of birth, from your original birth certificate?' Louise was asking him, even though her heart was plummeting with disappointment. He was more than a year older than David. He was not David. That fantasy had just been shot down in flames.

'Yes,' he said, puzzled. 'As you know I haven't traced my mother but I know her name.'

'It's nothing,' said Louise, but her eyes had filled with tears.

'I suppose I was having a little pretence that you might be my long-lost son.'

Suddenly Andrew remembered the strange way in which she had told him that she and Colin had had no children. She'd had a child, a boy, but by someone else.

'You did have a baby,' he said. 'While Colin was away. You gave him up.'

She did not answer, looking down at her lap, pleating the fabric of her grey skirt between her fingers. Then she had to get up to find a tissue, and while she was in the kitchen he came up behind her and turned her to him, holding her. She was so small, and very thin. She was trembling.

'It's all right,' he said. 'I'm not him, but we can do some pretending, unless he really does turn up to find you.'

He did not leave until nearly nine o'clock. Discovering that she had had no lunch, he found a tin of soup, and made some cheese sandwiches, which they ate in the sitting room while she told him most of the story, but not Richard's name.

He could not wholly grasp why she had not left Colin at various stages in the intervening years. It was difficult to accept at face value her plea of being weighted down by guilt.

'Guilt can make you behave badly to the person you have wronged. You punish them for what you've done yourself,' he said. 'But you were good to Colin. You stuck with him.'

'I wasn't good. I didn't love him. I cheated him,' she said.

'He cheated you first,' said Andrew staunchly. 'And what was he doing abroad?'

'He said he was making a lot of money, but he brought very little back,' she said.

It sounded very dodgy. Colin's past would bear investigation.

Andrew stayed with Louise, getting her to talk more positively about Croxbury and the people she had met. She seemed better and calmer by the time he left her.

'It's not for long,' he said. 'I'll ring you up tomorrow, and I'll be down again with Nicky at the weekend.'

What have I got myself into, he asked himself, driving off; he had saddled himself with an obligation which could be demanding. Too demanding? She had been, like Desdemona, cruelly wronged, and she had truly loved the father of her child, protecting him by her concealment of the birth. What a desolate and fearful time she must have had. The man had had an eminent career, she had revealed; what if he were a prominent politician? What a story. She might tell him, one day.

21

After Andrew left, Louise felt very restless. She could not settle, and if she went to bed, the strong coffee they had drunk would keep her awake.

She put on her coat, tied a scarf around her head, and set out into the raw, damp night for a quick, short walk. Louise noticed the weather here more than she had in Kenston, where their house had caught little of any sun that might be shining but seemed to attract heavy rain to batter on the windows. As she walked along, two cars passed her travelling at a normal speed, and another went by slowly, then accelerated, but on a Sunday night there was not much local traffic.

Andrew was not her long-lost son. They had talked about the rules governing adoption, then and now. The deal had been that the mother gave up all rights to the child, and this included tracing him or her in later life. Andrew had said that he accepted this and was grateful to his adoptive parents whom he genuinely loved and who had given him security of the kind that, regrettably, he had been unable to give Nicky.

'I feel so sorry for these children, moved about between their parents,' he said. 'Surely they need to feel safe? I always did. I never had that fear that my parents might separate.' And these faithful, loving people were not his blood parents.

'Nicky knows you love him,' Louise had said. 'And I'm sure his mother loves him, too. That's not affected by the differences between you. I'm sure you've both told him so.'

'What if you and Colin had had children of your own?' Andrew had asked her. 'Would it have made a difference?'

'To me, yes. All the difference in the world. He said he never wanted them, but he changed his mind – I think he may have thought children would keep me busy, stop me being such a disappointment to him.'

'He was a disappointment to you,' Andrew had pointed out.

'People expect too much from marriage – from other people,' Louise said. 'If you had been my son, I'd have disappointed you, too.'

'I'd have been proud to have you as my mother,' Andrew said stoutly. He meant it; he liked her, but, were it true, she might have expected a miracle of happiness as a result of finding him and could have been disappointed. 'But I'm sorry you can't find out about David.'

'It's right, really, that I can't. I made that undertaking, knowingly. But with the child able to seek out the mother, imagine what could happen to a marriage when suddenly in walks a child that was never mentioned. It could wreck everything.'

Andrew agreed. 'There's counselling,' he said. 'They try to avoid that.'

He knew that in some cases there was the need to know. He might develop it, in time.

Louise, walking round the village, went over their discussion in her mind. She'd see him and Nicky again at the weekend and Andrew had said they could look for other furniture she wanted.

She'd need beds; then, taking it slowly, she could suggest that he and Nicky should stay occasionally, in the summer, when it was hot in London. They'd come often if she made them welcome and learned which were their favourite foods. Nicky would get friendly with the boys next door. That was something to look forward to, and she must plan what to do in the garden; soon she could start working in it. Dorothy would be back before long and she would feel less isolated, but she mustn't cling to the older woman; she must be self-sufficient. If she lived quietly in Lilac Cottage, reading and gardening, and eventually finding a job, she would be content. She could not expect to make a lot of friends, not at her age, not on her own. People went around in couples, even discordant couples, and most of those that parted seemed to set about finding a new partner immediately, as though being alone was to be a social outcast.

She would make a success of it, Louise vowed, as she approached Jackdaws. She had decided that the man's voice she had heard when Lavinia came to the door must have been the radio, but now, once again, the curtains were drawn across the windows and a light showed upstairs.

She hesitated. It must be ten o'clock, or later. Should she go home and telephone Dorothy, ask her if this was in order? She had not spoken to her since she went away. To ring at such an hour might alarm her needlessly. Surely this was proof that her lights were set on timers giving the appearance of occupation and a neighbour was coming in to draw the curtains. While she stood there, wondering what to do, a car came down the road and she waited while it passed. Pausing on the doorstep, she touched the front door, and, to her astonishment, it gave beneath her hand and opened. She remembered Dorothy giving it a good bang when she closed it, saying the wood had swollen; Lavinia must have failed to bang it hard enough when she left after her last visit. A light, not visible from the road, was burning in the hall. Louise could shut the door properly now, or she could enter the house and check if all was well.

She stepped inside the hall, pushed the door to without quite shutting it, and looked into the sitting room, where a lamp was burning. It was empty, but the cushions on the sofa were dented. That was not like Lavinia, surely? Worried now, she hesitated, then went slowly and quietly up the stairs. She had not been upstairs before, and moved cautiously along the landing looking for the lighted room. Its door was ajar, and as she approached she heard sounds, gasps and a long moan, which at first hearing puzzled her, but then, almost subconsciously as she pushed open the door, Louise recognised their nature, expecting to see invading youngsters engaged in sexual exploits in Dorothy's bed.

A bedside lamp was on and the bed was occupied, but these were no youngsters. Louise saw a man's broad, hairy back as she demanded, quaveringly, 'Who are you?' before, swearing, he heaved himself off the woman and turned to see her.

Louise, rooted to the spot, more outraged and indignant than afraid, had now recognised the woman rearing up behind him: Lavinia. The man lumbered heavily towards Louise. She was small; he was tall, and, acting instinctively, naked as he was, he gripped her by her shoulders, spun her round and marched her along the passage, where Louise tried to turn to face him, bravely remonstrating.

At this, the man hit her hard across the face, striking her nose so that with the sudden stab of pain she stepped away from him at the stairhead, found no footing, and hurtled down the narrow stairs, rolling over, the sharp agony of newly fractured ribs all she was aware of until her head struck the polished quarry-tiled floor.

* * *

Judith found Louise.

Dorothy Kershaw had telephoned at half-past nine on Monday morning, and, as Judith was out, left a message on the answerphone. She said that she had called Louise at different times the previous week, and on Sunday morning, but she was never there. She was out herself on Sunday night, spending the evening with some friends who lived not far from her daughter's house. She had thought it too late to ring when she returned, but this morning she had tried three times, at intervals from eight o'clock when she knew Louise would be up, with still no answer. Judith did not get the message until she came in for lunch after making several visits in the parish; there were three churches in her care. She dialled Louise's number and it rang on and on. The telephone might be out of order, but if so, the engaged signal was the normal response.

Sighing, Judith put her coat on again and walked up the road to Lilac Cottage. She saw at once that something must be wrong. The curtains were pulled across the windows, a bottle of milk stood on the step, and there was no answer when she rang the doorbell. She walked round to the rear of the house and found the back door locked, the kitchen blind down.

Judith called out to Louise, without result. She had no key, and knew of no one who might have one. Louise could be lying ill inside the house. Judith pushed open the letter box, intending to call out from there, but then, peering through it, saw a sort of bundle on the floor.

She ran back home to call the police. Then she rang Dr Gibbons, who was still at the surgery. He came straight away, broke the kitchen window and climbed in, opening the front door to the police when they arrived soon afterwards. Judith had followed him into the house through the kitchen door, which he had unlocked for her. He would not let her move in further.

'She's dead,' he said. 'She's lying at the bottom of the stairs. She's wearing her coat and has on heavy shoes. There's nothing to be done for her. She's quite cold. The police won't want anything to be touched.'

In the middle of the controlled activity which followed, the telephone in Lilac Cottage rang and a policeman answered it. He took the caller's name and number, and said that Mrs Widdows could not come to the telephone; there had been an accident.

It was Andrew on the line. Driving back to London the previous night, he had become anxious about what Colin Widdows might be doing, and whilst it was difficult to believe that he knew where Louise was, he had shown such guile that if he really meant to harm her, he might somehow manage to track her down. Andrew felt that she should be warned that Colin had gone back to Kenston. However, the police officer who answered the telephone was not prepared to give him any details about what had happened at the cottage. Frustrated and alarmed, he remembered that Louise had said the woman vicar had been friendly, and he rang her, getting the number from directory enquiries. By this time Judith, having told the police what she knew, was back at the vicarage, and she had telephoned Dorothy who, horrified, said she would abandon her daughter's house to the mercies of the workmen and return at once.

It was no good trying to persuade her to stay where she was, though she could do nothing, now, to help Louise; she would be better among friends herself.

'Drive carefully,' urged Judith. 'We don't want another accident.' For it had to be an accident. Louise, wearing her coat, ready to go out, must have gone upstairs to fetch something, slipped and fallen. Or she had had a sudden heart attack. 'And come to the vicarage, Dorothy,' Judith added.

Dr Gibbons hadn't liked what he had seen. He was not the police surgeon, though he could certify that Louise was dead, and had been dead for some hours, for rigor was setting in, but he had noticed blood and bruising on her face and there was something about the way she lay that bothered him. She was stretched out, face down on her stomach, limbs extended, skirt and coat covering her legs, which lay neatly together. People didn't fall so tidily, particularly down stairs. Yet she lived alone. What could have happened? There was no sign of a break-in, apart from his own. It did not look like a straightforward accident, and he pointed out his misgivings to the police. In any case, there would have to be a postmortem and that would reveal the cause of death.

Judith had not known of Andrew's existence until he telephoned. He did not tell her he was a journalist, simply saying he was a friend of Louise's and had been to see her the previous afternoon, not leaving until around nine o'clock. Judith had to tell him she was dead.

'You might have been one of the last people to see her alive,' she said.

'The police need to find the husband,' Andrew said. 'He's been looking for her back in Kenston.'

He was unable to take in what had happened. It was too startling. He had driven away full of pity for her, wanting to support her yet fearing over-heavy involvement if her life in Croxbury became difficult or she became dependent on him. She had been a sleeping Cinderella throughout most of her existence. Now whether she could have overcome the past remained unknown.

Judith had told him Louise was dressed for outdoors. She had said nothing about going out when he left, and she had no dog needing exercise, but she might have wanted to clear her thoughts after their intense discussion, and in such a quiet village she would have felt safe at night, unaware that Colin was searching for her.

He had found her.

Andrew was certain that Louise had been murdered and that Colin was her killer. He told Judith he would come over straight away, but before leaving he rang WPC Rogers in Kenston and told her what had happened. As a result, and because Judith had told the local police that Louise had left home after her husband had disappeared, the wires began to buzz before anyone dismissed Dr Gibbons' cautious words, decided that her death was an accident, and carelessly obscured evidence. The scene was cordoned off; the forensic pathologist was sent for before the body was removed; and, when he saw, superficially, the nature of her injuries in relation to the position in which she lay, he was sure she had not fallen where she was found.

A general call was put out for Colin Widdows, who, already wanted on a charge of theft, was to be arrested on sight.

Andrew reached Lilac Cottage as Louise's body was being taken away. He saw the undertaker's van departing for the mortuary, where the postmortem would take place as soon as possible.

Detective Inspector Scott was at the scene. Andrew explained that he had heard the news, and thought the police might want to know that he had seen Louise Widdows the night before.

Scene of Crime officers were still examining the interior of the cottage. Scott asked Andrew if he would go to the police station to give a statement, and he agreed, following behind the detective's car, back to Durbridge.

Scott questioned him very thoroughly, noting times. Andrew had to explain how he and Louise had originally met. He said she had been depressed the night before, and seemed frightened of her husband, whom she suspected had been the driver of the car that had knocked her down in Kenston.

Andrew was obliged to disclose his occupation, and a deal was struck about what he might report to his paper. As he had been in Lilac Cottage, his fingerprints were taken for the purpose of elimination.

He could not believe that Louise had died as the result of another accident, and nor did the police. This was Colin's doing, and he, Andrew, might have prevented it by staying with her overnight, or doing more to alert the police.

Dorothy was very shaken when she arrived at the vicarage after her drive from Wiltshire.

'What can have happened?' she asked.

'She had her coat on. The most likely answer is that she decided to go out for a walk. She had been walking a lot lately, because there wasn't much that she could do until her arm got stronger, and she was building up her stamina. Enjoying her freedom, too, I suspect,' Judith told her. 'Then she crashed out with a heart attack either before she went out or after she had come back. A fall down the stairs is much less likely.' She took a deep breath. Dorothy would have to know the score. 'The police aren't certain, though,' she said. 'There may have been an intruder.'

Even in apparently quiet Croxbury, such a thing could happen. There had been several burglaries in recent months, and no one had been caught.

They were still discussing possibilities when Andrew arrived after his interview with the police. Before entering the vicarage, where Judith was running open house, he had used his mobile phone to file his story. It was a scoop, and its release might help the tracking down of Colin.

'Manslaughter,' he said slowly, and enlarged upon his theory. 'He'll get off.'

'But how? Why? Where did it happen? Why was she in her outdoor clothes? Did he waylay her when she went out and follow her back into the house?' This was Judith.

By now Billy had come back from school. Walking down the road from the bus, he had passed Lilac Cottage which was still cordoned off, with two police cars parked outside. He had imagined a burglary. When he heard the news, he was incredulous and shocked, but he said he had looked out of his bedroom window at ten o'clock or thereabouts the night before, and had seen Louise walk past on the far side of the road. He was sure it was her; he was sitting at his desk, struggling with some homework. His room was in the gable end of the vicarage, with a clear view, and he often noticed what was going on outside when he was at his desk. After dark, he frequently left his curtains open so as to enjoy any distraction.

So Louise had gone out after Andrew left.

Apart from the officers making routine door-to-door enquiries in the village, two detectives had come to the vicarage to take statements from Judith and those present who might have relevant information, and they took note of Billy's contribution.

Possibly other village residents would have seen Louise, some-one out with their dog, for instance. The timing and the route of her final walk might be narrowed down.

Revived with coffee and sandwiches, for she had had no lunch, and having made her statement, Dorothy decided that she had better face up to things and return to her own house, so Andrew went with her. Judith invited both of them to come back to supper, and offered Andrew a bed, but he said he would have to get back to London.

'What does that guy do, Judith?' asked Billy when Andrew had gone out to his car, saying he would follow Dorothy back to her house.

'I don't know. He's a friend of Louise's,' Judith said. 'Why?'

'Oh – nothing. Only he was on his mobile phone when I got back from school,' said Billy. 'Talking away, he was, like anything.'

'Probably speaking to his office. He must have had to take time out to come down here,' Judith said. 'He was really upset when he heard what had happened.'

'How did he hear about it?'

'I told him. He rang me, because he rang Louise's house and spoke to a policeman who said there'd been an accident but wouldn't tell him any more,' Judith told him.

Andrew hadn't explained how he and Louise knew one another. She had shed everyone from her past life, but not this man. It was odd, and Judith could see that Billy was busy casting him in the role of murderer since it was clear that the police thought there was reason to suspect Louise had been deliberately done to death.

Andrew, at Jackdaws, was now telling Dorothy why he had been anxious.

'I don't see how her husband could have found her,' he said.

'She had covered her tracks so thoroughly, but I know that someone telephoned a former neighbour pretending to be her half-brother when she hasn't got one, only a stepbrother. He – the husband – is wanted by the police for theft,' he added.

Dorothy was having too many shocks, one after the other, and she decided that a brandy would be medicinally restorative. She poured one out and offered one to Andrew, who, though tempted, declined because he would be driving back to London later.

They had both parked in the road outside the house. Dorothy had a garage behind her cottage, but in bad weather she tended to leave her car in the road, though it was sometimes difficult to find a nearby space as so many households had two cars, and only a few had off-street parking. Lilac Cottage had a small wooden garage, empty now.

Entering Jackdaws, Dorothy draped her coat over the banisters. A neat stack of mail was on the hall table, together with some flyers and the free paper, but there was a brown, uninteresting-looking envelope on the mat inside the door. Andrew, following, had bent to pick it up to save her stooping, and she laid it absent-mindedly beside the waiting post as he shut the door. She told him to give it a good bang, and sure enough, it needed one before it snibbed securely. Now, going to collect her brandy, she glanced at the waiting post and frowned.

Andrew noticed her expression.

'Something's bothering you,' he said.

'I'm thinking that my cleaning woman must have come in over the weekend to pick up the post,' she said. 'How very thorough of her. I didn't ask her to. Wednesday is her regular day.'

'Everything looks spotless,' Andrew said. 'She must be a jewel.'

'She has her merits,' Dorothy said drily.

She poured out her brandy, added a splash of soda, and took a hearty swig.

'Now tell me how you met Louise,' she said.

22

Colin had watched them.

He had seen a porch light come on at Lilac Cottage; then the door opened and a woman left the house. He had no difficulty in recognising Louise in her old raincoat, with a scarf over her head like some peasant. He saw her walk along the road. Driving slowly, at a distance, he had followed her to the main street and past the few shops, until she came to a house at the end of a terraced row, where she stopped to gaze up at a window. Colin saw that a faint light showed around the curtains. Then Louise walked towards the door.

It was a late hour to be calling. She was hesitating in that silly way she had, so awkward and gauche still, even in her sixties. His heartbeat quickened: he felt rage at her deceit, and triumph at his own success in finding her. He drove on. He would wait for her at Lilac Cottage, ready to pounce when she put her key in the door. Before he dealt with her, he needed an explanation of why she was living here. Was she staying with a friend? What friend? She had none; he had seen to that.

Back at Lilac Cottage, having parked a short distance away from it, he walked up the path and rang the doorbell. It echoed through the house but no one answered, so any friend was also

- 231 -

out. Maybe the owner was away and had lent it to Louise, or perhaps she had a post as a housesitter. There were such people. Colin walked all round the building, testing the windows, trying the back door, hoping he could enter and confront her when she returned, but the place was well secured and he could not get in without breaking a window.

He'd have to wait for her outside. She'd soon be back; bed no later than eleven was her normal practice. Returning from where he had seen her earlier, she would have to pass his car, so he settled in it to keep his vigil. It was a very long one, lasting several hours, during which he began to wonder if she could be visiting a lover, but, apart from her age, given her nature, that was impossible. The mere notion was disgusting.

When a car's lights came up behind him, he slid down in his seat so that he could not be seen. The car passed him and stopped outside Lilac Cottage. Colin, peering cautiously from behind the steering wheel, saw two figures emerge; the driver, a man, opened the gate of Lilac Cottage as the other, a woman, came round to join him. Then the pair reached into the rear and hauled out a third person, whom they supported between them as if she were drunk or ill. Colin knew this must be Louise. They dragged her to the door of Lilac Cottage where they seemed to have a minor altercation, though Colin heard no sound – by now he had wound down his window. Seconds later they reappeared without their burden and drove off, quietly and slowly, not accelerating while the red rear light was still in his sight.

Colin waited for quite a time. Everything was silent; the inhabitants of Croxbury seemed to be sleeping peacefully, and no cars passed. At last he judged it safe to get out of his car; he walked quietly to Lilac Cottage, opening the gate again and going up the path.

Louise was lying on the doorstep. Her scarf had fallen back and he saw her short hair. It shocked him.

There was dried blood on her face and she was very obviously dead.

Colin had not anticipated anything like this. In his scenario, she had visited some friends who had taken her home, intoxicated. He adjusted quickly to the revised situation. She must have had a key to let herself back into the house, but there was no handbag visible. If her skirt had a pocket, that was where it would be, for she was always afraid of losing it if she put it in her coat. Skirt pockets, she had said, were safer. He reached beneath her coat to find it, awkwardly, for the task was distasteful, and he had to remove his glove. After an unpleasant search, he found it. Colin opened the door, dragged her quickly inside, pulling the door to, and spread her out below the staircase which was right in front of him. He wasn't going to fumble in her skirts again so he put the key in her coat pocket. Then he looked round for the switch controlling the porch light and switched off both it and the light that had been left on inside the house, wiping the switches with his glove while waiting for a controlled few minutes before he left. When he drove off, it was half-past three in the morning.

Unfortunately he hadn't taken the number of the other car; it was too far away for him to read it. Its occupants had saved him a job, however they had done it and for whatever reason, and he had made sure that Louise would not be found at least until the morning, by which time he would be on his way across the Channel.

The fact that rigor had set in was no immediate help in establishing the exact time of Louise's death, for it would be affected by the temperature in the house, and she was wearing warm clothing. It indicated, however, that she had died during Sunday night. A more precise timing would be established after the postmortem.

Before she was moved, Judith had been summoned back to Lilac Cottage to identify her officially. She had rung Leonard earlier to tell him what had happened, and at least this had saved a special journey to the mortuary, Leonard grimly commented when he came home and heard that part of the story. Someone had to do it, and there was no relative; who better than the vicar? The poor woman had had no time to make close friends.

Judith had put potatoes to bake in the oven and there was cold gammon left from the large piece they had had hot on Saturday night. Leonard had made a casserole for Sunday lunch, his usual weekly task. When, after their talk, Dorothy and Andrew returned to the vicarage on Monday night, meal preparations were under way; everyone, despite their distress, was hungry.

It was Dorothy who thought that Jonathan Barnes should be informed, without delay, of Louise's death. She might have interests to be guarded. She said this during supper at the vicarage, and after some discussion it was agreed that as she knew him personally, she should ring him up at his home.

By this time the postmortem had been carried out, and the preliminary report had shown that Louise had been struck hard across the face, with resulting brief nosebleeding before she died. Death must have come soon after the blow, or there would have been more blood. She had sustained other injuries, including a fractured skull, a dislocated shoulder, and fractured ribs, but the most significant discovery was that she had been moved after death. Hypostasis – blood settling at the lowest points of the body – established that she had been lying on her side when she died. This reinforced the obvious fact that she had not fallen into the orderly position in which she had been found. The main cause of death was internal bleeding; this time her fractured ribs had pierced a lung, but shock and the skull injury had been contributory factors. After further tests and calculations, the pathologist hoped to narrow down the likely time of death.

Billy's evidence had established that Louise was alive at about ten o'clock. The pathologist's estimate was that she had probably died not more than two hours later, and maybe sooner. Digestion of bread and cheese, and what was probably soup, was well established and she had drunk coffee with this meal, which tallied with Andrew's statement about what they had eaten. Mr Barnes had learned some of these details by telephoning the police, and that Louise's death was being treated as a suspected murder. It was dark now, but investigations in daylight round the cottage might provide more evidence, for as her attacker had moved her from wherever she had died, death might have occurred in another room in the cottage.

Jonathan Barnes came down to the vicarage to tell the Brights and Dorothy Kershaw what he had been able to find out, and there he met Andrew Sherwood, possibly the heir to Louise's small estate.

'What a shame she hadn't lived here any longer,' Billy said, the full horror of it coming home to him quite suddenly. 'She was all right,' he added, refusing to give way to tears.

'She was happy, though, in Croxbury,' Andrew said. 'Content, at least. She'd had a wretched time. The police know about the husband,' he told the solicitor. 'In my book, they need look no further for the man responsible.'

Jonathan was inclined to share this view, though, prudently, he did not say so. Malice, greed, revenge and jealousy were all powerful motives for murder.

Andrew told him what Louise suspected about her accident, and again Mr Barnes circumspectly held his peace; she had mentioned it to him, but that was confidential, and Andrew had already pointed the police in Colin's direction.

'He's skipped off with some money, too. He's wanted for that in Kenston,' Andrew said.

This was news to Jonathan.

'Not a nice customer at all,' he allowed himself to say. 'It's very sad,' he went on, less dispassionately. 'She had a chance to create a whole new life here. She'd have managed.'

'I hope so,' Andrew said. 'She was a bit "little girl lost", you know.'

'She was still recovering from her injuries and from the upheaval in her life,' Mr Barnes pointed out. 'A little like after a bereavement – there's shock and also there's exhaustion, and for some there's a sense of unreality. Time puts that right, or enables an adjustment to be made.' Dealing with the aftermath of death, as he so often did, he saw a lot of this. And now there were more pieces to pick up.

The two men left the vicarage together, and, standing beside their cars, Andrew asked the solicitor if he knew Louise had had a baby.

'He was adopted. David,' Andrew said. 'She wanted to find him but the parents of adopted children can't. Now it's too late, if he – David – wants to find her.'

'She did tell me,' said Jonathan.

Now he would have to try to do it. It could be a mammoth task, and if he failed, passing the estate on to this man would not be straightforward. He foresaw further discretionary trusts having to be set up, lest David surface in ten or twenty years.

He would have to find out what powers existed to discover his whereabouts. If he were to advertise, imposters might appear, he thought, sighing, reflecting on the Tichborne case. It would be wise to get samples of Louise's blood, for DNA testing, to detect bogus applicants. She had not revealed the father's name, and no one, now, would ever know it, for she had told him that the man himself was dead. Jonathan always tried to distance himself from his clients' personal sorrows, but sometimes it was difficult.

Andrew Sherwood's story about Louise's death was featured in his paper on Tuesday morning. *Foul play suspected* – not his own headline – appeared above his edited words. Details followed of Louise's recent move to Croxbury, with the established facts about her accident and the disappearance of her husband, Colin Widdows. Though the inference was there, nothing libellous was printed, and now the police press officer was busy fending off other journalists, but he had confirmed that a woman, Louise Widdows, had been found dead in her cottage and that the police were treating it as a murder enquiry.

Andrew, knowing it would be in the paper and to prevent Nicky from hearing about it by rumour, or even seeing the paper, telephoned him before he went to school. He told him, bluntly, that he had some very sad news and that nice Mrs Widdows had died suddenly. He'd come and see him as soon as he could to tell him what had happened. Then he spoke to Hazel and explained.

'And I suppose you got the story?' was her comment.

'Yes,' he had to say.

It was a short conversation, leaving Andrew sad and angry.

He had a job to do, and part of this one would be hounding Colin Widdows, making sure he didn't get away with it.

After that, he telephoned Clare Fairweather at her home.

'If it wasn't for the husband being such a dodgy customer, we'd have had to take a look at that Andrew Sherwood,' said Detective Inspector Scott. The man's prints were all over Lilac Cottage. Sherwood, however, had no motive: the police were unaware of the terms of Louise's will, which would have provided one if the adopted son were never traced, but it would have been a weak theory. In any case, the spouse or partner was always the prime suspect.

Colin had left prints. He had taken his gloves off to feel for Louise's key, and though he had remembered to wipe the light switches, he had left clear thumb and forefinger prints on it, and more on the fob to which it was attached. Recognising that this was not an accidental death, Detective Sergeant Walker, assigned to the case, had made sure that these were examined, although some colleagues thought they must be those of the dead woman. That, however, could be checked as hers were taken at the postmortem. Kenston police, investigating Colin Widdows' thieving activities, had prints which were likely to be his, though it had been difficult to isolate them. Colin had destroyed the records of the charity funds he had stolen, but the aggrieved officers of the British Legion and the other organisations concerned, when interviewed on Tuesday, were only too anxious to be helpful, and three of them produced letters signed by Colin which, when tested, yielded prints other than those of the recipient. Eventually a match was found with those on the key, and another clear set on the door-frame at Lilac Cottage. Colin Widdows had been there, and it looked as though he killed his wife, perhaps outside, then moved her indoors while he got away.

Door-to-door enquiries in Croxbury produced a resident in Church Street who thought she had heard a car drive past in the middle of the night but did not know what time it was. A milkman, approaching the village on his early round, had met a car driving fast towards Durbridge, a rare sight at such an hour, though there were vehicles abroad at any time. He couldn't say what sort of car it was, for it was going in the opposite direction, but it wasn't large – a medium-sized saloon, he'd guess. It hadn't dipped its lights, and chuntering along in his van, he'd been dazzled.

This rang no connecting bells to link it with the dazzle that had blinded Louise when she was run down; the police working out of Durbridge had not had the report from Kenston of her accident. Besides, headlight dazzle was a very common phenomenon.

By Tuesday morning, while the news of Louise's sudden, tragic death was being made known to a largely heedless public through the press, it had spread more personally around Croxbury. Colin, however, was soon in France; his new passport had passed muster during the cursory examination on the Eurostar train. At Waterloo, he had had a thorough wash. While he was in Manchester he had grown a moustache, and a small beard which was quite white, and now he shaved neatly around them both, and slicked down his hair. He wore a dark suit – it was old, but it was his own – and aspired to look like a company director, which was what his passport proclaimed him to be. He should have been one, of course, had things worked out differently.

His troubles had begun while he was a young man, before he did his National Service in the army. He had been stationed in Germany, working in the paymaster's department of his regiment. This experience had equipped him for his future in accountancy. His call-up had rescued him from life above and in the shop – a butcher's – which his parents ran in Sheffield, and from the consequences of a night out with Stan Brown during which a woman had been killed. It had been an accident as she resisted Stan, and she had not been missed for several weeks, by which time Colin was doing his initial training. No one testified to having seen Colin with her; and she was never found because Colin had bound her up with sacks, weighted down with stones, and, borrowing his father's van, had driven across country to dump her in a lake where, if anything remained of her, she lay until this day. The problem of his father's wrath over taking the van without permission was as nothing compared with facing criminal charges.

Then, some years later, when he had left the army, there was Rene. Stan alone had killed her, but someone other than Colin had known about it.

At that time Colin was working in the shop, in the role ordained for him from his cradle, but he hated the smell of animal flesh and animal blood, and the messy sawdust on the floor which he had to strew and sweep up. He hated having to scrub the counters and he hated having to wear a starched white hat while being pleasant to the customers. His father's manner was obsequious and Colin loathed aping it, though in later years the same false unctuousness became second nature to him in his public role. Louise was his target when he dealt in its obverse, the cruel sarcasm and taunts. He hated women, and when his authoritarian mother died, he did not mourn. She had done the books, sitting in a small cubicle fenced off from the shop floor, guarding her ledgers and her pile of invoices. He, with his financial expertise, had expected to take over from her, but his father appointed a handsome widow with a young son and daughter in her place, and very soon they married.

Colin saw that he would be dispossessed. He was planning to leave before the second prostitute – as he had thought Rene was – had been killed and he had again disposed of the body. Leaving a note to say he was emigrating, Colin – then Bruce Atkins – had, like the victim, disappeared. In time he took on a new identity, becoming Colin Widdows, and later, when he met Louise, hid himself away in wedlock.

It had been a big mistake. He could have gone abroad, lived in Canada or Australia, been rich by now, instead of being bled by blackmail.

Leaving Croxbury, he had sold the Ford for cash to the first likely dealer he saw on his way into London, waiting in a side road until it opened. From there, he caught the tube train, losing himself among the passengers. He left the Eurostar at Lille; there, he took a train south. Marseilles was a large, anonymous, cosmopolitan city. He would hole up for a while, living frugally. Louise had sometimes wistfully suggested that a holiday in France would be agreeable, but the Widdowses rarely took holidays, and when they did, they went to a private hotel in some seaside resort where, invariably, Louise spent hours walking on the beach or staring at the sea, and watching any vessels on the ocean. Colin spoke no French, but Louise did, he knew – not fluently, but reasonably well, having benefited from a better education than his.

Now he was going to be at a disadvantage. Perhaps he should have gone to Germany, for he had picked up some German all those years ago. And didn't the Gemans speak English, every one of them, whereas only some French people did?

In Spain, however, where he'd planned to go eventually, finding opportunities for making money from the ex-patriates who had gone there for the sun and low cost of living, things would be easier. He'd move on there as soon as he could.

Only when he was sitting in the fast train heading south did he really start to wonder how Louise had died. Who were the man and woman who had dumped her so inelegantly on the doorstep of the house where she was mysteriously living, and whose house was it?

He'd thought she was drunk and had passed out, but there had been no smell of alcohol when he moved her. At least he'd taken her indoors, where she was out of the public gaze, and he'd laid her out in a dignified position. As he didn't know her circumstances, he could not guess when she would be found. In any case, her death – an elderly, nondescript woman in a remote village – would be of no interest at all, and the police would be looking for the man and woman who had been involved with it, not for him, for why should they connect him with it? Probably she was the victim of an accident, as that first one was, which had set the whole pattern for the years that followed, and dictated the entire course of his life.

In Marseilles, he found a room in a small hotel which seemed respectable. He'd changed some money at Waterloo; that wasn't difficult. After all, he'd been abroad since he married Louise, though many years ago, and not to Europe. Still, it had given him some valuable experience, and funds he had urgently needed at the time, silencing the blackmailer.

23

After Louise Widdows had fallen down the stairs, Ken Morris stood at the top, frozen. Her body made a lot of noise as it bumped from tread to tread, and she gave one shrill cry. Then there was a thwack as her head struck the floor.

'Oh, my God,' cried Ken, and he ran down to the foot of the staircase to where she lay in an unmoving, crumpled heap. He stood staring at her, horrified.

Lavinia had pulled on Mrs Kershaw's warm dressing gown, which she had not taken with her to Wiltshire, where her daughter had a spare one. She came down the stairs after Ken.

'What have you done?' she cried, then went straight to the front door and banged it shut. 'That's how she got in, the nosy bitch,' she said. 'It wasn't properly shut. You know it needs a bang. Didn't I tell you to make sure it caught?' She stooped down and put her fingers against Louise's neck. 'Christ, I think you've killed her,' she said.

'She shouldn't have come marching in. You said it was safe here. And I hardly touched her. She backed away and tripped,' said Ken. He was shaking.

'It is safe. The old woman's away and no one else has a key.

How was I to know that stupid cow would come trying the door and that you hadn't shut it properly?' Lavinia was ranting at him like a termagant.

'For God's sake, what are we going to do?' Now he was sitting on the stairs clutching his head, ready to weep. 'We'd better call an ambulance.'

'It's too late for that. She's dead,' said Lavinia.

'Are you sure? Mouth to mouth,' he said.

'I tell you, she's dead. Look at her,' said Lavinia. 'And pull yourself together. We've got to get her out of here.' Her mind and her heart were racing as she tried to work out what to do.

'Who is she? Do you know her?'

'Of course I know her. She's Mrs Widdows. She's a friend of Mrs Kershaw's. What was she doing, walking round the place at night?'

Despite the horror of the moment, Ken found it strange to hear Lavinia, who was often foul-mouthed, one of her attractions, refer to Mrs Kershaw and her friend by these formal titles.

'Couldn't sleep,' he said, and began to shake with half-hysterical laughter.

'Christ, you are a useless git,' said Lavinia. 'For God's sake, pull yourself together. And keep your voice down. We don't want next door to hear us. These old places may be solid, but they're not soundproof.' Jackdaws, on the end of the terrace, had only one attached neighbour, and Dorothy's bedroom was next to the thick outer wall; activity within, unless extremely loud, would not be overheard. 'She's not going anywhere. Get some clothes on and we'll think what to do.'

But Ken was already on his way upstairs, rushing to the bathroom, where Lavinia heard him vomiting. What a jerk he turned out to be, she thought.

She had met him two months ago in a hotel bar. He was staying there on business, and she was with several other women having an evening out. All were divorced, all wanting relaxation, most ready for adventure; two others had not been seen that night after leaving the bar. Lavinia had got talking to Ken, who had asked for her telephone number and had rung her the next day. Their affair had started at once, in the back of Ken's car. He was a sales representative and married. When Mrs Kershaw went down to Wiltshire for a fortnight, the chance to meet in greater comfort than in his car and more safely than in a hotel room, at no expense, was too good to miss. He was often away from home; his wife was used to his absences and she could reach him on his mobile phone. They had spent several nights at Jackdaws. Lavinia's two teenage children, old enough to be left from time to time, were told that a friend of hers had had a major operation and that Lavinia was taking turns, with others, to care for her during her recovery after leaving hospital.

Now, before Lavinia's eyes, Ken had turned from being excitingly masterful into a craven coward.

Lavinia dressed, stripped the bed and put on clean sheets. She ran downstairs, stepping over Louise's body to fetch a bin liner from the kitchen into which she stuffed the used linen. She'd wash it at home, a precaution she had taken after each visit just in case the old woman returned early. Then she went round the bedroom with a tin of Sparkle, spraying and polishing off fingerprints that might be Ken's or Mrs Widdows' – she must at least have touched the door. Her own, if found, would not be questioned. She dared not use the vacuum cleaner in case the neighbours heard its whine but she would come back tomorrow and sweep round thoroughly.

When Ken had pulled himself together and dressed – she took his clothes to him in the bathroom – she cleaned up there.

Then she sent him into the kitchen, telling him to touch no surfaces. To reach it, he had to step over the body. At last Lavinia joined him. He was sitting at the table, head in hands, a terrified, deeply shocked man.

Lavinia put the kettle on. She made some strong coffee.

'We've got to wait,' she said. 'We'll move her – take her back to her own place – but we'll have to stay here until everyone around is asleep. We can't risk being seen.'

'We can't do it,' Ken said. 'Someone will see us.' While she was cleaning up, in his mind he'd been arrested, charged, convicted, his wife and children lost to him. They would never visit him in prison, his life would be as fatally destroyed as that of his victim, but he made one last effort to save himself, and his family. 'You'll have to call the police, but I can leave. It was an accident – I needn't have been here at all – you can tell them some story. You've a right to be here. She came in because she saw the light on, then fell. After all, it's the truth.'

'She might not have fallen if you hadn't rushed at her and grabbed her,' said Lavinia. 'You hit her.'

'I know. I panicked. I didn't really think – I just struck out.' And he was already in a violent mood, responding to Lavinia's demands. But he'd let go of her before she fell. She'd stepped backwards into air. 'Perhaps I sort of thought she must be Mrs Kershaw,' he said, lamely.

'If she had been, I'd have lost my job,' said Lavinia.

'That's better than a murder charge,' said Ken bitterly. 'You can't go on working here now, anyway.'

'And why not?' she demanded. 'Mrs Kershaw would want a reason. Besides, she needs me,' she added, defiantly.

She was very attractive when she was fired up. A slag, of course, who liked a bit of rough, something Ken had not encountered before. He had despised himself for being drawn to her so irresistibly; now he wished to God that he had never met her. And she wasn't thrown, even with what had happened; here she was, coolly planning how to save them from detection.

'Get that coffee inside you,' she said. 'We'll wait until it's quiet. Then we'll get her out as if she's drunk. She's small enough – that won't look suspicious, but if we're seen carrying her out in a plastic bag on our way to dump her in a ditch, we'll never get away with it.'

Lavinia would not even contemplate Ken's suggestion that he should leave and she should call the police. Why should he get away scot-free, when it was all his fault? In her mind, there was no choice. After they'd had the coffee, she washed up, wiped round, found some rubber gloves and made him put them on, then took him into the sitting room where she switched the television on, with the sound very low, to occupy them while they waited. She felt really turned on, on a high, after what had happened, but, looking at him, she knew that passing the time in a more exciting way was impossible. He had literally gone to pieces; as a cop movie unfolded on the screen in front of them, he began to sob, and had to go out to the cloakroom where she heard him vomiting again. Once more, she did a cleaning operation and after that, she found him some of Mrs Kershaw's brandy, which pulled him round.

It was hours before she decided it was safe for them to go, and before they did, she looked up and down the street. Not a thing was stirring; no lights showed, and no car approached. Lavinia lived in Durbridge, travelling to work at the various houses which she honoured with her services in a small white Fiat. It was too conspicuous to be left outside Jackdaws all night, where it might be recognised by the neighbours, so on these dates Ken had picked her up at a crossroads near her small modern house. His company car, a Vauxhall Calibre, might also be noticed, so he had left it up the street. Lavinia, with her key, had entered the house first, leaving the door on the latch, and he had followed a few minutes later.

And tonight he hadn't pulled the door to after him.

She sent him off to fetch the car. Luckily there was a space outside Jackdaws. They waited another ten minutes, and then they heaved Louise upright – though dead, and dead weights are heavy, she was manoeuvrable – pulled an arm round each of their shoulders, holding her sleeves – not her hands, which were already cold – and Lavinia put her free arm round Louise's waist. They dragged her to the car and pushed her into the rear seat where she lolled against the back like some top-heavy doll. Lavinia went back to close the door of Jackdaws, inserting her key in the lock and turning it before pulling it to, so that it did not bang, testing it to make sure it was shut properly. Then she got into the passenger seat of the Vauxhall and directed Ken where to go.

Cars were parked more sparsely in Church Street than near Jackdaws and after they passed one saloon there was a clear area outside Lilac Cottage. Before getting their burden out of the Vauxhall, they waited to make sure that no one was about. Ken was desperate to be gone. He had begun to think this crazy plan might succeed. Then, just as they heaved Louise out of the car, he said, 'How are we going to get her into the house?'

Lavinia had not foreseen this problem.

'She must have a key,' she said, and at the door of Lilac Cottage, she rummaged in Louise's raincoat pocket, but found nothing.

'We'll have to leave her,' she said. 'Just dump her.'

And they did, dropping her on her doorstep, where the porch light shone down on her pathetic body.

As they drove off, Lavinia said, 'Pity we didn't force some gin down her throat. Or pour it on her coat. Then people would think she'd passed out, drunk.'

'God, you're a callous bitch,' said Ken. Now he couldn't wait to get rid of her, to drive away and find some clean fresh air to breathe.

'You liked it, though, didn't you?' said Lavinia.

He knew she meant the sex, not what had happened tonight. Or did she?

Ken was not familiar with the steely nature of Lady Macbeth, or he might have thought that here was someone cast in the same mould. But Lady Macbeth, eventually, was haunted by her evil acts. Lavinia was made of even sterner stuff; it was Ken who would have the nightmares.

He left Lavinia at the usual spot, driving off without waiting to watch her walk down the street. What had happened to him? How could he, however badly scared, hit a woman, and a small, old, thin one at that? Eventually, on a country road, he pulled into a gateway, switched off the lights, and bowed his head over the steering wheel, giving way to further shuddering sobs, thinking first of himself, in fear of what might happen to him, and then, when the spasms eased, of that poor woman abandoned so unceremoniously, and without dignity, on the threshold of her house. How long would she lie there before someone found her? Would it be the milkman in the morning? Did she really die immediately she fell, or could she have been saved? Her face had been bloodstained from where he had hit her. He had never been violent to a soul before he met Lavinia, yet in a few short, intoxicating weeks he had plumbed depths of which he would not have believed himself capable, and he could not lay all the blame on her. He was a consenting adult. Now he longed with desperation to put the clock back. In the dark, he thought of suicide. If he had a length of hosepipe he could do it, easily enough. But he had no hose, and what would happen to his children, and his wife, Nancy, whom he had deceived? If he died now, it would all come out. As it was, the woman's death might be put down as a heart attack.

He drove on as the sky was turning pale before dawn, and, in a public lavatory, did what he could to tidy himself up, washing, shaving, and putting on a clean shirt and underclothes. Following the other nights he had spent at Jackdaws, he had left at half-past five, after a bath in Mrs Kershaw's guest bathroom and had been on his way to his day's calls in good time when he had taken Lavinia back to Durbridge. He'd always stop for breakfast somewhere, ravenously hungry after such an interlude. Today, he thought he would never eat again, but he would stop for coffee.

It was he who had caused the woman, Mrs Widdows, to fall: not Lavinia. He was the guilty one.

But no one would find out. It would be an unsolved mystery.

Lavinia put Mrs Kershaw's bedlinen in her washing-machine as soon as she reached home. Her son and daughter both slept heavily and were not disturbed by the noise; they were accustomed to their mother's antisocial hours and they knew she had a new boyfriend because she had been better tempered lately. She never brought men home, which was a relief to both of them; it could have been so embarrassing. Her daughter, fifteen, had decided that boys were a pain and she didn't want one hanging round her when she had exams ahead; she intended to go to college as the first step to a powered career. Lavinia's son, nearly seventeen, was saving up for driving lessons and could think of little else but cars; he had a Saturday job at a filling station and did a morning paper round before school. Their father had remarried and his second wife, with whom he ran a pub, was calm and plump; he was generous to his children and they liked visiting him, which had been easier since they were old enough to travel on their own, or to meet him at a given rendezvous, rather than his fetching them from their mother's house. Both children were protective of their mother but worried about how she would manage when they left home, which they were determined to do as soon as possible. She was a good mother; they were well fed and their clothes were always washed and ironed. However, she was perpetually finding fault with them, and with most of the world. She wanted only the best for them, but her standards were exacting. They both understood that she required a man as an accessory, apart from any other needs, and they wished that someone rich would come along and marry her.

On Monday morning she was up before them as usual, with tea already made. She insisted that Jason should have a mug before he went out, particularly on these dark, cold mornings. Sandra slept in later; Lavinia took one up to her in bed.

That done, she removed Mrs Kershaw's linen from the tumble-drier; there was just time to iron it before Sandra came downstairs. She would take it round to Jackdaws before going to her Monday job, which was in Durbridge at the home of a working couple who left before eight; they were never back before seven o'clock at night, so that she could fit in their hours to suit herself. She often stayed on there, eating her sandwich lunch in their smart lounge with its black leather suite, watching television or reading her employers' shiny magazines.

Lavinia wanted to make certain that no traces of the night's events remained at Jackdaws, and, after putting the linen away, she spent two hours there, hoovering and polishing. Mrs Kershaw had cancelled her newspaper but the post arrived while she was in the house, and she picked it up and looked through it, wondering if there was anything of interest before she added it to the waiting heap.

The house gleamed and smelled of lemon-scented spray when she departed, confident that there was not a speck of evidence to link Mrs Widdows, or Ken, to the house.

Everything seemed quite normal in the village as she drove back to Durbridge. She was tempted to make an excuse to stop at the shop to see if there was talk of Mrs Widdows being found on her doorstep, for surely someone must have seen her there by now, but the less Lavinia knew about it, the better, so she went straight past. Then, when someone told her in the normal way of things, she could register shock in a natural manner.

She spent a pleasant day at the house in Durbridge, giving it an extra spray and polish before sitting on the sofa looking at television. There was no item about Croxbury on the local news, but then, Mrs Widdows' sudden death would not be worth reporting. She wasn't in the least important.

24

Ken tried to forget what had happened as he carried out his Monday calls. He did his best to concentrate on making points to various customers, but his mind kept wandering. Surely, when she was found, the bloodied nose and bruising on the woman's face would indicate that she had been attacked?

Lavinia had said that he must get his suit cleaned and wash his shirt at once, but he had been naked when he bundled Mrs Widdows along the landing, and he was not holding her when she fell. For that was what had happened. He hadn't pushed her; she'd backed away from him after he hit her and simply run out of floor, then fallen. And in his right mind, he'd never have done something so cruel and fierce, but since meeting Lavinia he had become brutalised. He often got angry in the car, when he was running late and there was a traffic hold-up, but he'd never resorted to open road rage, though many times he'd fumed in frustration and banged the steering wheel. Lavinia had unlocked part of his nature that he did not want to acknowledge, and it must be reinterred at once, never to be resurrected. He would have his suit cleaned, and he would see that his shirt and socks and every other stitch he wore were laundered. Lavinia had been imagining the worst case, when they would be suspected of involvement and their clothes would be tested to see if anything had been transferred between them and Mrs Widdows, but how would anyone suspect they were involved unless they had been seen?

Why hadn't he kept cool, grabbed a towel or a sheet to cover himself, and apologised profusely?

Because he was doing wrong, and had been caught and was frightened of the consequences. If that had been Mrs Kershaw, she would probably have called the police from the telephone downstairs when she realised there was someone in the house, whereas Mrs Widdows, having heard them, had come up to investigate.

If it had been Mrs Kershaw, no one would have died, but Ken could have been charged with anything from breaking and entering to theft. And he wouldn't put it past Lavinia, in an attempt to save her own skin, to accuse him of assault and rape.

He'd been mad. He'd been through a phase of utter, obsessed insanity. They'd spent hours in the house on the previous Sunday, while his wife thought he was on a course in the Lake District. Someone had come to the door while he was there, but Lavinia had said it was nothing and after that he'd lost all sense of time. Then he'd gone there again this Sunday, having told Nancy he had a conference.

He'd take her some flowers tonight, and be extra nice to her. She, after all, had done no wrong, and he loved her, in a mild and tender way.

There had been nothing tender in his dealings with Lavinia. She couldn't get enough of it, and nor could he, when he was with her.

* * *

Ken listened to the radio news throughout the day whenever he was in the car. When Mrs Widdows was found – by the milkman, or the postman, or a passer-by – what would they do? Call the police, of course – bang on the door of the neighbouring house and ask them to do it, and then a small crowd would gather as an ambulance and police cars arrived at the scene. In his mind's eye, he could see it all. When each bulletin went by without a word, he told himself that the sudden death of a woman in a country village would not be reported unless there were suspicious circumstances. The fact that there had been no announcement meant that Lavinia had been correct and it was being accepted as a sad accident. So he consoled himself, driving west, past Swindon where his head office was, towards home in a village much smaller and more rural than Croxbury.

In a late bulletin which he heard before arriving, it was mentioned. A woman had been found dead in a house in a village near Durbridge. The death was thought to be suspicious, and the woman's husband, who had disappeared some weeks ago, immediately after she had been injured in a road accident, was being sought by police.

Ken couldn't make sense of that at all.

There had been a police guard on Lilac Cottage throughout Monday night, and in the morning there was considerable activity outside, where a search of the garden and the short path was made, as well as within the house. As the day wore on, and news of what had happened spread round the village, small posies appeared – early daffodils and polyanthus plucked from gardens and left as close to the building as the police permitted. Later, more bunches of flowers arrived. Greg, from the post office, brought a spray of rosemary.

Dorothy had not gone for her walk on Tuesday morning. A terrible thing had happened, a dreadful deed had been done, and a woman who at last had a chance to make something of her life had been brutally and senselessly killed. It was such a waste. Why hadn't she suggested taking Louise to Wiltshire with her? Louise might or might not have been pleased to come, but Dorothy had not thought of it. Anyway, she had not wanted to become too involved too fast with the new arrival. However, it was no good repining. She would not miss Louise, since she had scarcely known her, so it was shock she must recover from, not a bereavement, and at her age she was used to both. She must not falter, or Barbara, on her return from the Alps, would come muscling in, deciding how she should reorganise her life. As it was, she would have to explain her desertion of the Wiltshire house. Barbara made use of her mother when it suited her, but at other times was prone to treat her like a child. Dorothy's defence was to remain in control, never showing weakness.

She was weak enough today, however, to go down and make a cup of tea and take it back to bed, drinking it while listening to the *Today* programme on the radio, where the heckling of speakers and the interruptions by the interviewers never failed to irritate her. The paper had not yet come: when it arrived, it would keep her occupied for a while, and later on she would walk down to the vicarage. If Judith were there, she might have some news about the police investigation, and she would be company.

Thankful that today was not one on which Lavinia came, Dorothy got up more than an hour after her normal time. She had lain awake for hours during the night, and when she finally slept, it was not for long. Andrew had taken her home from the vicarage and had then driven off to London. He must have an office to go to, she supposed; she still did not know what work he did.

They had discovered this at the vicarage, however, as Dorothy learned when she called in that afternoon. Someone had stopped Judith in the street to ask about the tragedy; Andrew's exclusive story had been reported in their paper, though not in Judith's *Independent*, which she seldom had time to read, nor in Leonard's *Times*, which he took to work, nor was it in Dorothy's *Telegraph*.

Judith was in, and made tea. Dorothy, who normally appeared cheerful no matter how she felt, looked tired this morning, and every day of her age. They settled down, warm and snug in Judith's untidy study, where piles of papers and magazines were stacked.

'He's not a traitor,' Judith declared, when Dorothy suggested that Andrew would soon write a story about all Louise's friends and her short period in Croxbury. 'In fact, Jonathan Barnes told me he'd befriended Louise on a train journey when she was attacked by some hooligans.' She had learned this earlier today, for she had telephoned the solicitor at his office as soon as she had heard about Andrew's journalistic scoop.

'To write about it, I expect,' said Dorothy, snorting into her cup.

'Not at all,' Judith insisted. 'Jonathan said that Louise seemed fond of him and his son; they were becoming real friends. But I suppose the story was too good to let go. Someone else would soon have picked it up. And he has put the police on to the husband. He made it clear last night that he thinks the husband was responsible. If his paper helps to find Colin Widdows, that will be good.'

'The end justifying the means? I'm surprised at you, Judith,' said Dorothy, but she laughed. Some colour had returned to her face.

Judith knew she would have to speak about Louise in her

sermon on Sunday. She could not ignore what had happened. Even if, by then, the police had made some progress, what could she find to say? There was no comfort in this sad business, except that Louise had seemed content during her brief sojourn in the village, yet they had not been able to protect her. She said some of this, now.

'You can't protect anyone if an evil person is determined to destroy them,' said Dorothy. 'Look at suicide bombers.'

'It doesn't sound as if Colin Widdows was a suicidal homicide,' said Judith drily. 'Just a callous, cruel, all-controlling man.'

'What about the funeral? Who's the next of kin?' asked Dorothy.

'No one, really. The stepbrother and stepsister, I suppose,' said Judith. 'Jonathan knows where to find them. I imagine he'll notify them. Otherwise, it's Colin. But she can't be buried yet, not until after the inquest. They'll open it and then adjourn it, while the police investigate, but Jonathan doesn't think the coroner will give permission for the funeral for ages, in case Colin, when he's arrested, wants another postmortem to try to prove she died of natural causes. Like shock at seeing him – which might have happened, though it doesn't explain the bruised face and the nosebleed. If they discover where she died, they may know if she did meet Colin.'

'She wouldn't have met him voluntarily,' said Dorothy.

'He may have waylaid her, when she went out walking after Andrew left,' said Judith. 'He might even have been watching the house and seen her leave. We know she did go out because Billy saw her. He could have caught her when she returned.'

It was a tenable theory. It was frightening.

*   *   *

Cooperation was now under way between the police investigating Louise's death and those in Kenston who wanted Colin for theft. At the same time, the Kenston CID still had their own murder to solve, and they had begun to connect it with Colin Widdows. The Kenston victim, Lesley Timson, had been killed at the time that he disappeared, and Widdows had been seen in The Golden Horn, with another man, just before she died.

Who was the other man? What was known of Colin Widdows? Laboriously, detectives were seeking to unravel his past.

Andrew's work on the paper was with the weekly magazine, but his coup over the Louise Widdows murder gave him clout and though not the crime reporter, he had a head start here because he knew the victim, and his editor detailed him to cover the story. He wrote a piece about their meeting on the train when she had been assaulted. He revealed that she had inherited a dream cottage, and had been killed just as she started a new life. Her past, and Colin's part in it, he was keeping for a later instalment when the man had been arrested. Meanwhile, he wanted to track down some early photographs of her, if it could be done. Jonathan Barnes might be able to get some from her stepfamily. As no one had been arrested for Louise's murder, so reports and conjectures about her life could be freely aired. Once a suspect had been charged, the case would become *sub judice* and public speculation in the media would be contempt of court.

Andrew had the monopoly, but so far he had unearthed nothing new, and not a word about Louise's son had been disclosed. He meant, for the present at least, to keep her secret, which, as far as he knew, she had shared only with the solicitor. Clare Fairweather had been very shocked by what had happened, reduced even to tears when Andrew told her on the telephone. She took a day off to go with him to Croxbury on Thursday, catching an early train to London, where he met her, the reverse of Louise's trip when he had taken her to Waterloo. They drove down together, and she put daffodils on the pavement outside Lilac Cottage, where there were now ten or more bouquets.

'It's a strange thing to do,' said Dorothy, who had resumed her morning walks and had seen the forlorn display as she went past early on Thursday morning. 'All those flowers, some still in their wrappings, left there to wither.'

Judith, anxious about her, had called in on her way to see an applicant for the post of organist, a position which had been vacant since Judith's arrival. A retired schoolmaster had been helping out; he did not want to be landed with it for the rest of his retirement.

'Yes. It's spontaneous and good, in many ways,' said Judith.

'Personally, if someone dies among my friends, I send flowers to the bereaved who can appreciate them,' said Dorothy. 'But in this case, there's no one to receive them.'

They discussed this comparatively recent phenomenon for a while. Both had seen sad little heaps left at roadsides where there had been fatal accidents.

'People can't deal with grief,' said Judith. 'It was better when there was a ritual to be followed.' She sighed. 'By the time we can hold Louise's funeral, she may have been forgotten.'

'Not if the murder is still unresolved and Colin still at large,' said Dorothy.

'You make him sound like a prowling panther,' Judith said.

'A panther would be a better companion,' said Dorothy, then added, 'Andrew Sherwood telephoned earlier. He's coming in later with a young woman who knew Louise. A librarian from

Kenston. I have a feeling he has a romantic interest in her – the librarian.'

'That would be good, if she's a nice librarian,' said Judith. 'I suppose he's really coming to see if he can ferret out any more information. Perhaps he can tell us if the police are any nearer finding Colin.'

'He'll be abroad somewhere by now, sunning himself on a beach,' said Dorothy dourly.

'Then Interpol will get him,' said Judith.

'I hope so,' said Dorothy. 'I suppose no one in the village is talking about anything else.'

'People are very shocked,' Judith said, soberly.

Lavinia, the previous day, had not mentioned it, so Dorothy had asked her if she'd heard about the sudden death of Mrs Widdows.

'You may not have met her,' she had said. 'But she moved into Lilac Cottage very recently.'

'I did hear something, on the radio,' said Lavinia, and she made no further comment.

She had been in an odd mood, polishing and scouring as if her life depended on it. When she arrived she was surprised to see her employer back so soon; she had asked Dorothy about her daughter's house and the renovations but had not listened to the answers. The fact that she had asked was remarkable, for normally she worked in total silence, grim-faced, occasionally giving monosyllabic answers when Dorothy enquired about her family. Yesterday she had spent a long time cleaning the bedroom, in which Dorothy had slept for only two nights since her return. Dorothy had thanked her for putting on clean sheets and Lavinia had barely acknowledged this remark. She had been almost surly, yet she had carried out an extra, unasked for action, and Dorothy would have considered herself at fault if she had not acknowledged it.

She told Judith about this curious reaction.

'Ah – your treasure,' Judith said. 'I suppose she hadn't met Louise, and living in Durbridge, she doesn't feel involved.' She had not met this paragon and could do with one at the vicarage, but she felt she should not employ a cleaner, though with Leonard's salary they could easily afford one. She said this to Dorothy.

'That's silly. I should find someone, if you can,' said Dorothy. 'You'd have more time then, for your wayward flock.'

'They're not very wayward, those I've got,' said Judith. 'I might be able to round up a few black sheep, perhaps. Do you think Lavinia would have time to come to me?'

'I can ask her. But I'm not sure it's a good idea,' said Dorothy. 'She'd know too much about what goes on at the vicarage.'

'One of the young women in Jonquil Crescent works for an agency – DustAway or some such name,' said Judith. 'The boss lives near your old house. This young woman came to see me last week about getting married – a bit after the event, as there's a child of two and another on the way, but better late than not at all.'

'Same father?' asked Dorothy.

'Oh yes.'

'And the child will be a bridesmaid. Or page.'

'Probably.' Judith began to laugh.

'She'll think the path to salvation lies in keeping the vicarage clean,' said Dorothy. 'You engage her, once you've enrolled the child.'

'I'll think about it,' said Judith. 'Send Andrew and his girl-friend down to me if you want to get rid of them.'

'They'll probably come anyway,' said Dorothy. 'I suppose

one can't blame him for wanting to cash in on the story.'

'He'll be kind to Louise in what he writes, at least,' said Judith. 'We can be sure of that. And probably accurate.'

Louise's stepsister produced a number of photographs, including a wedding group, with Louise looking very young and defiantly proud, and Colin, smug as ever, clean-shaven. Mr Barnes reported their existence to Detective Inspector Scott and they were transmitted on the Internet to airports, ports, and to Interpol. Some were released to the press, and several papers printed the British Legion photographs with their shots of Colin.

Among the many people who saw some of these photographs. was an elderly lady living in Lyndhurst. She was Richard's sister, who had known about his brief romance in Portsmouth, though she had never met the girl concerned. Shortly before he died, Richard had told her more about it, confessing the guilt he felt now, a lifetime later, at having left Louise without a word when he received his new posting and promotion. She was married; it was better to leave it, and he was ambitious. The last thing he wanted was a scandal. She might mope a bit, he flattered himself, but she'd get over it when her husband, whose name was Colin, returned. Richard, who had subsequently had a number of affairs but failed to make a lasting commitment, had chortled in a self-satisfied way, saying that he thought her sex life with her husband had not been very good and that their little fling had done neither of them any harm, but he knew he had behaved badly.

Because he had not said some sort of goodbye, his sister had thought him craven, even cruel, but men did walk away. It had always happened, and it always would. She had remembered Louise's name, however, and when the murder was reported, even in *The Times*, she felt a shock. This might not be Richard's Louise Widdows, but her husband's name was the same. The paper said he was wanted by the police to answer charges on another matter. What sort of life had she had since Richard abandoned her? The sister, widow of a judge, bought up several papers every day to follow the story.

Press interest faded, because there were no immediate results and no arrest, but Louise's history slowy emerged. A reporter made contact with her stepsister and learned that she had led a peripatetic life, with Colin often changing jobs. He had worked abroad, and for a spell she lived in Portsmouth, cooking at a school. Richard's sister knew this must be the same woman, Richard's mistress.

But no one mentioned that she had a child; the newspaper reports made a point of saying she was childless.

Jonathan Barnes followed these developments with attention. His father's files about her mother began only when Susan had inherited Lilac Cottage and did not record Louise's early history, merely her mother's anxiety about her, and Louise had not told him anything in detail.

25

Colin had been robbed.

It had happened in a side street in Marseilles, as he was walking back to his hotel after having dinner in a café near the harbour. He had bought an English paper to read while he ate his meal, laying it on one side while he mopped up the sauce left from the fish dish he had eaten. Ordering from the French menu, he had not known what to select, but had pointed to another table where a diner was eating with enjoyment, indicating what he had chosen, and it had been a good stratagem.

He was accustomed to adapting to new environments, and he was used to living on the edge of fear, but now, in his later years, he had begun to know real terror as it seemed that he could avoid retribution no longer. When, all those years ago, Stan had killed the two girls, Colin had escaped the aftermath, and he had continued to dodge fate throughout his life, paying for the silence of the only individual whose evidence could testify to his involvement. Now, if he were to be caught and convicted, not only for the frauds he had committed but for being an accessory to murder, he would not survive his sentence. How dreadful it would be to die in prison. All these years, feeble as she was, Louise had kept house and looked after him efficiently, though he had never been weak enough to tell her so. Keeping her up to the mark had been his aim, and in return, he had put a roof over her, fed her, and given her the protection of the married status.

It had not been too difficult to find office jobs after each move, and when he failed, he had run scams, advertising various things – shampoos, cosmetics, herbal remedies – from bleak rented rooms where the orders arrived, with money enclosed. As soon as he had collected his spoils, he had moved to another base, and he kept changing his tactics. People were so gullible: promise them hair on their bald heads, sexual vigour, beautiful skin, and they would trustingly send for a discounted introductory sample.

While Stan was inside, locked up with a life sentence, and he had his new identity, Colin had felt safe. Then the demands had started to arrive. Someone knew a lot about the crimes. Prison inmates could acquire information, arrange raids, robberies, even murders, using contacts made inside or through their visitors. People could be traced, as he had been located, and blackmail was easy.

That first fatal night, so long ago, Stan, with whom Colin – then Bruce – had been at school and whose daring he had always envied, had been chatting up a barmaid in a pub where they had spent the evening. After it closed, Colin and Stan had waited outside to walk her home, as Stan had put it. They had taken her into some scrubland and Stan had gone too far with her. That was how Colin had described it to himself, in his mind, unwilling to think the word 'rape', even while, mesmerised, he watched. Stan had shoved a grubby handkerchief into her mouth, and when she struggled, he hit her across the face. Then he had urged Colin to take his turn, holding the girl down, but by now she had stopped resisting. Colin had not protested. The time for that had been when it became clear that Stan's intentions were not simply the bit of fun that Colin had been expecting. He hadn't wanted to lose face in front of Stan, so he had unbuttoned and straddled her, but he hadn't been able to do it. Then the girl had given a shudder and gone very still. Colin had got to his feet, doing up his trousers, but Stan had seen his humiliation. With a jeer, he had turned to leave, but Colin had grabbed him.

'She's dead – you've killed her—' he gasped, and Stan had stopped and looked down at her.

'She's fainted, that's all,' said Stan.

But Colin had seen too many carcasses not to know death when he met it again.

'She's dead,' he said.

Stan rallied. Bluster was his trademark.

'You had her last. You did it,' he said.

This was no time for Colin to say he hadn't. He had always been brighter than Stan, though envying the other boy throughout their school careers, where Stan had had a coterie and Colin had been an outsider. Now he, briefly, took charge, a heady feeling once Stan had fallen in with his scheme.

'I'll get the van. We'll put her somewhere,' he said. 'You wait with her. Let's move her a bit.'

They dragged the poor corpse further into the bushes, but when Colin returned with the van, Stan had gone. So he never knew where Colin had taken her, which, wrapped in sacking and weighted down with stones, was to a lake.

The girl – she was twenty-three – was soon missed.

Stan had been seen chatting her up, more than once, in the bar where she worked. He was questioned, but there was no body. Her disappearance was a mystery.

Within two weeks, Colin reported for his national service while the hue and cry for the girl went on. Then an anonymous telephone call to the police sent them round to Stan's home – he, like Colin, still lived with his parents. There they took away some of his clothes, and they found a handkerchief stuffed into a pocket of an old jacket Stan had thrust to the back of his cupboard. As, briefly cooperating, they had dragged the body under cover, Colin – and he didn't know why he had done this – had pulled it out of the girl's mouth, perhaps because it looked so obscene, and had pushed it, unnoticed, into Stan's jacket pocket.

Murder convictions without a body are rare, but this one stuck because of the handkerchief. Before the discovery of DNA fingerprinting, blood grouping could establish the possible source of stains; saliva on the handkerchief, matched with the girl's known blood group, had been enough to convict Stan, though he maintained his innocence throughout the trial, but as the years passed at last he admitted that the girl had died during consenting sexual intercourse. He could not lead the police to the body for he did not know where it was, and he did not admit rape. Then he became eligible for parole, and when he was eventually released on licence he went looking for Colin, who, thinking himself safe, was back in Sheffield. Stan had never named him during the investigation because Colin's evidence, if it were believed, would condemn him utterly.

But Stan had been planning his revenge.

He had waited for Colin outside the butcher's shop, taking him by surprise. Colin was still living at home, with his father's new wife looking after them, and was setting out for the cinema where he had arranged to meet a girl called Dora who worked in Boots. His stepmother frequently hinted that he must be thinking of marriage, but Colin was not well paid – after all, he received free board and lodging – and the idea of indefinite intimacy did not appeal. He did not like women, and his few sexual encounters had been brief, furtive, and of limited pleasure. What he had enjoyed was a fleeting sensation of power.

Stan, looming up in the dark, gave him a fright almost as bad as the terror he had known the night the girl died, but he wasn't aggressive.

'Let's have a drink for old times,' Stan said.

His release was a shock to Colin. Because of an incident during his time in Germany, when a soldier was accused of murder following rape, he now knew that the girl, Vicky, might have died of fright or a heart attack, so that a manslaughter verdict would have been possible. Stan knew it, too, but without a body it couldn't be proved, and only Colin knew where she was. By this time, decomposition would have destroyed the physical evidence.

The best thing to do, Colin decided, would be to go along with Stan and try to discover his intentions; then he could make a plan.

In a bar they met two girls, Sylvia and Rene, and both were on the game. Before long they were all in Colin's old Morris, in which at weekends and on summer evenings he went for long drives in the country. On Sundays he often sat in at services of any religious denomination, depending on where he found them. While in the army, he had liked church parade; the format was prescribed and simple, and there was no aggravation. Sometimes he longed to be back, leading that orderly existence.

Stan had insisted on driving Colin's precious car, pushing into the driver's seat, elbowing Colin, who had not wanted to make a fuss in front of the girls, aside. He drove towards the area where that first dreadful crime had taken place, and stopped in secluded scrubland. Leaving the engine running, Stan told Colin and Sylvia to get out of the car and look for their own spot. 'You'll know where to find the car,' he told Colin, and he accelerated off.

Sylvia was shivering with cold.

'Where's he going?' she wailed.

'Not far,' said Colin, his stomach lurching. He knew that Stan had driven a few hundred yards away to where that other girl had died.

'Let's get on with it,' Sylvia was saying, clutching Colin's arm. 'Then we can get back.' A chilly outdoor encounter had better be quickly concluded.

'You know who Stan is, don't you?' said Colin. 'He went down for that murder – she wasn't found – Vicky, her name was. It was years ago. I don't trust him. You don't want to be around now.'

'What're you doing with him, then?' the girl demanded. 'Letting him drive your car and all?'

'He made me,' said Colin, who knew that he hadn't the courage to stand up to Stan. 'And he's got a knife,' he added, inventing.

'But what about Rene?' asked Sylvia.

'I'll look after her,' Colin declared. 'But not both of you.' Then he had the wit to add, dramatically, 'If you never see me again, you'll know what happened,' for he had already decided to disappear.

He gave Sylvia ten pounds – a lot, in those days, and a satisfactory deal for her as she hadn't had to earn it – and watched her teeter off on her platform soles in the direction of the main road. She'd soon pick up someone on her way into town.

Then he went to look for his car. He found it at almost the exact site of the earlier death. There was no sign of Stan, but Rene lay dead, strangled, on the rear seat.

This time Colin knew where there was a building development with trenches taken out for foundations. He stole a spade from a garden shed at an allotment on the way, and he buried her, but he was sure she would soon be found. When she was missed, there would be a search with dogs who would smell her out, or the builders would find her, but Colin would have time to get clear. He couldn't risk being involved and having his part in the earlier crime revealed.

Because Sylvia and Rene had been seen with Stan, Sylvia was questioned by the police and she made a statement, by which time Colin, not wanting to be reported missing himself, had told his father and stepmother that he was emigrating. He had said his plans were already made, and he left within a few days. He went to London where he lay low while Stan was arrested and charged for a second time. Sylvia, who had been with Rene in the bar, said she and a male friend, whose name she did not know – which, at the time, could have been the truth – had separated from the other pair outside the pub where they met, and after a few words of ordinary conversation, they had parted. She had spent the rest of the evening with someone else. No one came forward to testify that they had seen the quartet going off together in a car.

Rene was not found, but Stan, already on licence, was tried for her murder and the jury, convinced by Sylvia's evidence, found him guilty. He received a second life sentence. He really had committed cold, calculated murder; after the trial the jurors learned of his past record and were satisfied that they had returned a just verdict.

Stan had tried to implicate Colin, but failed. He and Rene

had been seen together in the bar, they had been seen leaving together. Sylvia's statement and the fact that other witnesses had seen Stan with Rene were enough to get his licence revoked, and when the police failed to find Sylvia's companion, whom others in the bar had identified as Bruce Atkins, they learned that he had gone abroad and did not try to trace him.

Colin, then Bruce, was forced to sacrifice his precious car, for it might contain evidence of the murder. He removed its number plates, and in a quarry where scrap was dumped, set it alight. He carried the registration plates to London in a holdall, from which he took them one dark night, dropping them off Battersea Bridge into the Thames. They had never been dredged up.

He did not risk being caught trying to leave the country. Instead, he set about establishing a new identity, but he was always afraid that Stan would get out again, perhaps by escaping, come after him, and set him up more successfully. After only a few years, the blackmail had started and he could not change his name again because by now he had saddled himself with Louise. He had always tried to avoid being photographed but it had happened at his wedding and on a few other occasions. Private detectives could be very clever, and, by paying for it, they could obtain information. Luck could also play its part when tracing someone, and he had been identified from a wedding photograph in a syndicated newspaper. In the end, when he had made the promised big pay-off after his second trip abroad, he had come to an arrangement, agreeing to regular payments, and he kept on the move, each time hoping to leave no trail, but his blackmailer always found him.

And now, years later, other bodies had been discovered, battered barmaids in towns where he had lived, and finally the one in Sheffield which, after tests, had been identified as

Rene. Colin could be brought down. So he had fled, and in a sudden parting gesture had decided to shut the mouth of the one individual, his wife, who had been his gaoler all this time and could institute a search for him, at last committing murder.

Finishing his meal, Colin picked up his English paper and began to read. On page three he saw the fatal photograph of the wedding group, the one that had led to his identification, with Louise in that stupid white dress and a lace veil that she said had been in her family for years. The paper, two days old, stated that Louise had been murdered and that he was wanted for questioning. His youthful features were circled and enlarged in an inset, and there was another head shot, much more recent, taken in Kenston at a British Legion fête.

But he hadn't killed her. He had moved her indoors, out of the cold, placing her in a decorous position after finding her in an undignified heap at that house. He could not believe it was happening all over again. He had expected his financial acquisitions, as he phrased them in his mind, to be discovered after his disappearance, but he was convinced that the sums he had manipulated were not large enough to warrant extradition. Now he was being blamed for something he had not done.

He touched his new, neatly trimmed small beard. He was well disguised. But he had best speed up his plans to move to a place where it would be easy to find a British community to absorb him. Spain, he had thought, would be best; Spain it should be.

He would leave that night, by road, if possible.

And then he was robbed: pounced on in the street and stripped of all his money, and his papers.

26

Nicky had been sad when Andrew told him what had happened to Louise.

'But why?' he had asked.

Andrew couldn't embark on a long explanation of the probable cause – the hatred and resentment that must have grown up through the long marriage – the flare-up of rage.

'At the moment no one really knows,' he said. 'The police are doing their best to find out.'

'Was it a robber?'

'It may have been,' said Andrew.

Hazel had been surprisingly sympathetic when he explained to her about Louise. She agreed that he could collect Nicky from school on Thursday and he reminded himself that she hadn't turned into a monster simply because she preferred Terry to him; nor, though much of her attention was taken up by her new partner's needs, had she become a bad mother. She had always been somewhat casual, but never uncaring.

There was still a lone police constable outside Lilac Cottage, and tapes kept the public away, but the forensic scientists had completed their examination when Andrew and Clare arrived on Thursday. She laid her flowers, unwrapped, on the footpath.

'Poor Mrs Widdows,' said Clare, who never thought of her as Louise. She wouldn't read the new Anita Brookner now, or the Carol Shields. It seemed so sad. 'I hardly knew her,' she said to Andrew. 'It was the books, really. She appreciated some I suggested and she read a lot.'

They exchanged a few words with the police sentinel and then they went round to see Mrs Kershaw.

'If it hadn't been for her telephoning and getting no answer, Louise might not have been found for several days,' said Andrew. He wondered how long it would have been before she was missed: a new arrival, with few acquaintances and her one friend away. It was dreadful to think of her lying there, cold and alone; what terror had she experienced before she died?

Mrs Kershaw had the answer to that.

'We've heard that she died instantly, or almost at once,' she said. 'She would have lost consciousness straight away.'

'Do they know how it happened? Do they think she was hit with a weapon of some sort?' asked Andrew.

'A blunt instrument, do you mean?' A faint smile lit Mrs Kershaw's wrinkled face, making Clare smile, too. She had noticed a row of detective novels on a shelf in the sitting room at Jackdaws. 'They haven't said. Maybe he surprised her – she would have been very frightened if that husband of hers rang the bell or had got into the house and was waiting for her, and hit her before she had time to understand what was happening.'

But there had been no sign of forced entry, and the toes, not the heels, of her shoes had been scuffed, suggesting she had been dragged along face down, the position in which she was found. However, as well as the fatal injury to her head, she had been struck across the nose.

'Could she have left the door on the latch if she'd just gone out for a short walk before bed?' asked Clare, an urban young woman who still cherished illusions about rural calm.

'No,' said Andrew. 'She was most particular about locking up when she came out with us.'

'Will they find him, though?' Clare asked. 'People vanish, don't they?'

It had to be admitted that this was true.

'They're often found in the end,' said Andrew. 'They give themselves away, or someone on a bus recognises them.' But all three of them could think of horrific murders where no one had been charged.

'The Kenston people he's swindled are keen to get him,' said Clare. 'Stealing from charities is despicable. But he won't come back.'

He had before, though, and someone had told him Louise's address.

On their way to Reading they stopped at the Incident Room in Durbridge to see what progress had been made with the investigation. Detective Inspector Scott said that there was so far no proof that Louise had been attacked inside Lilac Cottage; there were no bloodstains, no splashes anywhere on the walls or carpet, but there were faint marks on the path leading from the gate, suggesting that she could have been dragged along it, into the house.

'So she could have been attacked somewhere else, and taken back inside?' Andrew asked, and Scott nodded.

'By someone who used her key?'

'Yes.'

'And you've got a match? Some fingerprints?'

Scott looked at him, weighing up the advantage or otherwise of letting this reporter know that prints on the key fob had matched those found in Kenston on papers which had been handled by Colin Widdows. He decided to pass on the information, but it was for Andrew only, not for general consumption.

'I'm holding a briefing later today,' he said. 'We'd like help from the public, and we hope they'll respond, though he isn't a child killer, nor, as far as we know, a rapist.' Unless he was, as Kenston CID suspected, guilty of the murder there; the victim had been sexually assaulted.

That possibility had not occurred to Andrew.

'She wasn't—?' He was aghast at the possibility.

'No. There was no sign of anything like that. It's likely that she fell very heavily. Her injuries are consistent with that, and she might have hit her head on some hard surface as she landed,' Scott told him. 'Even if it was an accident, she was definitely moved after death.'

'And when you do get him, he might get off with a manslaughter charge.'

'If we get enough evidence to charge him at all,' said Scott.

'But you've connected him to the doorkey in her pocket. That's better than circumstantial evidence. That's fact,' said Andrew.

There were fingerprints on her shoes, too. Scott didn't tell Andrew that. Whoever had used Louise's key had laid her tidily down on the floor and had grasped her feet as he put her into position. Several hairs, not from Louise's head, had been found attached to her coat. They were not all from the same head, but if one could be matched to Colin, it would help their case, though a clever brief would be able to sow doubts in a jury's mind, for it could be suggested that in the course of their married life, the hair could innocently have become attached to her clothing.

Clare waited in the car while Andrew collected Nicky at the school gate. She watched them as they crossed the road and went into the nearby park, the stocky, dark-haired man and the boy whose build was a smaller replica and whose hair was also dark. Daffodils were blooming in the council's flowerbeds and the grass was showing green. Spring was on the way. Clare did not know where this friendship with Andrew was going, but she felt easy with him and she liked his laugh, heard all too seldom. He missed the boy. She had suggested that she should wait for him in a café somewhere, to be picked up later, but Andrew had said that as she had been a friend of Louise's, Nicky would want to meet her, and they'd have a meal before taking him back to his mother.

They returned to the car quite soon. Andrew looked relieved and Nicky did not seem to have shed tears. Children were very resilient, she reminded herself.

While they were gone, she had moved into the back of the car so that Nicky could sit in the front.

'This is Clare, a friend of Louise's and mine,' Andrew said.

'Hi, Nicky,' said Clare.

'Hi,' said Nicky. He didn't stare at her, nor seem curious. She wondered how many women his father had introduced him to since his parents had parted. 'Dad said you took flowers,' he added. 'We gave her some, didn't we, Dad?'

'We did,' said Andrew, making sure Nicky was fastened into his seat belt.

'She liked them a lot,' said Nicky. 'She was lonely.'

What could they reply to that?

They soon arrived at a pizza restaurant which Andrew and Nicky had been to before, with a street nearby where parking was possible. All of them enjoyed their pizzas and the talk turned to football. Clare, who had two brothers, turned out to be quite a fan. Nicky, cheese stretching like rubber from his fork, asked Clare if she had been to Louise's 'old' house, as he put it, and Clare said that she had not, but Louise had spent a lot of time in the library where she worked and was one of her favourite readers. After that, he didn't refer to her again.

'Kids are funny, aren't they?' Andrew said, when they had left him back at Hazel's. Nicky had run up the path and Andrew had held the car door for Clare to move into the front passenger seat. He didn't care if Hazel saw him with a woman. It was his turn. If she was really curious, she could question Nicky. 'He didn't seem much affected.'

'He probably is, under the surface, but she wasn't in his life, day to day,' Clare said. She was going to add, 'Like you and his mother,' but Andrew was no longer in Nicky's daily life. 'You do ring him up a lot, don't you?' she asked. 'Most days?'

'Often. Not as often as that,' said Andrew. 'He must settle. Once or twice a week, but now I'm seeing him every weekend, it's much better.'

'Chats help to bridge distances,' said Clare, who had had a good few telephone talks with Andrew lately.

While Lavinia had been in the house the previous day, Dorothy Kershaw had had the strangest feeling of discomfort. She had told Judith about the powerful cleaning that had gone on, and of Lavinia's casual response to the death of Louise, but there was more to it than that. The woman had been edgy, and much less remote than usual. She had even made coffee, a task

Mrs Kershaw always performed unless she was out, which, by design, was often the case.

On Thursday, after she had watched the evening news on television, something made Dorothy go up to her bedroom and draw the curtains early. Normally she did not make a special trip to do this, but now, as she did so, her neighbours, who travelled to work together, came home. They had parked on the opposite side of the road, presumably because there was no other space close enough. She paused, hand on the curtain, watching them get out of the car and lift out supermarket bags. It was all rush, rush, these days, she thought: a rush to get off to work, a rush to reach home with a hurried stop to shop on the way, and then the need to prepare a meal.

They could have seen her at the window. She raised a hand to wave. They were a nice couple, the wife quite young, the man older; a second marriage for him, she guessed – if they were married. They had introduced themselves by their first names only. She'd invited them in for a drink soon after they arrived, remembering to provide wine, which young people seemed to prefer to sherry, and they'd been pleasant, but she saw very little of them. Now, however, as she paused before drawing the curtain, she saw them exchange a few words, hesitating on the footpath, and then, seeming to make a decision, they crossed over and the woman came to Dorothy's door and rang the bell, while the man took the shopping into their own house.

Dorothy went down the stairs and opened the door.

'Mrs Kershaw – I'm sorry to disturb you – but I just wanted to ask—' The girl seemed breathless.

'Come in,' said Dorothy. 'Don't stand on the step getting cold.'

'And letting out all your warm air,' said the girl. Dorothy was racking her brains to remember her name. Jo, was it? Yes

– that was it – Joanna or Josephine, she did not know which. 'I'll only keep you a second,' Jo went on, coming into the hall. 'You've been away, haven't you?'

Dorothy shut the front door behind her.

'Yes – to my daughter's in Wiltshire.'

'Did you leave your lights set on timers?' asked Jo.

'Downstairs, yes. Why?'

'Not upstairs?'

'No.'

'We'd been wondering if we should mention it,' Jo said. 'But we sometimes saw a chink of light upstairs. Not every night. We didn't really think about it, but then, with what happened, we began to wonder.'

Dorothy was wondering, too.

'We thought we heard voices, once,' said Jo. 'But we tend to play music ourselves, when we're in. I hope we don't disturb you?' she added anxiously.

'No – not at all. And I hope I don't disturb you,' said Mrs Kershaw.

'Never,' said Jo. 'These walls are very solid. Sound doesn't really carry. Was everything all right? Nothing was missing?'

'No. Everything was fine,' said Dorothy.

'I expect you left a key with someone,' said Jo.

'My cleaner has one,' said Dorothy slowly. The couple who had previously lived in Jo's house had also held one, for emergencies, but Dorothy had not liked to ask that of their successors, and she was reluctant to inflict the responsibility on anyone else, though there was no reason why she shouldn't ask Judith, except that the vicar had enough to do already. 'No one else – except my family, of course, but none of them lives nearby.'

A small silence fell.

'Might your cleaner have come in at night?' Jo asked. 'Just to check up? We didn't see anyone,' she went on.

Lavinia might have come in an extra time or two, if she was passing, to keep an eye on things, but Mrs Kershaw had not asked her to do so.

Dorothy suddenly remembered the mail: the post and the free local paper all placed on the table. When she came home on Monday, there had been only a letter and a circular on the mat, and no free paper. It had already been picked up.

The two women looked at one another.

'Voices,' said Dorothy.

'I might have been wrong,' said Jo hastily. 'Sounds carry strangely.' They'd heard something on Sunday night and the upstairs light had been on when they'd returned after visiting friends.

Clean bed linen, Dorothy was thinking.

'I don't believe you were,' she said. 'I'm most grateful to you for telling me.'

Lavinia had been entertaining a friend in her house in her absence. Bidding Jo goodbye, Dorothy was sickened. While the cat's away, she thought.

Relying on the Yale, she never bolted the door at night in case she was ill and someone had to get in, but that night, she did, putting the chain across and snibbing the lock.

She would have the locks changed as soon as it could be arranged, and she would give Lavinia a month's pay instead of notice.

Neither she nor Jo connected this tawdry discovery with the death of Louise.

27

A well-preserved woman, who considered herself to be still only middle-aged, let herself out of a semi-detached Edwardian house in a respectable suburb of Birmingham. Her silver-blonde rinse was covered by a wide-brimmed fake leopard-skin hat, and she wore a smart black coat. On her feet were shoes with medium heels, for higher ones, however chic, killed them. Sylvia had done well for herself, and was always elegant, one of the more successful landladies in the neighbourhood, with a core of regular lodgers. She walked down the road to a telephone box in the neighbourhood shopping centre and there she made a call to the police. From the box, it could not be traced to her home address, and having concluded it, she caught the bus into town, where she met a gentleman friend for lunch and an afternoon's pleasure. Sylvia still entertained a few chosen clients, ones she had known for years.

She had read of the woman battered to death in Kenston, and when the police, no nearer finding the killer, went to the lengths of showing on television a brief reconstruction of a scene in The Golden Horn, she had decided to act, for she knew that Bruce Atkins, now living as Colin Widdows, had not killed this woman, nor Rene, for whose murder Stan had tried to frame him. Only her evidence – or lack of it – had saved Bruce then. This time, DNA testing might prove Stan's guilt and keep him locked up for good. This time there was a body.

There had been one in Redditch, too, but no one had yet thought of linking it with Stan.

The original murder for which he was sentenced, when Vicky had been killed, happened a lifetime ago. Later, there was Rene. Stan, who considered Bruce inept and lacking in guile, had been convinced that when her body was found, Bruce would be charged, but once again Bruce had successfully concealed a victim. His car, which might have held evidence to link him with the crime, had vanished as totally as he had, and until recently, Rene's body had remained undiscovered. Stan, the prime suspect, out on licence at the time, had been sent back behind bars, largely thanks to Sylvia's testimony. Thus, she had earned his enmity.

Stan had discovered Bruce's new name through Sylvia. While in prison, knowing she had left Sheffield, he had commissioned a fellow inmate whose sentence was nearing its end to trace her, promising rich rewards later, and on a home-leave weekend, Stan had been to see her.

She was running a successful bed and breakfast place, apparently prospering. She did not recognise Stan, who called on the pretext of wanting a room, which she could not let him have as she was fully booked. She recommended another address, several streets away, and he said he would try it, but first he asked her where he could find Bruce.

Only then did Sylvia realise who he was. He threatened her physical harm and the destruction of her house; he was a violent man, and he frightened her into revealing Bruce's new name, and his address, which at that time was in Redditch. She did not like to think of what he might have done if she had genuinely not known it; he could have hounded her from prison, had her beaten up, even killed. Stan, however, had worked on the premise that as Bruce owed his freedom to her evidence, the same evidence which had convicted him, they would have been in touch with one another. So they were, but only because Sylvia had paid to have Bruce found, and then there had been an element of luck about the success of the search. Not satisfied simply with information, Stan demanded money; he guessed Sylvia would have cash in the house, but if not, he would have forced her to get it. He used some of what he extorted from her to pay his informant.

Redditch wasn't far away, and Stan went there, but before seeking out Bruce under his name of Colin Widdows, he visited a bar. Later, a woman who worked there was found battered to death. Stan had time only to telephone Colin, and even so he was late back from his leave, which meant that his next one was forfeit, but officially he had been home to Sheffield, nowhere near Redditch, and he was not suspected of the crime.

Colin moved soon afterwards but now Stan knew the name he was using and he was able to keep track of him. In prison, contact with the world outside can be maintained. Sylvia, a blackmailer herself, was now on the receiving end of threats, but Stan's demands were not for cash. He wanted to be informed whenever Colin moved. Failure to comply would jeopardise her world; a fire at her nice house could easily be arranged, and how sad if her body were discovered in the burnt-out ruin.

Sylvia always knew where Colin was. He had paid her the large sum of money that had bought her house, and he was her source of regular, safe income. She had managed to put by a comforting nest egg.

When Lesley Timson was killed in Kenston, where Colin was now living, Sylvia knew that Stan, obsessed with the thought of vengeance, and out again on leave, was responsible. By now he had the taste for blood. If he successfully framed Colin, there could be other victims. This time there would be proof, one way or the other, and meanwhile the police appeal for help could not be ignored.

She was afraid for herself. She knew the truth, had testified against Stan and he had come knocking at her door again, forcing her to write, at his dictation, to Bruce in Kenston. It had been terrifying, but now there was a chance to end it.

Sylvia made her anonymous call and then went into town on the bus. There, waiting for her friend in the lobby of the hotel where they were to meet, she picked up a paper. On a centre page she read that Colin Widdows, wanted by the police for questioning about another matter, was also wanted because his wife had been found dead in suspicious circumstances.

Due to the television appeal, the anonymous message was taken seriously. The caller had mentioned Redditch as well as Kenston. Both murders, it transpired, had taken place during the home leave of the man the caller named. This last time, he was supposed to be staying with a woman he had met while she was visiting another prisoner, and who had returned to visit Stan; you could always pick up a new man in prison. Stan had returned from his leave only a few hours late, with plausible excuses about the friend being ill.

A DNA check was instituted, and while the police waited for the results of a comparison with that of the suspect, who was back in prison after his official break, an officer went to The Golden Horn with photographs of Colin Widdows and of Stan. Witnesses who had seen two men talking there the night Lesley disappeared identified them both. Colin was wanted for the murder of his wife, but he had once had another name which the anonymous caller had revealed. In the past, he had known Stan, but the caller had said Stan was the guilty one, and might have been responsible for the unsolved murder in Redditch. Stan could have become a serial killer, courtesy of home leave.

Life was so unfair. Colin could not believe his ill fortune. Robbed of all he had in the world, his false papers, and, above all, his cash.

What was he to do?

He thought back to what had gone wrong over the years. Nowadays there was the saying about being in the wrong place at the wrong time. That had been his fate when Stan involved him in his crimes of violence. His army years, when he had obediently carried out his allotted tasks, finding his true niche in the paymaster's department, were, he now knew, the happiest of his life. He was suited to the orderly clerical routine, with minimum drilling, and discipline which, if you kept the rules, as he did, was just. He thought, as so often before, that if only he had stayed on, made it his career, he would never have met Louise, and he would have been safe. Rene, too, might not have been killed. But here he was, fleeing again from a crime he had not committed.

He conveniently forgot the stolen money and his attempt to run Louise down.

He had grown used to providing for Sylvia. After the major payment, with money earned during his long overseas tour of employment with an oil company, her demands became more reasonable, for he had persuaded her that a regular, manageable sum on which she could rely was a wiser arrangement than trying to extort from him huge amounts which he would be unable to find legitimately. Sooner or later, he had explained, if he had to steal, he would be caught – as had happened now, when, with age, his failure to earn enough had meant he had had to resort to fraud. He had visited her at intervals in her Birmingham house, taking her what was due, and after a while they had developed a mutually dependent relationship, for she had said that she owed him for the ten pounds he had paid her the night Rene died. They had gone upstairs to her large, chintzy bedroom where she had introduced him to pleasures he had never imagined existed. In effect, she became his mistress.

With the move to Kenston, however, he had ended the personal part of their arrangement. With age, Colin, never a vigorous performer, had become totally impotent. However, he sent her banknotes by post, less than formerly, varying in amounts, but she accepted the fluctuations.

Then, in a letter, she had suggested a meeting, to discuss the future, and had appointed as its location The Golden Horn, a place over whose threshold he had never set foot.

In the pub, he found not Sylvia, but Stan, a mean, muscular Stan, old now, just as he was, but they recognised each other. Stan said he would get Colin; he would do it, he promised, not today, but when Colin – or Bruce, as he called him – least expected it.

Surely Sylvia would not have betrayed him after all this time? He was her meal ticket. But she had. Stan enjoyed telling Colin this, leaving out how he had threatened her. She had written the letter luring him to this appointment. In the intervals of this conversation, Stan started chatting to the barmaid, Lesley, and Colin seized his chance. He left the pub while they were talking and went straight home to pack, planning to leave the next day as soon as he could empty his various accounts. All that night he was afraid that Stan might seek him out at home, but he was too busy, and Lesley was never seen alive again. Colin's last-minute attempt to run Louise down had failed, and now, once again, he had to save himself.

A law-abiding citizen reports theft to the police. A British citizen who loses his passport abroad goes to the Consulate, requesting a temporary one and his fare home.

Colin had killed no one. He had merely embezzled a modest amount of money, not enough to warrant expensive pursuit. Now he had been robbed. With his new identity, established when he checked in at the hotel, no one would suspect his real one. He went to the police.

An alert gendarme decided not to fob him off with promises. He took details, for by this time Interpol had been asked to look out for one Colin Widdows, previously known as Bruce Atkins, wanted for murder. There were photographs and there were fingerprints.

Several detectives, regarding this aggrieved victim of theft who thought himself safe, considered that without the beard, he could be their man.

They let him go, and they gave him enough francs to get himself to the consul for help, but he was followed and watched as, on the way, he bought a newly arrived English paper. He sat reading it, with a coffee, paying with some of the francs the police had given him, and was startled when a voice spoke to him in excellent English.

'Well, Mr Widdows, how does it feel to read of your crimes?'

While waiting for computer data to reach his office, the French detective had taken a chance. He had scribbled a beard on to the photograph of Colin which had already been received, and he was confident enough to make an arrest.

Widdows would have to be extradited. It would all take time. But he had been found, and the Marseilles officer who had recognised him was covered in personal glory.

'So are villains brought down,' said Andrew. 'By one small slip. In this case, the ill fortune of being robbed and the conceit that he would not be recognised.'

Colin would be brought home and charged with killing Louise. The forensic evidence was strong enough to bring a good case, and there was no other suspect. Colin's past was gradually uncovered. Andrew learned about his connection with the earlier crimes for which Stan had been convicted. As soon as he was charged, his case would become *sub judice* and a media trial would be prevented. In the interval, Andrew found out a great deal. He would cover the trial; that was agreed. There might even be a book in it. His professional future looked bright.

Mr Barnes was dealing with Louise's mail. There was very little, but among the few business letters concerning the services – gas, water, electricity, and the telephone – was one in a thick white envelope, addressed in a firm hand.

It was dated the day Louise had died, and was from a retired senior civil servant living in Ringwood who said that he was the adoptive father of Louise's son, David. The authorities had been in touch with him because Louise had put her name on the register as willing to make contact.

Sadly, the man wrote, David had died of meningitis when he was four. By then, he and his wife had a daughter of their own – this so often happened after adoption, he mentioned in parenthesis – and later they had two more sons, but they never forgot David, whose original name they had kept, and they thought of him frequently. He would be happy to meet Louise and he enclosed a photograph of a small, laughing boy, taken on a beach. In his hand was a toy yacht. The writer's wife, David's adoptive mother, had died a year ago, and before that, both of them had wondered if they should try to find David's birth mother, as she was termed, because there had been heart-rending publicity about the anguish of women forced by circumstances to surrender their children. Whatever her reasons had been, she had a right to know what had happened.

Mr Barnes knew that he would have to see this man, and quickly, for he would have heard of Louise's death. However, his own eventual duty in the settling of her affairs was now simplified. In the fullness of time, Andrew Sherwood would become the owner of Lilac Cottage.

What would he want to do with it?

That was not Mr Barnes's problem.

On the second Wednesday following Louise's death, after Colin had been arrested in France, Mrs Kershaw was vigilant when Lavinia arrived. The two exchanged minimal greetings, and the woman was silent as she worked round the house.

Making their coffee, Mrs Kershaw remarked on the crime and the fact that the murderer had been apprehended.

'We must be glad of that,' she said. 'Did you notice anything, when you came here to pick up the mail and make sure that things were in order?'

'No,' said Lavinia. 'Why would I? I only came in on Wednesdays.'

'Really?' said Dorothy. She felt very calm. 'Strange, then, that the mail had all been collected up and put aside, when I came home early. Can you explain it?'

'No,' said Lavinia, but she put her coffee mug down abruptly and rose, saying she must get on.

Dorothy said no more, but before leaving, Lavinia told Dorothy that she was giving in her notice as she was going to work in a new hotel. In fact, Mrs Kershaw should not pay her today, since she was leaving without proper warning.

She got in first, thought Dorothy grimly.

'That's not necessary,' she said. 'You may keep your money. I'm afraid a week's wages isn't enough to take your gentleman friend out to dinner, but it will buy you some wine.'

She had the satisfaction of seeing Lavinia lose her poise and scurry away.

She knows that I know, Dorothy thought, satisfied.

Lavinia, leaving, told herself that though Mrs Kershaw had somehow discovered that she and Ken had been in the house, no one could have known that Mrs Widdows had found them there. If anyone had seen them on the Sunday, they would have come forward.

Who could have taken the body into Lilac Cottage? Colin Widdows had been arrested. Had he gone there looking for his wife, after she and Ken had left? What was he after? A reconciliation?

It didn't matter. The police thought he had killed her, so she and Ken were safe.

It was a good thing she'd scrubbed up so thoroughly at Jackdaws, but she'd been a bit too careful, tidying up the mail. Before everything went quiet after Colin Widdows' arrest, it had been alleged that he was mixed up with two murders long ago, and the killing of the barmaid in Kenston, where Mrs Widdows came from.

It was dreadful. Such vicious people should be locked up for good and the key thrown away, and it served Colin Widdows right to get the blame. She hadn't heard from Ken, nor did she want to; their safety lay in keeping apart and forgetting what had happened that night. After all, it was a complete accident because the stupid cow had come blundering in where she had no business.

Colin could not believe that he was to face a charge of murder.

He had not killed Louise. He had found her on her doorstep, dead, and he had taken her indoors, then gone. He said so.

What was he doing in Croxbury, and at night? For he had not been there when Andrew left.

He was going abroad and wanted to say goodbye.

Why was he going abroad?

Because Stan had killed Lesley Timson in Kenston and would attempt to implicate him, Colin admitted to having disposed of both Stan's earlier victims. To be charged as an accessory was better than facing a murder conviction for something he had not done, and he told the police where to look for Vicky, the first victim. The lake he described was searched by frogmen and they found her remains. A watch on her arm – reduced now to bones – and a silver ring, were proof, bitter solace to her remaining family; her parents were long since dead.

Several weeks afterwards, the judge's widow, Penelope, and Hugh, an old friend, were having Sunday luncheon with her brother and sister-in-law in their country house near Winchester. During the meal, Penelope asked them if they remembered Richard's girlfriend with whom he had had an affair during one of his early Portsmouth spells.

'I never knew who she was,' said the brother. 'But it was pretty intensive while it lasted. Helped him over that business when Rosemary jilted him.'

'I suppose it did,' said Penelope. 'He took that rather badly.' Rosemary was an admiral's daughter to whom her ambitious brother had been engaged.

'He broke a few hearts himself, later on,' said the brother.

'She's been murdered – the girl. Woman. Richard's mistress,' said Penelope, and her words had the remarkable effect of briefly depriving her elder brother of the power of speech. His wife, however, was less affected.

'How do you know? Who was she?' she asked.

'A woman called Louise Widdows. She seems to have been trapped in a sad marriage to a man who killed her just when, thanks to a legacy, she had escaped. Didn't you read about it in the papers?'

Her sister-in-law had dimly been aware of short reports of a rural murder in *The Times*.

'But how do you know it was her?' she asked.

'Richard told me about it, not long before he died,' said Penelope. 'He told me who she was. Her husband was working abroad, making lots of money in Dubai or somewhere. She was living in a dreadful flat and cooking in a school. He met her when she sprained her ankle in a field. Her name was Louise Widdows.'

'And she's been murdered? This woman?' This from her brother.

'Don't you ever read crime reports?' asked Penelope.

'I haven't your interest in it, not having your connections,' he answered in a waspish tone. 'But do go on.'

'There was a lot of coverage in the press,' said Penelope. 'She was found in her house – one she had inherited and lived in for only a few months – weeks, even – and she had wounds to her head, but she had died elsewhere, so it was said.'

'Do they know who did it?' asked the brother, a retired merchant banker, now a consultant.

'Her husband, it seems. He who went to make money abroad, while Richard had his wicked way with her,' said Penelope.

'It was all so long ago. Does it matter?' sighed the banker, hoping some escapades of his own would not be posthumously discovered. 'No one knows about it, do they?'

'I don't think so. Richard just walked away from her when he was promoted and got a new ship after that course. He never got in touch. I think he was rather ashamed about that, which was why he told me,' Penelope said. Then she turned to Hugh. 'Sorry, Hugh,' she said. 'This family scandal must be boring for you.'

Hugh, a retired civil servant, had been listening incredulously to every word, as he took in the fact that Richard could have been the natural father of his beloved, dead adopted child.

'On the contrary,' he said, with practised civil service calm. 'I find it intriguing. When was this affair?'

Calculating back to Richard's numerous appointments and promotions took them a little while, and there were various assertions and contradictions, but at last, between them, they established agreement.

Hugh knew the date of David's birth; it was about eight months after Richard left Portsmouth.

Those present had known Hugh and his wife for years. They

had hoped for marriages between some of their children, but these had not materialised. Penelope and her family were aware of the sudden and tragic death of little David, a beautiful child whom only Penelope had met, but they had not known that he had been adopted. Meningitis was still a killer disease, easily missed on diagnosis, but if prompt treatment was administered, nowadays there was a good chance of recovery.

Hugh looked round at the faces of his friends: Penelope genuinely cared about this unknown woman, but her brother seemed to think it was all rather a joke. Hugh, however, had now met Jonathan Barnes, Louise's solicitor, and he knew as much as Jonathan had deemed it wise to reveal.

'Have you any idea of the heartbreak involved in this business?' he demanded, suddenly fierce.

They stared at him, astonished. What had got into this quiet, cultured man?

'I think you will find, when the case comes to court, that Louise Widdows endured years of misery with her husband, and she had just managed to escape when she was murdered,' Hugh was saying.

'How do you know that? The press haven't reported it,' said Penelope.

'I met someone who has followed the case. A journalist,' said Hugh. He had wanted to learn more about David's mother, and cautious Mr Barnes, approaching Andrew separately and obtaining his consent, had put them in touch. Louise had willed Lilac Cottage to David, but now, Hugh was aware, it would go to Andrew Sherwood, a pleasant man with a young son who had also known Louise. Andrew had told Hugh all he could about her. Later on, Hugh would go to Lilac Cottage to see where she had spent those last few weeks of her life. To him she was an ethereal presence, a ghost. He was glad she had never known her son had died so young. She had kept her dream, just as she had kept Richard's secret, for of course this was the truth.

After a while, it would seem to the people of Croxbury that Louise had never lived in the village at all. She had been there so short a time that it was her death, not her life, which had made an impact. Hugh knew that Andrew had not decided what to do about the house. If he were to live there, he would be nearer his son, and there was some girl, a librarian, he seemed keen on. Perhaps she had a voice in the matter.

He looked at the red, complacent face of Richard's merchant banker brother. For a moment he wavered. Should he tell them that if they were right about Louise and Richard, then his adopted son David had been their nephew?

It would be a conversation stopper. What could they say?

He could always tell them some other time.